'Every sentence is full of informa
thoughtfulness and precision and, li
unexpected . . . this sophisticated lit
unpacking meaning as fast as we tu

'Dana Spiotta's writing is a perfect mix of addictively weird characters, slightly skewed history and art within art . . . *Innocents and Others* will have you forgetting that the bath has grown cold as you read long into the night.' Lena Dunham, *Lenny Letter*

'An extremely clever novel, about art, identity and ideas, but Meadow-esque intellectualism is always combined with Carrie's sense of humour and warm heart.' *Financial Times*

'A wonderfully gifted writer with an uncanny feel for the absurdities and sadnesses of contemporary life'

Michiko Kakutani, *New York Times*

'A thrillingly complex and emotionally astute novel about fame, power, and alienation steeped in a dark eroticism and a particularly American kind of loneliness' *Vanity Fair*

'It's difficult not to descend into hyperbole talking about Spiotta's work . . . it's rare to find a novel that is so much fun and, at the same time, seeks emotional truth with such intellectual rigor' *LA Times*

'The visionary liberty and daring with which Dana Spiotta has crafted her brilliant new novel *Innocents and Others* is both inspirational and *Elle*

‘Spiotta’s omniscient intelligence is employed in layering ironies and superimposing themes of memory, identity, reality and representation . . . We can edit versions of ourselves forever, [*Innocents and Others*] suggests, but there is no super-cut that can erase the pain we cause.’ *Wall Street Journal*

‘Highbrow and lowbrow have cohabitated before, of course, but rarely with this ease or this empathy. Spiotta – like Didion, DeLillo, Nicholson Baker and Bret Easton Ellis – understands that the interaction between her art form and the popular isn’t an agony but an amity: a peopled life.’

Joshua Cohen, *New York Times Book Review*

‘Immensely clever . . . while the novel’s form is promiscuous, its moral dimensions feel vast . . . Meadow considers how to create a “glimpse of the sublime.” Considering the limits of her medium, she asks herself, “Can an image convey something unnameable, impossible, invisible?” The quiet miracle of this novel is that it does just that.’ *Washington Post*

‘Brilliant . . . masterly . . . Recalling the recent past has a way of exposing present-day anxieties: Who, in these Insta-times, hasn’t dabbled in a little self-invention? . . . she nails a devastating irony: The more reachable we are, the more screens infiltrate our lives, the less there is that genuinely connects us.’ *Vogue*

INNOCENTS AND OTHERS

ALSO BY DANA SPIOTTA

Lightning Field

Eat the Document

Stone Arabia

DANA SPIOTTA

INNOCENTS AND OTHERS

PICADOR

First published 2016 by Scribner, an imprint of Simon & Schuster, Inc.
1230 Avenue of the Americas, New York, NY 10020

First published in the UK 2016 by Picador

This edition published 2017 by Picador
an imprint of Pan Macmillan
20 New Wharf Road, London N1 9RR
Associated companies throughout the world
www.panmacmillan.com

ISBN 978-1-5098-3914-8

1 3 5 7 9 8 6 4 2

A CIP catalogue record for this book is available from the British Library.

Printed and bound by CPI Group (UK) Ltd, Croydon, CR0 4YY

For Agnes

"What is a course of history, or philosophy, or poetry, no matter how well selected, or the best society, or the most admirable routine of life, compared with the discipline of looking at what is to be seen?"

Henry David Thoreau, *Walden*

PART ONE

WOMEN AND FILM

Home/Explore film and TV/Reviews and Recommendations/Articles

"HOW I BEGAN" INSTALLMENT #32: MEADOW MORI

This is a love story.

My boyfriend used to, used to. Now he is. Enormous. He says he worries about exposure, books, articles, lies, truth. Everything.

"Trust," I say. "Trust. One day I will be old."

"You will be the one to leave me," he says. "You'll see."

"That is such a cliché," I say. He laughs.

"Yes," he says. "It is. We are."

I climb around him. He is very good at one thing. Everything happens slowly. He watches me, and I climb atop him, feeling his eyes. He laughs, and his laugh is deep and I feel it shake his body.

"Smoke," he says. I light up a cigar. I sit, on the wrecked bed, in a camisole and panties, and I puff a little breath at the red coal.

"It smells awful," I say.

"It smells delicious," he says and laughs again. Sometimes I help him get dressed. I button his endless shirt. He wears a black shirt, black pants with an elastic band where a zipper should be, and a black sports jacket if he is going to meet someone. He is always going to meet someone, but I don't go. He has a table at Ma Maison, by the door, and people have lunch and make deals there. People stop by, there is some talk, he makes them laugh, he tells them stories, and maybe something will come of it.

While he is gone, I roam around his house. It is a three-bedroom bungalow, with a bean-shaped tile pool in the back. His having lived there will one day be something a real estate agent talks about. The rooms are overfilled with things, mostly papers: notes jotted on envelopes, sketches, marked-up play booklets from Samuel French, storyboards, letters unopened, letters opened, photographs, screenplays—so many screenplays, towers of screenplays—receipts, newspaper clippings, unused sheaves of hotel stationery from Prague or Paris or Denver. I don't clean or organize anything. He prefers I not touch things and misplace them. He will use his cane and start hobbling around, looking for this or that. He will find something else, a cocktail napkin with some scribbles, a matchbook with a phone number. If he finds anything funny—say a drawing, one of his cartoons—or if he finds something pretty—a postcard or an origami flower—he offers it to me, kisses my hand. He is generous, although I understand he doesn't have money, but in that peculiar Los Angeles way of not having money where you still have nice things: a Mercedes, Cuban cigars, a housekeeper, a cellar full of wine from Échezeaux and La Tâche and Romanée-Conti. But I see the bills. He does whatever he can to make money. "Must keep the balls in the air," he says. I say I will look for work, and I mean it. He insists that I do not. He wants me to stay at home, even if he isn't there. I accept this, and I like having days of solitude and nights with him. I like it.

It is another day and he is doing another voice-over. My boyfriend is a disembodied voice on a very popular TV show. He is old and fat, but his voice is rich and strong. He sounds like the voice of America, of a confident, glistening, win-soaked America, full of possibility and ambition and verve. He sounds that way still, when he wants to, and everyone loves to hear that voice. It makes them think, Oh yes, weren't we. And then it makes them sad, but sad in a pleasing way. His voice does all of this to people. Still.

He lies on the bed, propped up by pillows, watching me. I am wearing a short butter satin robe that gently opens when I move. There is a tray of food in front of me: a steak with grilled potatoes, a portion of haricots verts, a large glass of red wine. The wine lingers, silky and warm in my mouth, and after a few sips, it makes me laugh. He watches me eat the steak and drink the wine. I like his watching. I like how fascinated he is by my everything. He sighs.

"What?" I say.

"Old age is a shipwreck," he says. He doesn't stop looking at me as he speaks. "De Gaulle said that. The French know everything, and they know that too, even if you don't."

Other times, after he has done a talk show, a voice-over taping, a phone conference, a lunch meeting, other times he is not in the mood to watch me. We go to sleep. Tonight, things must have been quite grueling. When he comes in he looks gray and worn. This is what age is to me—that naked, worn-out face. Because a young person, if she feels bad, fed up, she must really make a show for you to get it. But old people, the only thing that keeps their faces from looking hopeless all the time is a lot of moving and a lot of expression, a lot of what my boyfriend calls flimflam. The minute they stop working at it, they look like hell.

He goes right to bed. Sometimes when he is like that I stay up and watch a movie on my own. But tonight I decide I should lie in bed beside him. He sweats and I can feel how restless he is. It is hard to move on the bed, his body sags and pulls him. He turns on his side, his face red and washed in sweat. He takes leaky, noisy gulps at the air.

"Do you want more room? Should I leave?" I ask.

"No, no." He looks at me. Whatever was building in his breath seems to pass. At last he whispers to me in the dark: "I just panic sometimes, which makes it worse. This body, this flesh—I feel like Fortunado in 'The Cask of Amontillado.' Do you know the story?"

I shake my head. I wipe my eyes with the back of my hand.

"Oh, it's marvelous," he says. "An elaborate murder by immurement, by being walled in. You see? I am not exactly suffocating, but being slowly immured behind a wall built of flesh. Brick by brick, until I am obliterated. Do you know how many stories and fairy tales concern immurement? Or being buried alive? It is the most elemental of fears."

He pauses, and I can hear him taking noisy breaths in the dark.

"You must stay, darling. See how just talking to you calms me down," he whispers.

I move up on the pillows, I put my hands on the sides of his face. I make him look into my eyes. His eyes are dark and wet. They look like a boy's eyes with laugh wrinkles at the edges. He presses his cheek against my hand. He presses his lips against my hand. I kiss his forehead, I pull his head in close to my chest. He rests against me and goes to sleep at last.

I told you this is a love story.

One day, one of the very last days, it will be a different story. But before I tell about that part, please let me tell this part. The very beginning part. The how-we-met part. I was just finishing my senior year at Wake School, a private arts high school in Santa Monica. It was 1984. I was a very good student; I had no need to rebel and actually felt comfortable at school. I did my senior project on him. It was a kind of stunt. I have always liked stunts (and also, as you may have guessed, pranks, hoaxes, games). I had read how he said he learned everything he knew about filmmaking from watching Charlie Chaplin's *City Lights* twenty times. My project was called, "A Response to My Favorite Filmmaker's Response to Watching *City Lights* Multiple Times (From Emulation to Extravagance)." Short official title (as it was too long for the school course credit form): "(From Emulation to Extravagance)." It consisted of me watching my boyfriend's most famous film—his brilliant, wunderkind, iconic film—twenty times over three days. That is, consecutively except for when I slept. The school let me set up in a room with a couch/bed where I could be comfortable, and I had meals brought in. (It was that kind of school.) I kept a record of my thoughts as I viewed the film and posted the pages on a large bulletin board in the adjacent hallway. People were welcome to watch the film with me, or simply watch me watch the film. My notes were the record of those twenty viewings and I still have them:

Viewing 1:
Fantastic, this is gorgeous. I can't wait to see it again.

Viewing 2:
The composition is so self-conscious.

Viewing 3:
The person who is narrating always occupies the lower right quadrant. It is a code, a secret code that can be charted. Windows must be passed through, seamless and yet with bravado. It is brash, revolutionary, yet very controlled and orchestrated.

Viewing 4:
Actually, not entirely consistent in the composition and cinematic tropes. Occasionally arbitrary?

Viewing 5:
Maybe not arbitrary, maybe the broken pattern is deliberate, the thing that makes the film live.

Viewing 6:

There is a kind of purgatory that happens on the sixth viewing. You are bored of the repetition, and then you go through it. You are liberated from the narrative, the story. But it is only because you know it so well, and then you can absorb HOW the story is told.

Viewing 7:

Agnes Moorehead. Paul Stewart. George Coulouris. Everett Sloane. Joseph Cotten.

Viewing 8:

He did not watch City Lights *twenty times. You don't need to watch a film twenty times to discover all it has to teach. Maybe eight times, maybe, but no way twenty.*

Viewing 9:

Dialogue, I'm just listening to the dialogue. My eyes are closed. Music and dialogue.

Viewing 10:

I've memorized this whole film. I could recite the entire movie. I'm going to say all the lines with the actors as they say them.

Viewing 11:

I did it, I did it. Just think of how this can impress and amuse people. I'll always have this.

Viewing 12:

I turned the sound off. Light—gorgeous silver light—and those tactile gray planes, almost abstract.

Viewing 13:
I am dreaming through these viewings. My mind wanders; I try to pull it back to the film. It is like trying to meditate. I have to let go in order to focus.

Viewing 14:
I've had it with this film. I'm growing to hate it. I'm listing every continuity error.

Viewing 15:
This was a bad idea. I have ruined the movie. It wasn't meant to be looked at like this. No film is. It is meant to be magic, not endless brain wallpaper.

Viewing 16:
I'm frankly ignoring this film now. I block it out. I endure it. I am just holding out for the hours I get to sleep, unmolested by images and sound.

Viewing 17:
Now when I sleep, I dream of this movie. I've become a part of the film now. This movie preceded me and colonized me and will outlast me.

Viewing 18:
It really is good, you know.

Viewing 19:
I never realized how funny it is; I am crying from laughter. My laughter echoes in the room. Now every line seems to wink and turn on itself. We are in some private, exclusive world, just me and the movie.

Viewing 20:
Done.

I used a spotless 16 mm print I acquired through Jay Hosney, the cinema studies teacher at my school. This print was a gleaming object of 1940s light and shadow. I had a projector and reels that had to be changed, making it hardly a seamless dream. But the reels were so physical, and as I handled them, it was almost as if I were touching not just the object but the film itself, mingling with it in some deep way, overcoming its implacable borders. In the end, I talked to the screen; I stood in the stream of dusty shades and shapes; I watched the projection flicker across my body; I hallucinated.

At graduation I was awarded the senior prize. The summer was suddenly upon me. I found his address on a map of the stars' homes. I sent him a copy of a school article about me and a letter explaining "A Response to My Favorite Filmmaker's Response to Watching *City Lights* Multiple Times (From Emulation to Extravagance)." I told him how in homage to his watching *City Lights* twenty times, I watched his most famous film twenty consecutive times. I also told him how an idea of him came to me as I watched: that he was everything Americans were, writ large. Written in giant, bold, back-lit sans-serif letters. I realized, as I sat in the dark, that he conjured up our past and our future, the glory and the disappointment. We lived in it, but we didn't like it. In fact, we hated it. We hated him. So now he was trotted out for quips, and sometimes he said disturbing things, uncomfortable things. He couldn't help it. He never learned, and I loved him for it.

He wrote me back right away. He said he would like, very much, to have lunch with me. I came to his modest Brentwood home. A middle-aged woman served us grilled fish by his pool. He didn't talk at all about movies. But he did talk about Brazil, about voodoo, about the paranormal, about extinct animals and the etymology of the word *chivalry*.

Then he said, "It wasn't *City Lights*, you know. Although *City Lights* is a very fine film, one of my favorites, I believe that I said I had watched *Stagecoach* over and over to teach myself how to make movies."

John Ford! Not Chaplin. I felt my face get hot. Had I misread that? It didn't seem possible that I could have made such a mistake. He pushed butter into the soft center of a roll. He bit into the roll, all the while watching me. I took a sip of ice water and watched him back. At once I knew what to say, but I took another sip of water first, placed my glass on the table and leaned back.

"It doesn't matter," I said slowly. "You were lying about all of it anyway, right?"

"Yes, that's right," he said.

"You didn't watch any film twenty times. It's a lie."

"I don't think of it as lying. I think of it as a little story I told about me, or what people want to think of me." He took another bite of his roll. It was nearly finished, only a dainty piece remained between his meaty fingertips. He slowly chewed and swallowed. "I've already disappointed you."

"No, you haven't at all," I said. "It is much better as a lie."

He barked a laugh at this; he laughed so hard his eyes closed. His body shook. He finally stopped laughing. "Just marvelous," he said. "I feel sorry for the college you're going to attend."

"I don't know. I don't know about going to college," I said. "I don't like the way everyone expects certain things of me because I am . . ."

"A bright young person," he said. "Possibly the best thing in the world one can be." The middle-aged woman, who apparently was the housekeeper, cleared the plates. At first I imagined she might be a wife or girlfriend of some kind but then I realized how unlikely it would be that such a person might wait on us. I watched her disappear through the sliding glass door.

He patted my hand, and then I leaned over and kissed him gently, pressing my lips against his. Understand, I was no groupie, no seeker of famous men. He seemed to me, for whatever reason, a chagrined innocent, a man I could trust. So I kissed him, then pulled back and waited for it to change my life. He shook his head, and he laughed again, a lower, softer laugh that trailed off into something else. He looked at me like he couldn't believe his luck. People, if you have never had that, that kind of look, well, it is worth giving up everything for. I sat back down. We ate crème brûlée. He had a beard. I never liked beards before. But I had never liked anything before, I realized.

I never left. I did return once to my parents' house—only a few miles away on the other side of Sunset Boulevard. I drove my graduation gift, a dark blue VW Rabbit convertible (this makes me sound spoiled, but it was used, a 1982, and you should see what some of my fellow graduates got as gifts), up into the winding streets of Bel-Air. We lived in a recently built very large one-level house that hugged the edge of a scrubby canyon. Sliding glass doors in every room faced the landscaped yard: the pool and the hazy view beyond the pool of other houses with pools on the opposite side of the canyon. Some of the walls in our house were lined with suede panels and other walls were lined with mirrors. My parents liked the effect of juxtaposing contemporary surfaces with an elaborate collection of French and Italian antique furniture. My mother considers herself a person with interior design skills, or at least a very strong sense of her own taste, and I admit that it worked in a way that at least felt deliberate. I didn't mind looking at the fine Louis XIV gilt-painted wood table set unexpectedly in front of the palm trees and cactuses visible through the glass panels. But I myself would have preferred a Mediterranean-style Craftsman bungalow decorated in Art Deco tubular furniture with the chromed curves and the squeak of leather promising a life of gliding modernity. That's me all right: out-of-date modernity with its edge of future promise unfulfilled, even failed. Which I admit contains a smug kind of nostalgia, but you can't help what you find beautiful. I so loved the clothing style of the 1930s that my prom "dress" was a slim, high-waisted vintage men's suit (in those days I liked to dress like a man, albeit a kind of louche, fem-stylized "man") that I had rented from Western Costume, something a minor player wore once in a long-forgotten silvery black-and-white film. But my mother was different from me. She liked things hypernew or very antique. None of this freighted recent past for her. "Vintage?" she would say when we went into the expensive, retro-stocked stores that now dotted Melrose Avenue. "That's what they call this garage-sale attic junk?" Or she would make a sound of hard-pushed air in her throat, which I came to understand meant that she had a similar item once and had happily discarded it years ago. She had no tolerance for the sentimental revisiting of the 1950s that became so popular during my grade-school years. She never understood our desire to dress up in sock hop outfits for " '50s days" and felt that watching *Grease* was ridiculous (not to mention inaccurate, i.e., "The fifties weren't fun, by the way"). My father did not have such strong feelings, but he went along with my mother in matters of decor and in almost everything else.

I sat them both down together but it was to her that I addressed my explanation of why I was leaving. Immediately.

I told her that I planned to take a road trip with my friend Carrie. I picked Carrie because she in fact was spending the summer driving across the country. She was going with her boyfriend—my going with her was something that I made up on the ride over to my parents' house, but it would be easy to cover for because it worked for both of us. Carrie could tell her mom she was with me when she wasn't, and I could say I was with her when I wasn't. I told my parents my plan as they sat on our cream velvet Empire couch and I sat on the rug in front of them, holding a can of Diet Dr Pepper and taking frequent sips. The sips helped me buy time, as I was making this up as I spoke, or at least partly, the general ideas taking shape on the drive over, but the detailed contours of the plan coming to life as I formed the sentences between sips.

"There is a film collective in upstate New York," I said. Sip. I was thinking of the great director Nicholas Ray and the weird upstate New York collective he formed with his students in the '70s after he had been forgotten by Hollywood. (I have always been attracted to afterlives, codas, postscripts, discursive asides, and especially misdirection. Note this.) I had never seen the film Nicholas Ray made with his students, but it was legendary, at least to me.

"Where in upstate New York?" My mother's brow furrowed. She was raised in Long Island, but she had developed a West Coast revulsion for the extreme temperatures of New York, and to her "upstate" seemed like a tundra of snow and forgotten factory brick. I hadn't considered that I needed to be more specific than upstate. I thought of Syracuse, Buffalo, Rochester. I thought of Troy, Albany, Kingston. I thought of Binghamton, where Nicholas Ray taught. But that isn't what I said to them.

"Gloversville. They have an abandoned glove factory that gets used as a soundstage. It's incredibly cheap, and we have easy access to woods or lakes or old houses for locations," I said, and took another long swig of my soft drink. I was addicted to the slightly cooked peppermint-chemical taste of Diet Dr Pepper. The flavor had a wave of sweet followed by something bitter and then something metal; it was so close to repulsive, and yet I had grown to crave it. I tried to figure it out nearly every time I drank it. Is it marshmallow or peppermint? Is it a cola with a fruit flavor? With an undertaste of saccharin? Perhaps the blatant artificiality of it pleased me—it wasn't trying to taste like anything real, the way diet Fanta or diet Fresca attempted to have "fruit" flavors. I drank it constantly. Sip, sip.

"A film shoot in Gloversville, New York?"

"A collective. Like an artists' commune, so we can share equipment and ideas. In Gloversville, New York." Sure. Why not?

The town of Gloversville came to me from a coffee-table photo book of old movie theaters: the Glove Theater in Gloversville. It was a former vaudeville venue whose exterior sign was renovated in 1939 in high Art Deco. Perhaps the glove in both the town name and the sign made it stick in my head, and then it popped out while the soda sip still tingled my tongue. Later, when I finally saw the place in real life, my eyes filled and blurred. It was a decrepit theater, in grave disrepair, on a dying street full of empty storefronts. The door was open; I stepped in. A ghost town with a ghost theater, yet the former grandness still evident, the gold wallpaper peeling, the velvet seats in attendant rows, though ripped and ruined. Why did I cry? Not because it was a wreck, but because I felt the history. I knew that cinema had touched every small town in America. Cinema is everywhere. And to discover it in the most obscure places made me believe that it mattered. Its decay only meant there was room for me somehow. That is why I cried; I was full of joy and excitement.

"Sounds ambitious," my father said. Ambition pleased him. He was an entertainment lawyer, but he never talked about his work with me. He loved, though, to talk about me and my "work." He encouraged me to believe that my particular possibilities had no limits, and one strategy he apparently had for conveying that idea was not giving me any limits, financial or otherwise.

"What's the name of it?" my mother said.

"Of the film collective?" I sipped my Diet Dr Pepper. Swallowed. "Spectro Corps," I said. Both parents tilted their heads like they hadn't heard. "Spectro Corps. Like the Peace Corps. Or the Marine Corps." No one spoke. I was about to go on, but I saw my father smile and begin to nod, so I made myself shut up (which is hard for me sometimes).

"Where will you live?" my mother asked.

"I will stay in the collective's apartment so we can work all the time." My mother pursed her lips.

"You are going to make films. That's great," my father said. "That's what she wants to do, she should do it."

"You are going to make films with Carrie?" my mother said. My mother loved my best friend Carrie. It is ridiculous how an adult decides to take to one of your friends. A bit of eye contact and a thank-you from a teenager is a kind of miracle I suppose. I knew any harebrained scheme became instantly credible to her if I included Carrie.

"Yes, Carrie. And others." They looked at me and leaned in. They were saying yes, but they expected some detail, so out it came: inventing, as I had just learned to do, a story about myself. A lie of invention, a lie about yourself, should not be called a lie. It needs a different word. It is maybe a fabule, a kind of wish-story, something almost true, a mist of the possible where nothing was yet there. With elements both stolen and invented—which is to say, invented. And it has to feel more dream than lie as you speak it. I could see it ribbon from my head like an image in a zoetrope. "We are remaking lost and never-completed films. Like *The Apostle of Vengeance* by William

S. Hart. *The Dream Girl* by Cecil B. DeMille. *The Serpent* by Raoul Walsh. *The Eternal Mother* by D. W. Griffith. Maybe every Alice Guy-Blaché short made before 1920. There are a huge number of famous silent films that don't exist anymore. The nitrate ignited or they were just trashed. Destroyed. Only titles, descriptions, and some stills survive. I want to make these films. Enact—but also interpret, because what reenactment doesn't involve an interpretation—the films as described. That is the summer project of the collective." See? I made it up on the spot and I already wanted to do it. My parents had no further questions at this moment. Just the benign smiles they always got when I started talking in detail about films. Like they wished they found it interesting so they almost did.

"But you will be in New York City by the time school begins, of course," my mother said. I was supposed to start at NYU in the fall.

"Of course," I said, and maybe I believed it.

"Orientation is August twenty-fifth."

I nodded.

"When do you leave?"

"Today—this week anyway."

Later, as I packed a suitcase in my room, my father knocked on my door. Did I need anything, anything at all? I looked at him. An Eclair ACL 16 mm camera, 16 mm film, a Nagra IV-STC, a good microphone, a Magnasync Moviola upright editing console, a Betacam video camera, a Sony VTR tape-editing deck, and videocassettes. But I wasn't sure what I would do with the equipment, as I planned to return to the Brentwood house with the pool and the huge filmmaker. My father wrote me a check for these things, trusting me to buy them. And I intended to buy what I described to him. I cashed the check and stored the money in a sock in a side pocket of my suitcase. Someday I would get my gear. But now? I wasn't—as it happened—ready to make films. I was still just thinking, wishing, hoping. Pretending to make films.

Things I now had to figure out after my lie:

1. NYU at the end of August—Can I defer? By when? Would I just inform my mother that I had deferred, after it was done, a fait accompli? Yes.
2. Mailing address. My mother will want a mailing address. Can you get a P.O. box without being there in person? And then forward the mail?
3. Ditto for phone number. However, I can say there is no phone, I will call you from a pay phone once a week.
4. Not to be seen lurking about Los Angeles by parents, friends of parents, friends.

I moved into his Brentwood house with one suitcase, five notebooks, a box of videocassettes, and a stack of paperbacks (including *Spectropia: Or, Surprising Spectral Illusions Showing Ghosts Everywhere and of Any Colour*, a reproduction of an 1864 novelty book of optical illusions that gave my film collective its name). I parked my Rabbit in the garage, closed the garage door, and didn't take it out again for nine months.

I had my own room, because of the times he needed to sleep by himself. But I spent many nights with him. He worked, mostly writing screenplays and treatments, and I read on the couch, screenplays or whatever I found on his shelves. I read *Red Harvest* by Dashiell Hammett and I read all the plays of Shakespeare. I read *Swann's Way* (in translation), several Booth Tarkington novels, and I read a tattered paperback of

Jealousy by Robbe-Grillet. There was only one thing I missed. I wanted to watch movies with him. The Brentwood house had a mini screening room, with a projector for films but also a VCR and a videodisc player. People sent him packages of movies, and many of them sat unopened. He rarely wanted to watch films. Later I would come to understand why, but at this stage in my life I needed to watch everything. This small difference in appetites was my only real complaint. He didn't stop me from watching them on my own, but I wanted to do it with him. I longed to watch movies—black-and-white movies, Technicolor movies, glistening silent movies, short and long movies, old and contemporary movies, funny slapstick movies, deep subtitled movies, glorious American movies—in the dark, with him. I wanted to share that love with him.

On one of those special nights when he did want to see a film, we watched a hand-marked videotape of Terrence Malick's *Badlands.* He asked me if I'd seen it and I pretended I hadn't because I didn't want to spoil the fun of his introducing it to me. It's the story of two American kids, Kit and Holly, who calmly fall into a killing spree as if it were a Sunday matinee. We watched, but he didn't say anything as he watched. I was disappointed. I wanted him to point out what he thought worked so well in the film. I wanted him to say, instructively, knowingly, "See how he uses long shots? Kit gets farther away from us as the film progresses." But he did not.

There is a scene in which Holly uses a stereoscope and we get her point of view as she looks at photos. We hear her voice-over as she looks at the hovering vintage images of strangers and wonders:

> "It sent a chill down my spine, and I thought, where would I be this very moment if Kit had never met me? . . . Or killed anybody? This very moment . . . If my mom had never met my dad? If she'd of never died? . . . And what's the man I'll marry going to look like?

What's he doing right this minute? . . . Is he thinking about me now, by some coincidence, even though he doesn't know me? Does it show on his face?"

This:
I used to have a View-Master with various "sets" of viewing reels that each contained twelve related photo slides. You pushed the plastic-and-cardboard reels into the View-Master and clicked through the illuminated photos. I had the Wonders of the World set. I looked at those a lot, but the ones I loved best were the slides of the Apollo landing. The capsule tiny and glowing on the screen. The men fragile and unprotected in their tinfoil suits. I imagined climbing into that capsule, and being the first person to do it, shooting past the clouds, the ship burning away, and then the world beneath me. Would I be brave enough to do it? What did they think about, the very first time they shot into space?

But also this:
Holly didn't love Kit anymore, and the movie shows us that through Holly's fantasizing about her future husband, obviously not Kit. It shows us how dreamy and self-centered she is, and it shows us the flatness of her moral imagination. Part of it is in Holly's monotoned-but-childish recitation, and part of it is in the cheerful drum-churn of the soundtrack.

And this:
While I understood the art of Malick's construction, I felt—like a revelation—that I was Holly, unrealized, my future uncertain, all possibility and no accomplishment. I had only dreams and the child-

ishness of yet, yet, yet. My dreams not of future husbands, but of making a film like this one, a film that implicated the viewer even as it delighted her. I blinked and tears blurred my view despite the fact that the filmmaker had gone to great lengths not to create a feeling of emotional sympathy with Holly and Kit. I blinked but I did not wipe my eyes; my boyfriend didn't need to know I was crying. What a mystery the way things act on us, like secret messages just to you as you sit in the dark. We watched the film together, but my feelings were private, unshared and unspoken.

We saw films together only a handful of times. Much more often I would see a movie on my own after he fell asleep. Sometimes I watched a video or I would watch what was on the Z Channel. But just as often I would get stoned and look at reruns of Rod Serling's creepy '70s TV show *Night Gallery.* One night, when very stoned, I watched a plant-loving Elsa Lanchester grow out of the ground after she refuses a developer's insistence that she move. He kills her, and her revenge is to come back as one of her plants. It terrified me and I had to sneak into his room. I startled him as he slept. My plan was to sleep near him, not wake him. But his breath caught and he sputtered awake.

"What's wrong?" he said in a stern rasp.

"Nothing, I'm sorry."

"It's the middle of the night, Meadow." He sighed.

"I'm so sorry."

"You can't do this to me. I'll be up for hours." He hoisted himself up on his pillows and rubbed his eyes.

"I was scared," I said, and I detested my own words as if someone else had spoken them. Then I stood there and waited for him to soften or explain. Instead he pulled the chain on his fringed reading lamp and picked up a book from his bed table. He opened it and began to read. I waited for him to look up or speak but he did not. Finally I went to my own room. That was the only time I remember him getting angry with me. Or that is the angriest he ever got, as far as I was concerned.

I'm not complaining, though. He was a great companion. He recited Shakespeare. He spoke it so beautifully in his deep, resonant voice. Words seemed to linger in the air after he stopped speaking. He had a precise, actor-trained memory—nothing I said to him was ever forgotten. He wove every moment into the last moment, never stopped connecting things. I think I will never get over what it was like to be with someone who remembered everything. He could make a fork disappear into the air with a wave of a napkin and the lift of an eyebrow. He talked as he worked his magic and he revealed his trickery, which only makes the trick work better. He never bored me.

One of the best things about him was his letters. He wrote love letters to me. I found them in my books. He would leave for the day, and I would read about my lips, my laugh, my gentle touch. My long legs in shorts and loose socks. Yes, mostly they were about my body, but a body is part of you, there is no getting around it even if you want to. Besides, I liked the attention to my body details. Strange as it seems, I hadn't had that before. All my life I had felt like a brain with two incidental arms and two useful legs growing out of it. For whatever reason, boys my age never approached me.

He wrote me letters nearly every day. Sometimes I wrote back. I reported on what I had read or seen or thought about that day. What I liked and why. I saved his letters in a small wicker box under my bed. I have no idea what he did with my letters.

We did this for nine months, the watching and the books and the tricks and the letters. I swam in the pool. I didn't rush into the future.

Once a week I took a deep breath and called my parents, spinning a story of a cross-country trip leading to the factory in Gloversville where I spent my summer and then winter making films. No, thank you, I didn't need more money, I had told them in late August, but I did need to defer college for a year so I could finish making these films. They protested feebly about delaying school but then insisted on sending money. (This is the type of parents they were.) Instead of making films, I lived with my enormous boyfriend. I inhaled filmmaking in the air I breathed. I ingested it; I took it inside me. I spent my days imagining films that I wanted to make while at night I loved my boyfriend.

Sometimes I wanted to go out into the world with him. To dinner or to a party. I was reckless like that. But he didn't let me. He did not want anyone to know about us, because he felt it would be misunderstood. He knew how people can be, and how much it can cost a person. "You have no idea what it feels like," he said, "I want to spare you that," and I believed it.

"I'm stronger than you think," I said, but I wasn't so sure. I tried out the idea as I spoke it. Maybe I really was.

Mostly we were happy, in the way you can be happy when you know something won't last forever. The way you can clutch the moment deeply and without holding back. "I love you," I whispered to him. "And I love you, darling," he said. "That is what this is, love," he said, as if he couldn't quite believe it.

Then the last day came—ready or not—but of course I didn't know it was the last day at the time.

We have lunch by the pool. The sunlight sparkles on the water. He looks pale, and somehow almost frail. He hardly eats or drinks, and lately his face has become gaunt, as though his full cheeks were hanging down from his bones. I should have guessed what was coming, for he surely does.

"Wonderful news," he says.

"What?"

"My picture will be financed. Things are falling into place. I just have to stay alive long enough to make the damn thing."

"Stop that—you'll be able to do it. You are ready."

"Yes, I am. I feel as if I can make my greatest film. I know exactly how I want to do it. I've been dreaming of it for years. And at last, I get a chance."

I see him momentarily perk up, excited at the thought.

"After all this time, I am finally making another film," he says. But as he exhales, I can see something else, some trickery below the surface.

He never made the movie. We all know that now. But about that very last day, the very last night:

He is going on *The Merv Griffin Show*. He will talk about the new project, get things heated up. He has some backing, but he still needs more. They use him, the wonderfully witty and entertaining old has-been, and he will use them back, sneak in his agitprop on his own behalf. "That," he says, "is how this town works, and I have always understood how this fucking town works."

I watch him on TV. He is eloquent and generous. I watch him and feel lucky.

It doesn't go the way he expected. He comes home from the studio, white-faced and damp. He shambles in on his cane, falls back onto the couch with a moan.

"How did it go?" I ask.

"A disaster. I went in to do my song and dance, but instead I was a dignified old man, elegiac and stinking of the grave."

"Nonsense," I say. "I thought you were magnificent." I sit down on the floor at his feet. I undo his shoes. His heavy wide feet are white and swollen. I take one foot in my hand: I feel tender toward this heavy small thing, the weight of a lifetime always pushing down on it. I press it with my palm for a minute, one and then the other. His feet are oddly soft and uncallused, but they also seem useless, abandoned somehow. I wrap my arm across his legs and push my face against his knees.

"I am sorry," he says.

I pull back from his legs and look up at him. His face is barely visible across the landscape of his body.

"What?"

"I have nothing I can give you, no money. I have ex-wives and a wife, actually, and children. And very little I haven't spent. It is possible you will get a window of attention, and you can do something with that. Believe me, the attention can hurt, so you must make sure you get something out of it."

I start to cry. He stops talking and places his hand on my head.

"Can you shut up? Please?" I say. He sighs and I help him to his bed.

You can guess the rest. What happened to him was on the news.

The housekeeper comes into my room and wakes me up. Her face is sweaty, and she seems to tremble as she speaks. She tells me she has called 911, and that the ambulance is about to take him away. I scramble out of bed and stop at the doorway, unsure what to do. I watch them take him out on a gurney. He is white and nonresponsive, his massive body already collapsing into itself, looking passed and dead to me. The housekeeper says, "I am calling his family." And she disappears into his room, closing the door behind her. Soon—within an hour—people will go to the hospital. Then they will descend on this place: a relative, an agent, the press. I pull on my jeans. I had slept in an oversized Mercury Theatre jersey, which I now use as a tunic shirt. I need, it seems to me, to get out of there fast. I pull a suitcase from the closet, the very same one I had brought over after a few days of living with him.

I look around my room. Here is what I take: my clothes, my videotapes, my notebooks, and a few little souvenirs he gave me (some lacquered balls for juggling, a deck of cards, a lobby card for the last of his great films, an annotated copy of *King Lear* with his small neat notes in the margins along with the *King Lear* screenplay he wrote but never shot, a long Nubian dress, and a vintage Mark IV viewfinder on a lanyard). I also take the wicker box filled with his love letters. Of course I do. I make the bed. I close the closet door. There is no sign of me in the bedroom or anywhere in the house. I walk to the back door in case someone is arriving. I hesitate as I pass his room. I push open the door. The bed is a mess; as they pulled him onto the gurney they must have dragged all the bedclothes off. I look at his dresser where he left his watch and his pocket notebook. His vest and scarf hang from a chair back, just as he left them last night. I pick up the scarf and hold it to my face. I can smell his hair oil and aftershave. I drape it gently across the dresser. I ought to leave. A tumbler of liquor on the end table by the bed. He couldn't sleep so he drank and read. Next to the book are some scribbled notes and his sturdy fountain pen. I pick up the pen—it is green resin, fat and substantial in my hand. Just one small thing of his. I put it in my pocket. I slip out the sliding back door to the patio. I open the garage, throw my suitcase into the backseat of my Rabbit, and go.

I drive to Brentwood Village and call my parents on a pay phone. "Everything is fine," I say. "I just wanted to say hello." The radio in my car is already reporting that my boyfriend was pronounced dead at UCLA Medical Center. I stare out the window and listen to the valedictory obituary, something carefully constructed long ago and updated each year until it would finally be read on the air. Nobody had really wanted to see him lumber onto TV sets to talk. They had been waiting to pronounce him dead, to bring to a proper close his long American story.

I head straight to the camera supply store with my father's wad of cash and pick out some gear. Then onto Route 15 and then 40, by myself, driving to New York. I drive until I reach a motel just over the New Mexico border. It isn't until I collapse on the motel bed and switch on the TV that I feel it. I watch the special report, and I see him young and beautiful. Close to my age, in fact. And out of that young man comes my boyfriend's voice. I cry and hold the motel pillow against my face. I see his face as he lay on the gurney, and it is that image that makes me feel how lost he is to me. How much I will miss him. How much I will always love him. I sleep.

In the early-morning light, I sit on the motel bed and examine the equipment I have bought. I read instructions; I put pieces together. I lift the camera and look through the viewfinder.

I will make my trip and I will also make a film diary of my trip called *A Film Made to Cover for the Lies I Told My Parents.* My first film since high school. I will make film after film that spring and summer. In the fall I will briefly attend the college with the excellent undergraduate film program. My life will begin to take an ordinary shape, as if the past nine months never happened. As if it were a dream, an unfinished film, a lost radio broadcast.

I am a hungry young woman, just like thousands of other young women. But I have some ideas. A directive, of sorts. I will work and I will work. I have said this is a love story, and indeed it begins that way: my love of cinema, as pure as any I have known. Making, watching, thinking cinema. I become a machine of cinema, a monocular creator. It is as though I had been a drawn-back rubber band my whole life, seeming to pull farther and farther away from the life I wanted, until I am released and then I come forward with a huge snap. I am no longer wishing; I am doing. What do I do? I make films that excite and please me, occasionally frustrate me, and for a long while that feels like enough. Later I will find this meager in a number of ways. Later I will see it as self-aggrandizing, problematic, not just useless but hurtful. Later I will quit.

But there is still a bit more of this inaugural story to tell, the end of the story of how I began. A narrative thread that I have left hanging. So here it is: a year after he died, I was working late and began to think about him. There had been a big retrospective of his work, and there was a flurry of articles in the paper. I knew more about him and his work than all of these people. I considered my future and my opportunities. I took the wicker box out. I read the letters. They were beautifully written: some were a little erotic, some were funny. They could be tastefully edited, in any case.

I took them out on the fire escape with me, and read them as I smoked. I could have shown them to an agent, published them, offered them to the highest bidder. That's what he had suggested—no, urged—me to do. If I approached it all in the right way, the interest in me could lead to a chance to make a film. One little chance to take that attention and use it to my advantage. It wasn't a sure thing, but it was like a puzzle for me to figure out: here was how I thought the world worked; here was how I thought I fit in it.

I also could burn them, one by one, like a girl in a black-and-white movie. Every last one.

But instead I perched on the steps under a shimmer of deep-night summer stars, and I started once again at the beginning. I read one, folded it, and put it away. I read another, then another, then another. When I got to the end, I put them back in the box, closed the box, and put them away, my secret forever.

I told you this was a love story.

—Meadow Mori, 11/5/2014

Meadow Mori was born in Los Angeles in 1966. She has directed and produced feature-length documentaries, essay films, shorts, and video installations including Kent State: Recovered *(1992), which was nominated for an Academy Award for Best Feature Documentary;* Play Truman *(1993);* Portrait of Deke *(1987), which won a BATT Silver Medal and the jury prize at the Seattle Film Festival;* Inward Operator *(1998), which was a jury prize winner at the Sundance Festival, and* Children of the Disappeared *(2001). Parts of* A Film Made to Cover for the Lies I Told My Parents, *the making of which is described in the post above, can be viewed* ***here****. Her reconstructions of famous lost films (made in 1984–1985) can be viewed* ***here****.*

Related links

Carrie Wexler, **A Conversation with Mira Shirlihan: Number 8**
Meadow Mori interview, **Sound on Sound, June 1999**
Meadow Mori film channel at **Gleaners.net** and **Vimeo**

Comments (866)

Mouchette Jan 6
This is so disgusting.

Sleepovergirl Jan 6
She was Carrie Wexler's best friend, but she barely mentions her here.

LegacyAdmit 12:15 am

What happened to the letters?! Did she finally publish them?

Eds 12:30 am

A Carrie Wexler interview can be read **here.**

Limpidpools 12:33 am

Is it just me, or is this a straight-up star fucking/sleep your way up story? Yay, feminism. Not.

Limpidpools→Mouchette 12:40 am

Like you said, disgusting.

Mouchette→Limpidpools 12:41 am

I meant a teenager sleeping with an old obese man. And calling that a "love story." Call it whatever you want. It's just sad.

dogyears→Limidpools 7:22 am

Nice to be so judgey about a great artist. Yay, female solidarity.

Limpidpools→dogyears 9:30 am

Who says I am a woman. #feminismfail

TheQualiaConundrum22→LegacyAdmit 9:33 am

She has never published them. She also stopped making films a few years ago. She had some sort of breakdown.

Eberhardfaber 9:37 am

I want to read the letters. I wonder if she will publish them now that she has told everyone about this relationship. I wouldn't be surprised if this was a setup for an announcement of a publishing deal.

deranger 10:02 am

So cynical! Don't you think the point of this is that she doesn't plan on exploiting the letters? That she got what she got on her own. His help to her was inspiration. What she did is unrelated to the famous boyfriend.

Makemoney 12:42 pm
I didn't believe it until I saw this with my own eyes! I work from home and make $1050 a week doing easy transcription and data entry. Go to www.workfromhome.com and stop struggling.

films4freedom 1:00 pm
If you like Meadow Mori's films, you should check out theendpoint dot net. We aggregate nonfiction and essay films that spotlight the struggle against corporate imperialism and environmental degradation. Many important documentaries all streamed for free.

RitaHayworth 3:30 pm
So she fucked Orson Welles. Who hasn't?

Rulalenska 3:37 pm
What happened with Carrie Wexler?

IrrealisMood→RitaHayworth 3:38 pm
You are killing me Rita. I laughed so hard I almost choked when I read this.

Canyouhearmenow→Rulalenska 3:39 pm
They don't speak because Wexler screwed her over. Neither Mori or Wexler will discuss it.

Limpidpools 3:45 pm
She hardly followed in his footsteps. Making those horrible films. Those distortive, pretentious documentaries. She is a tasteless, self-righteous defender of monsters. And it turns out she is the biggest woman-in-Hollywood cliché of all . . . expand comment to read more

deranger→Limpidpools 3:49 pm
I love when the mens start explaining how feminism works to the womens. Thank you. Whatever origins Mori has had, she came to be a fascinating artist. Why is it that only men get to have colorful pasts?

Limpidpools→deranger 3:51 pm
Men can't have opinions about female behavior, huh? Well the jokes on you, since I am actually a woman.

JennyW28 3:55 pm
The Children of the Disappeared is an incredible film.

rookiemistake 4:00 pm
I wonder why she never re-enacted Citizen Kane?

dogyears→Limpidpools 4:02 pm
No one cares if you are a man or a woman because you are simply a troll. #dontfeedthetroll

BarbiesCervix 4:02 pm
People, I am calling BS on this whole essay. Welles famously lived and died on Stanley Avenue in Hollywood, not in Brentwood. Everybody knows that. Even the death date is off. She is pulling your chain.

show more comments in this thread

PART TWO

JELLY AND JACK

1985

Jelly picked up the handset of her pink plastic Trimline phone and the dial tone hummed into her ear. She tilted the earpiece slightly away from her, and she heard the sad buzz of a distant sound seeking a listener. How many times had she fallen asleep after she said goodbye and not managed to get the thing on the cradle. The little lag when his phone was hung up but you were still on the line, in a weird half-life of the call, semiconnected, followed by the final late disconnection click, then silence, and then if you didn't hang up, sharp insistent beeps. These were the odd ways the phone communicated with sounds: urgent beeps to say hang up, long-belled rings to say answer, rude blasts of a busy signal to say no. The phone always telling her things. She pushed the eleven buttons—the 1, the area code, the number, zeroing in, the nearly infinite combinations ousted—her fingertips not needing to feel the grooves of the numbers, but feeling them nevertheless. So many distractions, unneeded and unwanted. She had to concentrate to keep the information away. There was a bird outside, trilling at her. It was at least fifteen feet from the closed window, but it still bothered her. It must be in the Chinese oak in the courtyard. The ring of another person's phone sounded so hopeful, and then it grew lonelier. It lost possibility, and you could almost see the sound in an empty house.

He didn't have an answering machine. Make a note of that. A distinction. You can let it ring all day. Is that true? Has anyone ever tried it? The plastic rubbed against her jaw and her ear. She tilted it away again. If she lay on her side and let the receiver rest on her head, using a hand only for balance, she could talk for hours.

"Hello?" said a male voice that cleared itself as it spoke, so the end of the word had a cough pushing through it. Then came another cough. Was it the first time he had spoken today? Or had she woken him up? Roused from sleep was a special, intimate opportunity. But it carried high risk also. The woken person could sometimes start out frightened or vulnerable and then grow angry as the reality of the call's interruption hit his conscious mind. It had happened to Jelly once: "Why the fuck are you disturbing my sleep? You have no idea how hard it is for me to fall asleep. And now. Well now I am awake for the goddamned duration, you bitch." Jelly couldn't get through a feeling like that. Not even Jelly. But this man just finished coughing and waited. She closed her eyes and focused on the white of ease, of calm, of joy. The pure and loving human event of calling a stranger, reaching across the land and into a life.

"Hello," she said. Her voice sliding easily through the "l"s, to the waiting, hopeful "o." She always takes her time. Nothing makes people more impatient than rushing.

"Who is this?"

"It's Nicole."

"Nicole? Nicole who? I think you have the wrong number."

This was a crucial moment.

"Is this Mark Washborn?"

"Uh, no. I mean, Mark. It isn't. Who is this again?"

"Nicole. I'm a friend of Mark's. I thought this was his new number."

"No. That's weird. I know Mark. I mean, he's a good friend of mine."

"Oh my. How awkward. I am so, so sorry I disturbed you, uh . . ." She rarely used "uh," but it was an important wordish sound that introduced a powerful unconscious transaction. Used correctly, not as a habit or a rhythmic tic, it invited another to complete the sentence. An intricate conjoining, it was an opening without content, just the pull of syntax and the human need to complete.

"Jack. Jack Cusano."

"Jack Cusano? Not Jack Cusano, the record producer?"

"Uh, yeah."

"Jack Cusano who composes film scores. The gorgeous work you did on those Robert DeMarco films."

"That's right." He laughed. His laugh cleared out his throat a bit more. She lay back on her pillow, held the phone so it barely touched her cheek. She imagined her voice going into the transmitter, sound waves being turned into electrical pulses, up the wires to the phone lines to a switching station, turned into microwaves speeding across the country with the memory—the imprint—of her exact tone, her high and low frequencies, her elegant modulations, to the switching station in Santa Monica, sending electric current up the PCH to a Malibu beach house and into Jack's receiver—undoubtedly a sleek black cordless phone. So fast too: instantly made back into a sound wave by the tiny amplifier near his ear. All that way, all those transformations, but no distortions. A miracle of technology. The sound was as clear as speech in a room. She could, she could—amazing—hear the ocean in the background. A gull, the sound of water pulling back from beach. She swore she could hear the sun shining through his west-facing windows.

JELLY AND OZ

Many years before Jelly called Jack, before she had begun phoning men for love (not work), and before she had recovered her sight, she had fallen in love with Oz. She met him in the summer of 1970 at the Center for the Blind.

Oz was bald and a lurching, lumbering six four. But his hands were soft and she liked the push of sweat with the air-faded tinge of clove that she got when he put his arm across her shoulders. Jelly was more than a foot shorter than Oz, and his arm across her shoulders was a natural fit. Later she would discover that the faint clove she got under—or right up alongside of—the sweat was from an old sachet that she found when she pulled open his undershirt drawer to put away the laundry she had washed and folded for him. It shocked her to see this girlish thing, an ancient silk square with a ribbon. She only saw it as a bruise of pink, but she could feel the slight catch that comes in the weave of older silk fabric. The sachet must have been in the bureau when he got it from the Salvation Army. Because Oz wouldn't buy a sachet of spices and put it in his drawer, would he? That seemed very unlikely. But surely he noticed the scent—his blindness made every scent noticeable. Distracting, even—one got so sensitive, and the overlay of scents could be deceptive, puzzling. Jelly had slowly stopped calling a smell "good" or "bad." Instead she thought of them as "real" or "cover" smells. She just wanted everything to smell as it was. Actually. An armpit should smell of sweat and hair and skin. A mouth should be clean but not minty. Hair should smell slightly vegetal, plantish. And a room should smell like old wood. A candle like melted beeswax. The street like rain and leaves. The backyard of grass, earth, flowers. Walking into a store and getting the rank sting of ammonia under fake pine could make her feel ill in a matter of minutes. She would leave gasping for air, clutching a hand to her nostrils.

Even the real smells overwhelmed her lately. She could barely walk past her neighbor's house with its ridiculous lilac tree. What kind of tree is this, with its heavy sudden bursts of overripe flowers? It too made her bring her fingers to the base of her nose. Just thinking about the rotting blossoms brought back the dense thickness of the odor. She had taken to crossing the street and pointedly facing away when she couldn't avoid walking in the direction of that house and that tree.

Oz gradually taught her the phone stuff. He had a kid's red plastic whistle that he got from a Cap'n Crunch box, and he showed her how to blow pitch tones into the phone. Oz had perfect pitch and on his own could whistle the unlocking combination: seventh-octave E at 2600 hertz. Short bursts achieved with tongue against lips and pushed over-and-out air, or by covering the second hole on the toy whistle. ("What's a hertz?" she asked. "A vibration," he said. "It is all waves and vibrations.") He could connect to anyone anywhere without any charges to his line. Jelly did not have perfect pitch, but she learned how to use the whistle. Eventually she even had a blue box to make tones, given to her by one of Oz's phone friends, the phone phreaks. The other phreaks were much younger than Oz and still in college. They had learned to make handheld boxes for what Oz could do by ear and mouth alone. Only Oz could do that. To hear him whistle a series of tones into the phone was impressive, but it was more than a trick. He could talk to her about the intricacies of the phone system like he was a line engineer: "single-frequency dialing system" and "hook dialing" and "Strowger switch." Or the thing that Oz explained made it all possible: the #4 (then #5) crossbar switch, the innovation to a mechanical electronic switching system all done with tone codes. The world connected by phone lines and Oz could go through it all by whistling. Sometimes he would get to a person deep in the network, an inward operator, and ask her to connect him to any line he wanted. But his favorite thing was reaching an electronic switching station. Then he didn't have to speak. He could use the sharp whistle tones to get wherever he wanted to go.

Oz had sat her down and showed her: seven short whistled tones. There was a click, another click. A distant ring, a connection sound. Another tone. Connected to a switching station in New York. Another series of whistles, and patched through to a switching station in London. Then Chicago. You could hear the response on the line—the gap, the distance—in the lag before the clicks registered. Then the other phone, Oz's second line rang.

"Pick it up." She picked it up. A distant click. "Hello, girl," Oz said into his phone. Less than a moment and it crackled on through the speaker by Jelly's ear. Thousands of miles, across a sea, contained in that slight lag.

"Hello, Oz," Jelly said.

"Your voice just went to London and back to reach me." There was no reason for it, just the fun of imagining sounds bouncing across the world in seconds. World whistling, he called it. Sometimes Oz was mischievous with his skills—he told her how he once walked past a man talking loudly on a pay phone. He did his sharp whistle and instantly disconnected the call. He could hear the man say, "Hello?

Hello?" But mostly Oz played with phones because he liked losing himself in the vast network of connections and he liked how he felt as a sound from his lips vibrated across the globe.

Oz sometimes patched into an open-sleeve conference circuit that allowed two or more people on a secret untracked and unbilled line. The phone phreaks—all those college boys—called this warbling. Chatting really, about phones mostly, with Ditto in Los Angeles and Mo in Seattle. David in England. They were united in the high of subverting Ma Bell. For its own sake, and also to find one another. Everyone used nicknames or fake names because this was illegal. Go-to-jail illegal, even though it felt like a harmless prank. So the warbling also concerned not getting caught, who got caught, who was being taped and recorded. Oz, whose real name was William, became the Great Oz because he was the first and the best, and Jelly, whose real name was Amy, was called Jelly Doughnut because Oz said she was soft and round and even sweeter on the inside. All the kids wanted to talk to Oz, but the funny thing was that Oz never had much interest in talking. He liked the tones and the mechanics and the distant clicks, whistling from one responsive line to another. But Jelly was different. Jelly liked to talk. Jelly could talk. She loved to patch into the open-sleeve circuit with the others. Their voices hanging in space; Jelly listening and laughing and recognizing. She was the only—the only—woman who phone phreaked. These were shy, awkward men. They gave her lots of attention, which she enjoyed, but they were never ever nasty.

Oz did not like the time she spent talking to other phreaks. At first he was proud of her, but then he became jealous. He wouldn't admit it, though. Eventually Oz started leaving the house when she got into a conversation and not returning until long after she had finished. He said that he didn't mind, but hearing the talking gave him a headache.

In the years after he had left her, Jelly would trace the way they unraveled in her mind. She thought if she could figure out the place they came apart, she could fix it and he would return to her. Being left was bottomless. Not only in the moment, but the way it gave the lie to all the moments that preceded it. Is that true? Is love real and true only if it continues? Was it revealed to be "not love" when it unraveled?

JELLY AND JACK

This was another crucial moment, and she knew that she could not initiate anything more. She had to wait for him to open it further. She could not get anxious. Jelly held the receiver with her left hand and leaned back on the pillows. She crossed her legs at the ankles, pulled her kimono robe over her knees. She was a little cold. She wanted to be in that room with the beach smell and the sun on the windows. She waited, closed her eyes. She listened to the quiet line. She heard him cough.

"So how do you know Mark?" he said. He sounded friendly and a bit amused now.

Jelly made an "em" sound in her throat, with a little push through her nose. It sounded thoughtful, vaguely affirmative. She knew that even if she had to say "no" at some point, she would say it low and round and long so it sounded as if it had a yes in it somehow. Or an up-pitched down-pitched mmm-mmm, like a hill. The hums take you for a ride, just under the nose with the mouth closed.

"We talk a lot. Sunday-morning talks, late-Monday talks. Middle of the night talks. Sometimes we talk for hours."

"Yeah? What about? Are you a girlfriend?"

Jelly laughed. These men all had "a" girlfriend, meaning several at any time. She never wanted to be one of a number. What Jelly wanted was to be singular. Not even "a friend." She wanted a category of her own construction. Something they never knew existed.

"No," she said. "Actually he talks to me about his writing. He reads me what he has written that day. I listen and tell him what I think. He says it gives him motivation, knowing I will call and he has to have something good to read to me."

"Really?"

"He never told you about me?" she said.

"No, but I don't listen to everything Mark says. He tends to fill the air with static. It is ambient noise at a certain point. You know, busy but easily ignored."

She laughed. He laughed. Jelly sat up, stretching her back straight, feeling her spine arrange itself in a line above her hips. She switched the phone to the other side and relaxed the tension in her neck. She took a breath. So much of this involved waiting, silence, timing.

"So I have to go, Jack. I am so sorry I disturbed you."

"No. I mean, no problem. I had to get up. I usually don't sleep this late. But I was working all night. On this piece."

"You probably want to make some coffee and get back to work."

"Yeah, but not really."

"Is it for a film score?"

"You know, it isn't. It is just a thing I had in my head and now I'm playing with it. Using the keyboard. It will end up in a film score at some point, I'm guessing."

"Really? You don't watch the film and then compose to it?" she said.

"Yeah, I do. But I also import melodies and musical ideas I have. On file, so to speak."

"Fascinating."

"So, would you like to hear some of it?"

"Really?"

"Sure."

"Oh wow, I would really love that. Yes, please."

"Okay, good." He laughed. "Hold on," he said.

Jelly closed her eyes again and leaned back. She called this body listening. It was when you surrendered to a piece of music or a story. By reclining and closing your eyes, you could respond without tracking your response. You listened. The opposite were the people who started to speak the second someone finished talking or playing or singing. They practically overlapped the person because they were so excited to render their thoughts into speech. They couldn't wait to get their words into it and make it theirs. They couldn't stand the idea of not having a part in it. They spent the whole experience formulating their response, because their response is the only thing they value. It was a way of consuming the experience or the work. Jelly had a different purpose in listening to anything or anyone. It had something to do with submission, and it had something to do with sympathy. She would lie back and cut off all distraction. The phone was built for this. It had no visual component, no tactile component, no person with hopeful or embarrassed face to read, no scent wafting, no acid collection in the mouth. Just vibrations, long and short waves, and to clutch at them with your own thoughts was just wrong. A distinct resistance to potential. A lack of love, really. Because what is love, if not listening, as uninflected—as uncontained—as possible.

But while Jack played his music for her she did not think about listening. She took a deep breath, relaxed, and let the music find her body. Jelly thought about things only after she got off the phone. When she went over what was said so she could remember it. She took notes on details, but the best way to imprint something in memory was to listen in the first place.

"So that's it," he said, and he let out a tight, nervous laugh.

Jelly opened her eyes, expelled a small sigh into the receiver. "It's wonderful," she said.

"Yeah?" he said.

"Yes," she said. "Thank you."

"Good," he said.

"There were these little leaps with each reprise."

"That's right," he said.

Only after she was done listening did she form her response. And it worked like this: find the words—out of the millions of words—that would describe the experience. That part, the search for the right language, was fun and almost like a puzzle. You thought of the word but then you felt it in your mouth, pushed breath into it and said it out loud. The sound of it contained the real meaning—she had to hear the words to know if she had it right. Then as it hung there she revised it, re-attacked it, applied more words to it.

"And it gave me a remarkable feeling of lifting. Not being picked up or climbing. Not even like rising in an elevator," she said. "Or an escalator. Not quite. More float in it. Maybe like . . . levitating."

Jack laughed. "You levitated listening to my little piece. Right on."

It did feel like levitation. Levitating through listening. Waves of sound. Waves on the ocean. Floating on the water. And floating on sound waves: levitation. What Jack didn't know was how easily this came to her.

"I have to go, Jack. I'm afraid I'm late."

"Oh no, really?" he said. She heard the hard fizzle of a strike and then a sharp breath followed by a blowing out: lighting a cigarette. She knew the sounds people made on the phone: the bottle unscrewed or uncorked followed by the pour of liquid over ice and the cracking of the ice. The sip—so slow it was painful, the delicate and distant sound of a swallow. And this sound, lighting a cigarette. But with a match, not a lighter. He was a constant smoker who used matches instead of a lighter, which made him a certain kind of person. Because a match had drama, a match left you with a flame to shake or blow out. And a match left a pleasant phosphorus smell lingering in the air.

"So nice to talk with you this morning, nice to meet you, Jack," she said.

"The pleasure, Nicole, is mine. So when can we talk again? Can I call you sometime?"

Jelly sat up. Held the phone back for a minute. She moved slowly in these moments. The giveaway was not in his request. The giveaway was in that he used her name. She had him.

"I do have to run. I promise I will call you soon," she said.

"I look forward to it. Anytime," Jack said.

"Goodbye," she said.

"Bye."

She would not call anytime. She would call on Sunday at the same time. Only Sunday, and it would only be her calling him. Parameters. Predictability. It was the way it worked best for both of them, for this thing they were building between them. He wouldn't understand, he would want to call her, have her number. He would want other times, more frequent talks. But she knew what was best, how to do this. Pace was important. She would make him her Sunday call, and as the weeks of talks would go by, he would accept her terms. He would begin to get great pleasure out of counting the days until Sunday.

JELLY AND OZ

Jelly first met Oz at a group session. He listened to her tell the group what she struggled with. Then she was quiet while various people made suggestions and said mildly supportive things. After it was finished, Oz came over to her. He had his dog with him, and he moved confidently through the space. She waited for him to tell her it would be okay, she would adjust to it all. Instead he told her his name was Oz, and then he said, "I dig your voice. I thought, I would love to hear that girl tell a story. A long sad story with children and animals in it. Like a dream you don't want to wake up from."

"Thank you," she said, and she blushed, a little unprepared for a come-on. In this place. Because that's what it was, wasn't it?

After he left, another girl from group told her about Oz: he had an IQ of 160 and a special genius for electronics. The next time she came to session, he approached her again.

"Hey, there," Oz said.

"Hi, Oz," she said. His high soft voice belied his big physical presence. He sat next to her, a large blur.

"Girl, what can I do to get with you?"

Jelly laughed loud enough for him to hear her.

"You like music?"

"I love music," she said.

"I'd like to listen to some John Coltrane with you. You should come over. We can order some take-out food and listen to Coltrane. You know, like *A Love Supreme*?" She was right, he was into her. It made her nervous. How old was he? She couldn't tell, not with her blurry view. Everyone looked like they had perfect wrinkle-free skin. It was funny not to know how old or how ugly someone was. She had to go on other things, like size and smell. But mostly the sound of a voice, and hey—even what the voice said.

"I don't think I have heard it—"

"Oh girl! Your life is missing something truly beautiful—"

"But I can't tonight. I'm going out with a friend. She is picking me up in a few minutes."

Jelly turning him down did not seem to bother or discourage him at all. Oz was always comfortable, always easy, which was unnerving and oddly seductive. And the next time she was at session, he asked her out again. She wanted to say yes, to date Oz and spend time with Oz and get close to Oz, but she hesitated for what she knew were stupid reasons. She was worried his blindness would make her even more ridiculous. She was on the continuum of blindness: a meningitis infection had nearly killed her and made her blind overnight, but then, slowly, she had recovered some sight. She could see shapes and light and colors, but her blurry vision was also tunneled to 90 degrees, which made getting around without the help of a cane difficult, although she tried anyway. Imagining the way two blind people would look walking down the street wasn't the only thing. Oz had no sight at all, never did. That was a different planet, "never sighted." There was something unbridgeable in it. But that was such a ridiculous idea, as if any human experience couldn't be bridged. How to build the bridge? You talk about it and find the things you understand in it. The pieces of your own experience in the other. That's the bridge, she thought. "Yes," she said. "I would love that."

She went over to Oz's apartment. They ate dinner, and Oz put on the promised John Coltrane LP, which sounded mystical and less romantic than she expected. He smoked a joint, which he assured her helped to make the Love Supreme, helped you hear the holiness in it, the God sounds in it, but she declined. "I'm nervous about getting home," she said.

"So sleep here," he said. She laughed. "What's so funny? It's cool."

"I know," she said. She made a loud exhale sound. "Does it get easier? I mean, I don't like to move from place to place. I could be a shut-in, I think."

"Girl, is this a group session?" he said, laughing. "Are there a bunch of weepy blind folks here?"

"I'm sorry," she said.

"Just relax. You are safe. Crash on the couch and you will have all day to get home tomorrow."

"Okay," she said.

She slept on the couch. Oz didn't offer his bed or even kiss her, which surprised her. She decided that although he was not handsome, he had a solidity that she wanted. He was all in one place, while she felt blurry most of the time. She was glad to sleep there and leave in the morning. The daylight was better for her—she needed contrast. For Oz it didn't matter. The dark was as safe a place as the light.

She asked him over to her place for their second date. She realized an apartment he didn't know would be more awkward for him, but he and the dog quickly found the chair at her little table. She brought him a glass of wine.

"Would you like to hear some music?" she asked.

"I would," he said. She put on *Blue Train*, which she had bought earlier that day. The record store clerk handed it to her when she asked what Coltrane album she should buy.

Right away Oz said, "I love this record," and she could hear the smile in his voice. They smoked some pot and drank some wine. They drank their glasses quickly and she poured more and then started to serve dinner. She realized how much she wanted to talk with Oz, to hear him talk about his life. Was blindness easier on people who never saw? How would Oz or anyone know? What were his dreams like, what were his thoughts when colors were mentioned? Could she ask him or would he just laugh her questions off? Girl, you ask too many questions. The wine made her brave.

"This is maybe too personal," she said, and the word *personal* sounded funny to her. A question about your personhood, your experience as a person. "But when did you realize you were blind? I mean, what blindness is, and that most other people are not blind. Do you remember?" Jelly said this as they ate spaghetti and a slow-cooked sauce that filled the air with basil, tomato, and almost-burned garlic. She had grown the tomatoes on her porch, on scaffolds and ties. More than the tomatoes themselves, she loved the tomato leaves in the early summer. She would water the plants and put her head close. She would inhale the burst of damp leaf with the faint tomato coming off it. A promise of fruit, the green bulbs just starting. As the summer progressed the smell grew more and more pungent. Sometimes she tore a leaf from the plant and took it inside her apartment so she could hold it to her nose and inhale. It relaxed her—such a fresh and earthy smell. How can something so new seem so deep? She knew Oz would appreciate the smell and the taste.

But Oz was not as interested in the food as she expected, as she was.

He was silent, and she was about to say that he didn't have to tell her or talk about this if he didn't want to. She was still figuring things all out, so she thought about it a lot. But instead of saying anything, she let her question hang in the space between them. She ate a bite of the spaghetti. She waited. At last Oz leaned in a little and she heard him let out a long breath.

"My mother," he said slowly, "my Italian mother made me the center of her world. My father was not around, and I was with her constantly. She talked to me, sang to me, and read to me all the time. That was how I learned what blindness was—from the books. We would read about what the little bear saw, and I would ask what that meant. She would try to explain. 'Some people can get the shape of something without touching it.' She didn't overdo it. She didn't tell me more than I needed. She would read a thing and then let me feel it. I didn't mind. At a certain point, she revealed that 'some' people were actually 'most' people."

Oz put his hand on hers. This was not an overtly sexual gesture. It was that being together and not seeing meant more touching, more body communication. The usual way Oz talked—affectedly easy, slangy, slightly stoned—seemed to fall away as he spoke. She knew that meant something. His voice was soft and low, so she had to lean in to hear him.

"But the big boom for me, the first fall in my life was not that I was missing this thing that most others had, but when I asked the question that she had avoided. It took me longer than you might have guessed for me to think to ask this, but it is hard to imagine your mother as really separate from you. It takes time, it takes a moment—a number of moments—of frustration when she doesn't understand you to even imagine that she is not part of you. That she isn't you." Jelly listened very carefully, but he hesitated, stopped telling her the story.

She watched the white blur of Oz pick up his wineglass and take a swallow. Wine was sour and red wine made your lips pucker and feel like they had an edge to them. Red wine found rough surfaces and emphasized them. A crack or dry spot on your lips, patchiness on the surface of your tongue. It surprised her that she was thinking of his mouth and what it would be like to kiss him. She didn't think she felt attracted to him, not yet, but she kept imagining this kiss. Their mouths would both be rough and sour from wine.

She could have said, "What happened?" or "Then what?" But her instinct told her to wait. She knew that would give him room to talk. She should not—could not—rush him.

"One day," Oz said at last, "I sat on her lap as she read. I could feel the words vibrate in her chest, and I felt the smooth pages in front of us. I realized that she got the stories from the page, the smooth pages that gave me nothing. I guess I had known that for a while. But now it all came together. I interrupted her, 'But Mama, can you see?' and she had to admit that, yes, she could see. She was not like me, and I was not like her. I was blind, and she was not."

Jelly reached out her other hand and placed it on his. Still she did not speak, but he understood her reaction to his story. He could feel it in the heat of her hand, hear it in the slight change in her breath. He leaned in so his face was next to hers, and they were breathing close, with their mouth and hair smells next to the food and room smells. He would kiss her, she knew, but for now they were almost motionless. She heard a murmur from one of them. Then she realized that it wouldn't just be a kiss, that they would keep going until they were naked and their bodies entwined. They would hungrily touch every part of each other, and she felt—even before the kiss—breathless and almost faint. She tried not to talk or even think. She tried to stop. She wanted to be still.

CARRIE TAKES THE BUS

1985

Carrie Wexler stood on the lower level of Port Authority and tried not to breathe in carbon monoxide. She waited in a line that snaked from the door marked 21, and beyond the door she could see and smell the idling buses. She put her backpack on her feet and turned up the volume on her Discman. She let the sounds of Rossini's *Il turco in Italia* be the soundtrack to the sightscape of Port Authority. This was the 1950 recording that she had wanted, and her father sent it to her with a note calling it one of her "odd little operas." Her going-to-college gift from him was the state-of-the-art portable CD player. That was a thing with him, "state of the art," and she was happy to play along even though it frequently skipped, unlike her cassette Walkman. Her father was crazy for new technology, and he liked to send his daughter extravagant electronic gifts despite the fact that her mother told her he had recently filed for bankruptcy. Carrie knew he had been broke or on the verge of broke since the divorce ten years earlier, but maybe the divorce was part of the reason he bought her things. He knew and shared her penchant for opera and musicals. Discard the cassettes, he said. He would replace them with the clear, perfect, undistorted Compact Discs. She now had a CD collection building in her dorm room, but many things were not available on CD yet, so she also kept a large collection of cassette tapes. Technological transitions are always messy. And you often have to keep multiple devices and formats. She had video as well as film cameras. In that case the video was distinctly inferior, but the film was so expensive—it limited what you shot, and you had to be so stingy about coverage. Part of the art was making blind decisions. Video is ugly but looser and more forgiving. You could experiment more. The technology would continue to change and improve. She would be drowning in overlapping gear and nothing would be perfect. She admired her father's commitment to the new. That was a strategy for handling it. Just go forward and don't look back.

A woman in the line ahead of her tried to get something out of her suitcase. It was overfilled and the top popped up when she unzipped it. As Carrie listened to the battling back-and-forth goofy frenzy of Rossini, she watched the poor woman trying to shove things back in so the zipper would close.

"Your eye is a camera," Zakrevsky told them in class. "Imagine where your camera would go and where you would put it. What would be outside the frame and what would be inside the frame." She did think of her eyes as a camera, especially when she had music flowing into her ears. It transformed the world into her soundstage. The music directed her eyes somehow. Something about that, how the music informs the looking. But of course films are scored and the music comes later, inspired by the images. The woman sat on her suitcase and her weight finally allowed the zipper a close-enough purchase to pull closed. Carrie checked for her own backpack and gear bag. She had brought a brand-new portable Betacam video camera that she had signed out from school, and she figured she could film some stuff in Meadow's "studio." She could edit what she shot when she got back to the city. Maybe she should have just brought the Super 8. Of course Meadow would be film-only, or whatever she was into now. Her homemade things, her projects.

A push from behind. The line moving. Carrie pulled the headphones down to her neck.

"Go!" the woman behind her hissed. Carrie lifted her bags and tried not to trip as she yanked her ticket out of her pocket while holding everything and moving forward. What is the damn rush? Wait to board after they take the tickets. Then wait three hours on the bus. Then off in Albany and wait for the next bus, which would probably stop in every empty town along the Mohawk River until it finally reached the stop in Fonda where Meadow would pick her up. All day was waiting.

The ride westward on I-90 turned out to be interesting. The highway ran along the rail line and the river, and Carrie could see the Adirondacks to the north and the Catskills to the south. She listened to Maria Callas singing "Vissi d'arte" in 1958. Her eye camera ran along the river in the foreground but then looked up to quilted farmland in the near distance and beyond that the long view of the cloud-dotted Adirondack peaks. The movement was glorious. You could see for miles, and no camera or lens she had ever used was very good at capturing the simultaneous long and short view. Nothing like her eyes.

She got off the bus in Fonda. Like most of the towns along the river, it looked quaint and pretty until you saw it up close. She took off her headphones and looked around. It wasn't just the empty storefronts and the peeling paint. It was the plastic signage glaring from a service station, which also appeared to be the only viable business in town. After the bus pulled away, she could hear the music from the speakers at each corner of the convenience store behind the rows of pumps. The two people who got off the bus with her headed straight inside as if lured in by the sound of the Eagles singing "Hotel California." Carrie followed them. What a strange overlaid place. Meadow had explained to her who lived here.

"Iroquois Nation people, fat white trash people, some leftover rural hippies, and sunburnt farmer people."

"Farmer people?" Carrie laughed into the phone. "You mean farmers?"

"Yes. Weird Germanic farmers. Palatinates, Moravians, some Amish. How and why did they get here?" Meadow said.

"How and why did you get there?" Carrie said. "I'm serious."

"The place I found is amazing. Wait until you see the Volta Cinematograph!" She spread the syllables out so it sounded very European: vol-ta cin-e-ma-to-graph.

"I can't wait."

Volta Cinematograph was James Joyce's failed cinema in Dublin. Meadow had a penchant for failures, a soft spot for them. And there were so many failures to chose from, weren't there? The Mohawk Valley was a collection of failures, or at least of the conspicuous obsolete. All of upstate New York was filled with cities that came to be for a reason, and still had to be even though the reason had long moved on. Syracuse, Buffalo, Albany, Troy, all slowly shrinking. New York City on the other hand was a collection of wins: crack vials and rats aside, make no mistake, the city story was a long march of win. No wonder Meadow liked it up here.

Meadow was late to pick her up, so Carrie wandered around the convenience store contemplating possible beverages. By the cash register was a rack with laminated prayer cards for Kateri Tekakwitha, the "Lily of the Mohawks." Carrie bought one and read the back as she sipped her pale coffee. Kateri was a Mohawk girl who converted to Catholicism. Later as they drove out of Fonda, Meadow explained that not only was there a shrine to Kateri, but also a huge shrine to two martyred seventeenth-century Jesuit priests who became the first American saints. The priests' shrine was on a hill on the south side of the Mohawk River, and Catholic pilgrims came from all over the world to visit it. But nothing beat the growing popularity of Kateri among supplicants. She was depicted as an Indian beauty, like Pocahontas in that kitschy Chapman painting, despite the fact that she was described as "disfigured by smallpox scars." Kateri was recently beatified, which put her on the short list for canonization.

"Is that really what they call it? A short list, like the Oscars?" Carrie said. Meadow drove an old Subaru station wagon. The back was filled with lights, microphones, gels, lens cases, and other shooting gear.

"Sure," Meadow said. "But the Iroquois have their own ideas about who was martyred. The Jesuits cut a swath through here, and there are competing histories standing right next to each other. When you buy a prayer card, you are picking a side, you know."

"Really? Is it offensive?" Carrie held up the card.

"It's complicated," Meadow said. "Did she have a great faith or in converting did she turn her back on her tradition of Long House spiritual practices? Is she the brave orphan who survived smallpox and had a genuine epiphany or is her elevation just the ongoing saga of the spiritual colonization of native peoples?" Meadow gripped the bottom of the steering wheel with one finger while she took a swallow from a can of Diet Dr Pepper. She smiled. "Probably both things are true: she had a conversion and she is a propaganda tool." Meadow turned up a road heading north, and moved up into the hills above the Mohawk. The air smelled of manure, and the fields were dotted with cows.

"But I must admit what most intrigues me is that her devotion manifested itself with—naturally—lifelong chastity and mortification rituals. They draw her as so pretty on that card, call her 'Lily.' But she must have been something in person, disfigured and then continually rending her flesh. This zealous scarred woman hurting herself with hot coals and cat-o'-nine-tails to feel closer to God. Now there's a woman you could build an interesting film around, right? Like Falconetti's screen-filling, deep-suffering eyes in Dreyer's *Joan of Arc*."

"You like it up here," Carrie said.

"Not Ingrid Bergman's glam little nun."

"Never! That hussy."

"Yes, I do like it," Meadow said. "Do you remember *Drums Along the Mohawk*?"

"No," Carrie said. "I haven't seen it."

"It's John Ford, 1939. Starring Henry Fonda and Claudette Colbert. So Fonda plays a settler constantly under attack from the Mohawks and the Tories." Farther up Meadow turned again, and they approached the town of Johnstown. Here farmland gave way to towns with no warning except a wooden sign. The sign said welcome, and then the farms stopped and houses appeared right by the road: a few sadly columned old behemoths, a prefab double-wide, a set-back stone mansion, and a stingy version of a gingerbread Victorian painted all white. The paint was peeling, especially on the sides.

"It's a very patriotic movie—from the settlers' point of view, of course—and the interesting part is that Henry Fonda's family is from that town, Fonda, his relatives were the European settlers who pushed the Five Nations out of there." Meadow looked over at Carrie. Carrie laughed.

"Really? The same Fondas?" Carrie said. The road bypassed the old downtown, and now the pasture was replaced by a commercial strip that could have been on Route 3 in New Jersey or in the Valley in Los Angeles. A Super 8 motel. McDonalds, Friendly's, Monro

Muffler/Brake, Big Lots discount store, multiple car dealers. Carrie felt the dulling effect of the familiar commercial architecture.

"Are there enough people up here to even bother building these things?" Carrie said.

"I don't get it either. This is the ugly arterial strip between Johnstown and Gloversville. But the downtowns are old and quite pretty, if deserted."

Sure enough, Main Street in Gloversville was a series of intact turn-of-the-century storefronts largely empty, ornate cornices attached to limestone back buildings. There were big brick warehouses with large multipane windows, many panes missing and some of the windows covered in wood boards. "It is great that they haven't torn down these empty warehouses." The impressive village library was also built of limestone. "Look how grand some of these buildings are. It is shocking next to the rest of this place."

"It takes money to tear things down. The preservation of poverty, they call it," Meadow said. "So. Not only the same Fondas, but get this. In 1980, Jane Fonda came up here. On the anniversary of her great-great-great-grandfather's death by Tory raiders, but also, apparently, to make amends for stealing all the Mohawk land. She may be helping some Mohawks who are trying to reestablish a community here."

Carrie couldn't stop herself from tilting her head and raising her eyebrows as she smiled to indicate a cartoonish level of skepticism. "Where did you hear that?" She was used to Meadow making things up, getting them slightly wrong, editing them or exaggerating them in the moment of the telling.

Meadow shrugged. "A Mohawk told me. He described it as a rumor."

"I thought you said it was the Iroquois?"

"Carrie, come on. Mohawks are Iroquois. The Iroquois Confederacy, or the Five Nations, is made up of the Mohawk, the Seneca, the Oneida, the Onondaga, and the Cayuga."

"Oh yeah. I guess I should know that."

"I've been filming trains."

"Trains?"

"All spring. Nothing but trains," Meadow said. "Do you remember that movie *Night Mail*? We saw it in Jay Hosney's class."

They pulled up in front of a brick warehouse.

"Of course. That tedious documentary about Scottish mail being delivered."

Meadow got out and Carrie followed, carrying her backpack and duffel of gear. Meadow went through the open exterior door and then unlocked an interior door that led to a stifling, dusty stairwell. After three flights, she pushed open a wood door with an opaque glass panel and a chain-hinged transom window above that. The studio space consisted of an open warehouse floor. The sun shone through the walls of tiny-paned windows, and the high-ceilinged, huge room was hot and airless.

"Not tedious," Meadow said. "*Night Mail* devotedly follows the mail train as it speeds across the land and through the night." Meadow had a slightly condescending habit of telling Carrie about movies even if she had seen them. As if Carrie needed them summarized and paraphrased to make sure she "got" it. As if Carrie watched things but had no relationship to them. But Carrie also understood that this was Meadow's way of thinking. Meadow was building an idea about something, and she liked to think through talking. Once Carrie understood that, she didn't feel condescended to. She instead felt a pleasing intimacy with Meadow and her great brain. Carrie knew how to be friends with Meadow.

"The train barely stops and we see all the automatic mechanisms to load and unload and sort the mail. It is a machine-age celebration of speed and technology."

"I remember. There is a poem."

"Right. An Auden poem, and music by Benjamin Britten. I have been thinking about it."

"I can see that."

"The poem and the music complicate the efficiency. Or counter it. Or maybe it is the long focus on only the train—anything looked at that closely becomes mysterious to us." Meadow turned on a large fan. Some papers blew around, but it felt great on Carrie's face.

"That's better! Thank you."

"It's a meditation. Or it starts out celebrating and marveling at this unstoppable train. Trying to meet the power of it. But then—as if the filmmaker himself transformed during the night—the film becomes progressively breathless and dark. After all, that 1930s devotion to efficiency did lead to dark places."

Carrie let the air cool her face, and then she walked around. "So you have been filming the trains as they come through?"

Meadow nodded. "I've shot a lot of footage while lying by the tracks as the train passes, filming at ground level. I've boarded the train in Amsterdam and stood on the joints between cars as they moved on the tracks. Filmed down through the spaces."

"Have you climbed on top?"

"Not yet. But I would love that. I'm too scared, though."

"I'm glad to hear that scares you."

"I want to strap myself and my tripod onto the cowcatcher of a locomotive and film a phantom ride across the United States in real time. Just the POV of the locomotive eating track as the world unfurls around it. Sixty hours of pure one-shot cinema."

"If only it were 1895," Carrie said.

"If only," Meadow said.

Carrie laughed. Meadow longed to be a barnstormer, a tightrope walker, an escape artist, an inventor. Or maybe she just liked the idea of film as a record of a filmmaker's feat. The making of the film as the art, and the film itself as merely an artifact of that artistic act, not the art itself. Meadow wanted her inventiveness noticed, which Carrie considered a "showman" style: the dazzling concept that just points back to the filmmaker no matter where the camera is turned. Carrie would like to make a film of Meadow making films. See the girl strapped to a train!

"You want to watch some of it?" Meadow looked doubtful even as she suggested it.

"Sure."

"Okay," Meadow said. "Excellent." But instead of making a move to one of the two projectors, Meadow walked over to a mini-fridge and pulled out two bottles of beer. She banged the bottle caps against the table edge: first one, then the other. She stood there and waited, holding a bottle out. Carrie walked to her and reached for the beer.

"Thanks."

Meadow took a long swig and smiled. Her hair was cut short, and she looked lean and boyish in her jeans and sleeveless t-shirt. She seemed even more boyish when she pulled a cigarette out of the pack on the table and lit up. She squinted as she took a drag, and her bangs fell in her face. She folded one arm across her chest and braced it under the other arm and hand that held the cigarette, exposing—or showing off—her defined biceps. She looked older and tougher than Carrie did, especially since Carrie had gained weight (12.6 pounds) from eating so much starch in the dorm cafeteria all year.

The door to the hall pushed open, and a young man stepped through. He looked young, maybe sixteen. His chin-length hair was blunt cut and dyed black. His dark-lashed eyes stood out against his pale skin. He was wearing eyeliner, which, perhaps because it was smudged, made him look androgynous rather than girlish. He wore the same outfit as Meadow: sleeveless t-shirt and narrow-cut jeans. And like Meadow, he was skinny but muscular. He smiled at Carrie. He was beautiful, Carrie decided, if odd-looking.

"This is Local Dave," Meadow said. He shook his head wearily. "Deke! A joke. His name is Deke, really. He's a son of Gloversville, an outcast, and now he helps me make movies." At the word *outcast*, Deke's eyes widened and he held up his large hands and waved his ringed fingers at Carrie.

"I'm Carrie."

"Hi," he said. He stood next to Meadow and their shoulders touched. He leaned slightly against her. Leave it to Meadow to find the one gorgeously odd kid in Gloversville and make him her soundman/boyfriend.

"Meadow and I grew up together in LA."

"He knows all about you, Carrie," Meadow said. "I talk about you a lot."

"You are best friends," he said.

"Yes," Carrie said. "We are." It was nice to hear it. She liked to think Meadow felt that way, even if she never believed that Meadow exactly needed anything from her. That night they ate thickly cheesed delivery pizza, drank wine, and watched a movie projected on a sheet Deke had hung on the warehouse wall. Meadow ran the projector. Meadow used their old teacher, Jay Hosney, to help her rent movies from MoMA and the New Yorker Theater and other film libraries. They watched a 16 mm print of Antonioni's *Red Desert.* Meadow rented it for a week, and she had already seen it five times.

Carrie watched Monica Vitti framed against the vast rusted hull of a ship. A good film to see if you are making films in the midst of industrial ruin, like a leather tannery or a glove factory.

And then Meadow showed Carrie her train film. Train *films*, rather. She had made a dozen of these short, odd documents. As Carrie looked at some very impressive and distorted close-to-the-tracks shots, Carrie wondered: what had it been like up here this past spring, with Meadow in a frenzy, in an obsession with something? Manic, possessed, as if she were enacting some cliché of an artist? All these repetitions and her relentless revisions of one idea were interesting, but what for? Who could even say what they were?

In high school, when Meadow decided films were her thing (and it was like that, a big decision, an announcement, as if her biography were already being written, as if the biopic were being filmed, bold-print supertitles appearing over her head), she began to obsess over old cinema artifacts: viewers, lenses, projectors, film stocks. She built a Mutoscope by hand. She bought old spectrographs, Kinetoscopes, and zoetropes and rebuilt them. She played with them. It was as if she had to go through the discovery of film step by step, all on her own. She had to invent it all for herself. Carrie often felt perplexed by Meadow's extremes. Making a film was already hard enough. Why not just step in and go from here? Why be so difficult and take the long way to everything?

After months of making Carrie watch silent films, Meadow moved on to specific filmmakers: John Ford, Nicholas Ray, Douglas Sirk, Orson Welles, Howard Hawks. Then it was the European New Wave, then she discovered Japanese filmmakers, then the American filmmakers of the '70s. Then the cinéma vérité documentaries, direct cinema, and kino-pravda. She had a passion for comprehensiveness that wasn't really possible. The dishonest part of it was the way she seemed to embrace things by rejecting what she had previously embraced. John Ford had to be seen as vastly inferior to Howard Hawks. It was Godard vs. Truffaut. As if engaging art became a conversion experience. Which felt juvenile and, well, reductive to Carrie. Carrie enjoyed a film even as she could see its flaws. She didn't need to be obsessed or disillusioned. That exhausted her. She consciously sought out films made by women. She didn't care if they were nakedly commercial productions or hardly seen lost films. She liked to think about Ida Lupino or Lina Wertmüller as well as Penelope Spheeris or Amy Heckerling. She liked the idea of taking a genre—say the high school film—and doing a really interesting version of it. Not breaking the form, but pushing it in subtle ways. You would get an audience, right? And there could be room for unexpected things. Even subversive things.

It was unclear, at the end of the night, where Carrie would sleep. Meadow hadn't thought about it, apparently. They went back to the apartment Meadow rented near the warehouse and Carrie slept on the couch under a sheet and with a throw pillow under her head. She heard murmurs from Meadow's room. She tried not to listen, and then she put her headphones on and listened to Maria Callas sing.

THE ARRIVAL OF THE TRAIN AT LA CIOTAT STATION

I

Meadow showed Carrie the train movies even though Meadow knew Carrie wouldn't appreciate what had gone into them. All spring Meadow had risen at five every day, not for any practical reason but for the feeling of immersion. She needed to feel the pain of her devotion. She drove the old Subaru down to Route 5s, which runs parallel to the Mohawk River. She knew it was a horse trail once, the one narrow pass between the mountain ranges if you needed to go west, and of course everyone always needed to go west. First the Erie Canal paralleled the Mohawk, then the railroad, then I-90. Meadow loved how each thing remained even as it was surpassed by new technology: the river, the canal, the railroad, and the Interstate lay right next to one another like a graphic depicting two centuries of progress. But her attention was drawn to the freight trains; their approach and passing were infinitely more beguiling than the semitrucks that monotonously thundered down I-90.

Meadow discovered that she could get to the tracks in a number of unprotected places in between stations. Sometimes she had to climb over a fence. At first she brought her lightweight Super 8 camera, but later she used her video camcorder. Other times she set up her expensive 16 mm camera and made Deke come to record sound. Oh, the sound of a train! The first rhythmic sounds of the approach, the wheels of the train clicking fast against the tracks. The way the rhythm gathered and the volume increased as the train grew closer. It created—a train approaching, that is—its own suspense. Not suspense, exactly. Momentum that intensified and created a need for satisfaction. And then, just as she anticipated, the sound built to a roar. The train went by in a huge rush: the clamor as it rattled the switch track, the whistle announcing its passing if it approached a station, the beeping alarm of the crossing signal if it cut through a road. The passing was a satisfying rush: you were in it, the longed-for moment, the powerful mechanical thing speeding by and dwarfing you. It overwhelmed you, but even in the midst of it you knew it would be over soon. The noise, the movement, the friction of metal on metal: it will all pass you by.

Meadow filmed the trains by lying in the cold wet mud and pointing the camera right at the point of contact of wheels on tracks. She also filmed pointing the camera up at the train from the same vantage. She filmed them from far away, like a train passing in an old country song. She boarded the passenger train in the tiny station in Amsterdam and rode it one stop to Schenectady, then boarded a westbound train back to Amsterdam. She spent the short rides kneeling in the joint between two cars. She stuck her camera close to the gap where she could see and hear the tracks as the train rushed over them. She saw a blur where the ties would be, and the camera lurched when the train lurched. She practiced keeping the camera steady. Then she held her body loosely and let the camera lurch with the train. The mechanical solidity and simplicity, the weight of the train on the track, the power of the constant friction—all of this she wanted to find a way to put in a film. And the longing of the train, the Saturday reproach of a train whistle in the distance that seemed to say, Why are you here and not on a train? Going, going, gone on a train.

Meadow sent her film to a lab in New York City on Forty-fourth Street. She collected the reels and watched them on the editing console in the studio she had set up in the Gloversville warehouse. She marked the film with wax pencil. She had two-minute or eight-minute segments clipped to a wire and hanging around her. She tried the sound out of sync, so that the noise didn't match the images. She tried it synced, then she varied the volume so the sound dropped in precise places. Then she abandoned the sound she had recorded altogether. Variables, so many of them that they overwhelmed her. Other times the possibilities excited her so much she got up in the middle of the night to work or take notes.

Meadow tried to add some of the Britten music to her films. Then she tried something more repetitive and tense, Steve Reich. Or something lush and melodic, Gershwin. Music can invisibly amplify, or music can be an ironic counterpoint to the images. Music can seduce or make you feel slightly off, uncomfortable. She always thought that a pushy film score was cheating, but she realized maybe she just wanted to eliminate variables to make things simpler. She was simple, plain. She knew nothing. She needed to see movies! How did they use music? Sound effects? Silence? There is true silence—which feels like negative sound, it almost sucks you out—and then there is movie silence with ambient sounds, like breathing and chair scraping. She paired her train images with music bright and nostalgic. Then just the sound of the river, which seemed so pastoral and almost invisible next to the train, but now suddenly had a fighting chance for her attention. She then filmed the outmoded, obsolete, obscure Mohawk River. The train in deep background. She filmed just the river—untrained or pretrained. She cut these together. The river disturbed and obliterated by the train. In a logical sequence. In a sequence of no logical chronology. The left and right expectations resisted. You lose logic, you lose legibility. It unnerves. Yes! She shot the untrained, unmanned world: birds, river, the wind on the leaves. The river roar made faint by the train roar. But then it returns after the train passes. If she took away the sound and let the train pass in the background without its steady clack clack clack, it still found its rhythm in your head. You supplied the clack clack clack from a hundred other movie or real-life trains. You could do that, play on the sounds already in people's heads. The memory of trains. But not even that: the memory of trains seen in movies. Was it fair or good or right to count on—even consider—an assumption of memory? But isn't that what all film counted on, a kind of shared memory of everything we have seen in the movies?

Notes:
My Memory of Trains

Night Mail, 1936, Basil Wright and Harry Watt. *Night Train*, 1959, Jerzy Kawalerowicz. The train ride in Hitchcock's *Shadow of a Doubt* in which creepy Uncle Charley tries to kill his on-to-him niece. Teresa Wright lets Joseph Cotten die by falling (or pushing him?) into the path of another train. *North by Northwest*'s train into a tunnel. *Strangers on a Train.* Just a private place for people to meet with no one the wiser. The spinning, unhinged carousel is really the central mechanical object in that one. Okay, no more Hitchcock. What else?

The Lumière Brothers. The forty-second film of a train arriving at La Ciotat Station. Entitled *The Arrival of a Train at La Ciotat Station*, 1895. People screamed and ran out of the theater because film was not understood yet, and the conventions of cinema were not yet invented. The technology was a stunning shriek of the new. *Pacific 231*, the short film that used Arthur Honegger's steam locomotive symphony, which itself was inspired by the train in Abel Gance's film *La Roue* (which makes it a memory of someone else's remembering).

La Bête Humaine, of course. *The Tall Target*, 1951, Anthony Mann. All steam gusts, night whistles, and steady clicks. The train chugging across the desert, blown up and raided, that a glorious Peter O'Toole climbs atop in *Lawrence of Arabia*, his white cloak billowing in the wind as he starts to walk and play for the camera. Lean shoots his film level to O'Toole's suede boots, defiant and above it all, as they walk. There were trains in other Lean films: *Brief Encounter*, *The Bridge on the River Kwai.* There is the train in *The Wild Bunch.* Or in *Once Upon a Time in the West*, 1968. Dozens of Westerns. Jean-Louis Trintignant having sex on a train in *The Conformist*, psychedelic trains in Vera Chytilová's *Daisies.* What else?

Oh! The great train scene in *Pather Panchali*, Satyajit Ray's film of poor children in 1950s India. The girl and her little brother are in a vast field of wheat or rice. No one in any direction but these little people. The far horizon is a blank except for the interruption of telephone wires, the only industrial thing in the landscape. They walk. No music. We hear only the wind in the grass. They are made tiny by the growth, lost in it. First the sister hears it. She stops. Then we hear it. The distant train. We see the locomotive in the far corner of the horizon, black steam pouring out of the smokestack. It is approaching. The children start to run toward the train, through the high grass. The girl trips, gets up. They run and run and make it to the train as it passes. The train is loud and Ray cuts to a wheel-level view of the children. We are on the other side of the train—it passes between us and the children, and we glimpse them through the gaps in the train's drive pistons and wheels. It is huge, and we see it as the children see it: massive, loud, fast. And then it is gone. The children have been passed by. We watch them watch it disappear.

THE ARRIVAL OF THE TRAIN AT LA CIOTAT STATION

II

Meadow woke up at five, drank coffee, and looked at the films she had made in the past two months. Hours upon hours of editing and here was how it read: nature dominated by industry. For Christ's sake, really? That's what it came to? Nature good, technology bad? The original cinema train cliché. She wanted to throw it all away and just watch how Satyajit Ray or Sam Peckinpah filmed trains. But she knew, somewhere, that where you arrived wasn't as important as how you got there. If it was hard earned, that mattered. She just had to show her work, put it together. Let it be organic. Take your time, let the weirdness come through. Maybe she can have that cliché and eat it too. Maybe.

JELLY AND JACK

1986

"Hey, babe," Jack said when he answered the phone.

"Hi, Jack," Jelly said. She was sitting on her couch. She had the trade papers—*Variety* and *The Hollywood Reporter*—on the coffee table in front of her. Next to the papers were a large magnifying glass and a bold marker. The rain was coming down hard and almost freezing. Later it would turn into wet, sticky snow. The news called it a "wintry mix," and it would freeze up and make the sidewalks ice sheets by morning. The weather was hard on her: if the sun wasn't out, it was low-lit, low-contrast gray with hidden ice. If she was lucky she would hear and feel the ice cracking under her feet as she stepped, but mostly it was unmoving slick surfaces that made walking frightening. Or if the sun did come out, it was high-glare, every surface a beautiful-but-painful shimmer of reflected brightness. Gleams that exploded in waves of white. The winter was different every day, and you had to plan and react and accommodate it. There were easier places for someone like her. For anyone, really.

"Congratulations on the Grammy nomination," she said.

"Thank you. To tell you the truth, it doesn't mean that much. Barely five people qualify in that category. Some of these things, if you submit and your name is known, you are automatically nominated," he said.

"But you have won before, and surely there is nothing automatic in that?" Jelly pulled her thick chenille robe around her. She had a cold, and she'd spent the morning sipping tea with lemon and honey. Her throat felt swollen and even to swallow her saliva caused a sharp pain, but it hadn't affected her voice yet. She held an ice pack wrapped in a dishtowel. As she listened to Jack, she pressed the cold compress to her throat.

"True," he said.

"And it is such a perfectly realized recording. The production is outstanding, anyone will recognize that," she said. She heard him light a cigarette.

"I watched *A Woman Under the Influence* yesterday," Jelly said. Jack loved John Cassavetes films, and he had sent her a private video copy, impossible to find.

"Yeah? What did you think?"

"I think it's my favorite one. Gena Rowlands is mesmerizing, the way her vulnerability just crushes everyone around her."

"I never thought of it that way," he said. "I love that scene where she's waiting for her kids to get off the bus."

"Yes, she's so excited she's jumping from foot to foot, looking down the street, asking people for the time."

"Yes! I love that. That's what I'm really like, way too much. When I was working at home and my daughter was little, I used to get so excited when it was three o'clock and she would get home."

"You?"

Jack laughed. "Nicole, inside I am Gena Rowlands."

"I believe it. I'm glad," she said. She made herself swallow a sip of tea. She felt the swallow in her ears. "So how did work go last night?"

"Shitty. I'm not feeling it these days."

Jack frequently stayed up all night working. Jelly called at 2:00

p.m., about an hour after he got up. He would have eaten his eggs and drunk his coffee. Read the Sunday *New York Times*.

"You say that, and then you have an amazing breakthrough," she said. "A few weeks ago you said you felt spent and uninspired, and then you wrote a perfect, haunting melody for that DeMarco film."

"That's true. I mean, I do usually feel shitty about it, but that's no guarantee that things will ever get better. And then I complain about it, which must be boring."

"You feel bad because you care deeply and you are hard on yourself. Maybe it is part of your process."

"What?"

"Feeling hopeless makes room for something, maybe," she said. She heard him exhale.

"You think I need to despair and give up so that I can get to something?"

Jelly cooed a sound that concurred with but did not interrupt his thoughts: "mmm."

"Maybe." A long drag on his cigarette. "Maybe I have to push all the obvious cliché crap out of my head. I have to exorcise it, throw it all out and then, when all the bullshit has been heard and rejected, there's only something new—or at least interesting—left." Jelly heard the ting of a spoon stirring coffee, a sip, and then an exhale. "Maybe that's true. But it is a hell of a way to do it."

"What you are doing works. You always get what you need in the end, inspiration comes."

"I really do do that, don't I?" he said. "Never thought of it like that before."

"No?" she said.

"I wonder if I could just be more deliberate about it? Know that I am clearing out the cobwebs, so to speak. Going through the litany of the obvious. The first wave of crap. Maybe I could be more efficient about the process."

"Interesting. And know that after you have rid yourself of it, the real work will start," she said.

"I could avoid the feeling of utter despair then," he said. "Just by telling myself a different story of what I was doing."

"You do get it eventually. But it also costs you a lot in gloomy moments."

"True," he said. "There really is a pattern."

"Maybe you can reassure yourself in the midst of it and it won't cost as much," she said. "Because you need—you deserve—the feeling of competence. You know what you are doing, and your bad moments are just part of a process."

"Now I feel a little better about working again tonight," he said.

"Wonderful," she said.

"You always make me feel better," he said.

"I hope so," Jelly said. She pressed the ice to her throat. "Shall I go and let you get back to work? I don't mind."

"No!" he said. Jelly laughed. Jack laughed. "Don't you dare hang up yet."

"All right," she said, but she usually didn't let herself get talked out of her instinct for exit timing. Most days when they talked, they talked for an hour, sometimes only half an hour. The times when she was on the line for two or even three hours were unusual but had happened more frequently lately. Jack would play music—his or someone else's—or they would watch a movie on TV together. He now regularly sent her VHS cassettes in the mail along with letters and other little gifts. She gave him her Syracuse address, and if he got the impression that she was a graduate student at Syracuse University, it wasn't from anything she directly said. She left gaps, and Jack filled them in. The contours were collaboration, built of his desires and her omissions. She didn't think of these as lies. He assumed things; she just didn't correct them. And she did feel like a graduate student. She had been helped by social workers when she really needed help. Jelly volunteered to work with blind kids at the center. Helped their parents. She was a kind of graduate student in sociology. She felt that way, just as she felt blond and supple and young when she talked to Jack. She felt elegance in her hands and wrists. Here is what she did not feel: she did not feel dowdy and heavy. She did not feel the doughy curve of her large stomach; she did not feel that the flesh of her thighs grew into her knees making them dimpled and lumpy. She did not feel knots of spider veins or calluses or stretch marks. Is it fair that she hadn't even had a baby, that mere quick adolescent growth had given her red stripes that had faded to permanent white breaks in the skin of her breasts, her upper arms and upper thighs? Did it make sense that before she had shown anyone her body, her body felt old and damaged? She did not feel like a forty-one-year-old woman, did not feel like being this heavy, invisible, unremarkable creature. She felt young and taut, a person who could beguile and a person who loved and understood men. That was the truth, and the rest was not of import to either of them.

"But I have to go soon," she said.

"No, Nico," Jack said.

Jelly wanted to hang up while he was still wanting her, long before he had had his fill. But Jack was hard to resist. She liked the way he called her Nico. The way he asked things of her so openly.

"No? Why not?" she said, her voice slightly creaking from her sore throat.

"Because your voice sounds so sultry today, and I need to listen to it," he said. His naked want worked on her. It skirted toward the sexual, but she never let it go there. She was reserved about overt sexuality, and the men she talked to got that somehow. Some women were butterflies in your hands. You didn't say crude things to them. You breathed gently and you didn't make any sudden moves.

However, it was also true that a few men she had called in the past didn't get her at all. They didn't understand her despite her guidance, her clear vision for them, her parameters. They weren't interested in her, not truly.

"You are making me so hard," said one unworthy contact apropos of nothing she had said. She hung up immediately and never called him again. This despite her elegant and subtle approach, her knowledge and the fact that she knew someone in his circle. Jack was polite, he cursed and he hacked his cigarette cough, but he was gentle. A gentleman.

"Maybe I don't have to go yet," she said. "Are you feeling sad? You sound a little sad."

"Maybe a little."

"It isn't just about your work?"

"I don't know. It's a nice Sunday sad, some old-fashioned melancholy. Sometimes I sit around and just feel sad about things. Is that odd? I am odd, you know I am. It isn't just loneliness. I miss certain people, feel sad about certain people, which is different, I think."

"Who?"

"I miss my Uncle Tom. He died a few years back, but I thought of him today. He was a funny guy. He didn't really understand me or what I do, but that didn't matter. We were family and he always liked me and made me feel that. Up until he died, he used to give me money every time I saw him. Even though he was a retired insurance salesman and I was making a lot of money, a successful guy, an adult with a kid, when he would see me at a family dinner or whatever, as he said good night, he would press a hundred dollars into my hand and say, 'a little gas money,' and wink. I would try to refuse, but it was his way to say he was looking out for me. An Italian thing, I guess. I miss that little jolt of family." Jack coughed. "I should have, I don't know, asked his advice or something instead of just talking to my cousins.

"And I miss my dog Mizzie. She was a mutt, with these droopy hound eyes and long velvet ears. I got her in my twenties and had her through my first divorce and second marriage. I never walked her as much as she liked, I rushed her or let the housekeeper do it. I grew impatient with her, and today I wish she were here so I could take her for a long walk."

"Oh, you are being very hard on yourself," she said.

"Not just that." She heard him light a cigarette and exhale. "Not just that. I miss my daughter and my mother. I mean, my daughter is still around, but—" Jack said. He laughed.

"What's funny?" she asked.

"I don't know. My spiel of regrets."

Jelly fingered her tender throat and listened to Jack smoke.

"It's difficult," she said. "So difficult."

"Do you miss anyone, Nico?" he said. "Maybe you are too young—"

"No, I do," Jelly said, talking before Jack finished, which is something she tried never to do.

"Yeah? Who?"

"My father died when I was sixteen," Jelly said. "He never lived with us, so I didn't see him too often. Once a week or so he would take me out. Usually we saw a movie and then went to a diner and had hamburgers. It was hard because he died suddenly of a heart attack, and I kept thinking about the last time I had seen him. I was in a bad mood, and I didn't want to go out to dinner with him. I wanted to be with my friends. So I went, but I sulked. I didn't want to see a movie and I barely ate my dinner. I remember peeling the label off the Coke bottle and that he kept asking awkward questions about my life. I found everything he said irritating and boring. Anyway, after he died, I felt bad about that dinner. I remember sitting on my bed and realizing I could actually count the number of times I had spent with my father. One night a week plus a full week in the summer. Times my age, or at least my remembered years, so let's say twelve. That's all we had, and yet I couldn't be bothered to even look at him the last time I saw him." This was a true story that she had never told anyone before. Part of her thought, Stop. What are you doing? She pushed that thought away. Jack would love her, she knew it.

"Oh no," Jack said. "I'm sorry. But you were a kid, he knew you loved him under the sulk. My daughter did this—all kids do this. I promise you he understood that."

"Yes," Jelly said. The word squeezed through her tight throat. She could feel patches of heat on her cheeks and her eyes started to sting.

"I mean, my daughter—I haven't seen her in months," he said. He made a loud exhale sound, half sigh, half noise. "We had a stupid thing a few months ago. We—I mean I—should be able to do better, but every day I don't." Jelly said nothing, just waited for what he would say or sound next. A sniff. "It's okay," he said, but it was still heavy in his voice. "It is good sometimes to feel this way, even if it fucks me up a little," he said. Jelly could hear that his voice had what gets called a catch: a failure of breath mid-word, and it undid her. Jelly's own throat caught.

"I know," she said softly, and she heard the unmistakable sounds of a person weeping, a man unused to it, and she let him get it all out. She could hear his breath, his sniffs, the little human sounds of feeling. "I know." She did know. The longing to love and be loved in a very deep way, not the usual way.

"Yes," he said. "I'm sorry."

"Don't be sorry, Jack. You're okay with me."

"Yeah, yeah. I am okay with you. I am."

She felt so close to Jack that she did something she had never done before. She stopped calling other men, her other phone dates. She gave Jack her number and let him call her whenever he felt like it. They began to talk every day. It was quickly escalating, and she tried not to worry about it or think of where it would lead. She tried, in her own soft, quiet way, to maintain a little reserve and slow things down. But it was hard because, well, she was in love with Jack. She felt connected to him in ways that made her feel happy all the hours of her day.

He trusted her and she trusted him, and when she hung up the phone she felt so loved. But then all at once her life—her real life, her harsh, real life—was all around her. She looked down at her hand holding the phone, at her legs in her robe, at her notebook full of notes about her phone conversations. She squinted up at her apartment, and imagined how she looked to anyone else. She tried to tell herself it might be okay, but the gap was so big. It made her gasp.

JELLY AND OZ

Sex was the easy part of being with Oz. They decided she would move in right away, just weeks after they started to date each other. The first few months were a daze of body longing and heat. Most afternoons Jelly would have to work her shift at the call center. In between making sales calls, she fell into reveries about sex from that morning or last night. She had never experienced anything like this before, having only one previous lover her last year of college, yet she understood that this intensity was too obsessive and unsustainable. She had some sense that later it would be important to remember feeling this way, so she went over everything they did from the very first night, getting the specifics exactly right and in order. Her reveries were arousing, but they were driven by purpose too. She kept track as if every orgasm were part of a story and she had to follow them in order. But that wasn't true: it was more like circling in and away, swings, than it was like a story. As time went by she collected favorite moments or sequences (Oz with his mouth by her ear, whispering to her as he came, then a cut to Oz slowly pulling her clothes off, then a moment when Oz reached under her skirt at dinner and put a gentle finger inside her as she spoke). Always Jelly wanted that heat to rise from her body, would rush herself to find the heat. Jelly made another sales call, then gave herself a moment to sit and dream. Daydreams, an indulgent combination of memory and fantasy, dreams that did your bidding. Jelly's vivid and detailed daydreams were almost as good as real life, like an edited, highlighted version of real life in which she saw herself in a soft, flattering glow. When she finally got home from work in those early months, she would practically run to find Oz and his body. She would put her hands and face against his chest. She would inhale, and the way he smelled made her tremble with want.

Jelly especially liked when she lay on her stomach and he got on top of her, covering her completely. She could feel the weight of his big body slowly pressing down, and it made her feel contained and safe. It was a lot but it wasn't too much; Oz was surprisingly graceful in bed. Jelly didn't like being on top. She had no rhythm, no coordination. She banged her shin on Oz's platform bed, she tripped against the coffee table. There was a recklessness in her limbs. She always had a bruise on her legs or arms. She could see it, barely, but everything looked bruised to her bad eyes. Oz could not see the bruises, but he could feel her flinch. Her awkwardness hardly mattered after a while. The very first time they slept together (which Jelly would remember over and over for its certain payoff in heat), Oz told her that she needed to settle down. They had already tried a number of positions. She was so aroused she nearly flinched at his touch, but he moved slowly. His patience just made her want him even more. Oz put his big hand over hers and pressed it between her legs. Her head was on his chest; she waited. His hand covered hers but didn't move. He said, "Show me. Make yourself come."

"I can't," she said. "I'm too nervous." Oz kept his hand on top of hers, barely pressing. Jelly was twenty-five, but she felt younger. She reminded herself that Oz couldn't see her, but he could in his way, he could feel every shudder and shake. Why was showing him so much more personal than when he was inside her?

"Try, please," he whispered. She reached her middle finger out to find the little bump under skin. The touch of her finger on it was too much. Sometimes that happened. She found a side spot that allowed for indirect pressure. So difficult—why is it so complicated, so particular from day to day? Not just from day to day, but from orgasm to orgasm. What felt good reconfigured moment to moment. Oz's hand lifted as she moved her finger, and his large fingers lightly traced her hand. She was moving faster. She knew that it would not take long. The gentle pressure of his hand excited her. Her eyes were closed, but she felt him breathing more quickly as she grew closer. She imagined it was his hand pulling this from her. Her finger thrummed in quick strokes while never losing contact and pushing down steadily. Her body clenched. She crested, Oz put his other hand on her face then, and the crest lasted for some seconds before she fell, relaxed and spent. Particular, yes, because seconds later she knew another one was possible, and she moved her finger until she found a lower, deeper spot. Oz was murmuring, one hand on her cheek and the other on her hand between her legs, when she started to come again. It was quicker this time, but it shook her body from the inside and then out and down her legs.

Soon Oz could do it to her with his mouth or his hand. She remembered the moment when she realized she no longer had to worry if she would climax—she knew she would always come. Oz liked to make her and he was very good at it. As the nights between them accumulated, she understood that she was particular in her details, yes, but not unreadable, not impossible. She loved Oz, loved fucking him. She had a sex life, right alongside the rest of her life, and it amazed her.

Eventually trying to remember every sexual act between them became impossible, so then she just thought of what they had done recently and let moments from the past leak in, every act reminding her of previous versions of the act, so nothing they did was distinct anymore. It was all part of their life, private things liked and repeated with tiny variations, the precision of pleasure eventually overcoming the hunger for the novel. She figured that was how it was supposed to go.

But other things between them were more difficult. Money was difficult. Oz lived off disability, which was a basic, rent-covering amount. Shortly after she moved in, he began to work part-time for an olfactory research project at the university that was trying to develop a truly neutral scent, the equivalent of white light for the nose. Oz's sensitivity enabled him to distinguish subtle variations between scents. He also didn't get olfactory fatigue, in which the perception of smell loses intensity with repetition. Which is why people can't smell themselves or the stink of their own house after constant exposure. Oz did not get desensitized to smell. They used Oz for only a couple of hours a week, which was okay because he often had a headache for hours afterward. It frustrated Jelly that Oz, who was clearly so exceptional in so many ways, couldn't find a real occupation. He had a college degree. He understood mechanical things very well. For instance, he fixed the washing machine in the basement. He listened to it run and located what was not working by ear. She imagined that he could listen to cars run and see where problems were. He couldn't do everything—he was blind, after all—but what he could do, he did exceptionally well. The trouble was the world wasn't willing—so far—to accommodate his limits to get to his skills. The world had no real use for this large blind man and treated him more like a freak: freakish high IQ, freakish flawless pitch, freakish ability to smell, freakish connection to machines. But the difficult thing was that Oz felt his own acute unusualness too. It had little to do with his blindness. Other blind people—even the congenital hard-core blind—found him unnervingly singular. He had a deep crust of self that was hard to penetrate. Even living with him, Jelly felt he operated in counterorbit from her and her life. The hardest part was that he just didn't seem to want to share much beyond her body. As close as they felt physically, most nights they would eat without talking, or at least without Oz talking. When Jelly spoke or told a story, Oz would listen and nod. But she could tell he just heard the surface of her voice. The auditory version of when a man didn't listen because he was looking at your face. Oz smiled and nodded when she spoke. Or he said, "Yeah," but it was as though he were listening to music he liked. He didn't seem to hear her. This made her talk more, but at a certain point she realized he couldn't or wouldn't respond. The early days when they had real conversations were gone. She wanted that feeling back—those moments when both of them were trying to reach each other. When stories were told, revelations made. It was like a window that was only open for a short time, but then slowly slid shut once they were truly together. If she only knew that back then, she would have asked more questions, gathered more of this person inside her. Why didn't anyone warn her that as you get comfortable with a lover, you can't hear or talk anymore? She tried not to worry about it. It wasn't just her—Oz didn't talk to anyone, as far as she knew. Maybe this was just what happened over time when you lived together. You didn't need to talk. But then why did she feel so lonely?

All of Oz's peculiar reticence about people didn't mean he had lost enthusiasm for his phones. Most afternoons she discovered him holding the phone, whistling tones and then listening with a compulsive intensity. Oz loved communicating with the phone machinery—he felt the pulses and clicks soothed his brain. "The dial tone is my lullaby," he said. Oz wanted to have two lines, and a big chunk of their paltry monthly income was spent paying for their lines. Even though they never paid for calls, the lines themselves were expensive. It wasn't sustainable, and Jelly didn't see why he couldn't do with just one. Oz was trying to figure out a way around this, a way to cancel one of the lines and then figure out how to reconnect it, to tap into an extra line without paying for it. He wasn't sure how far he could go in tampering with the phone company before they would figure it out. Jelly and Oz didn't discuss it, but the prospect of always just barely getting by weighed on them. As the high of their new relationship wore off, they were left with a meagerness that started with their lack of money and then seemed to seep in everywhere.

Oz applied for jobs in electronics when they came up, but he didn't get them. Once he came close—he got an interview for a job at the huge Carrier factory that designed and manufactured air conditioners. After the interview, they didn't call him. He presented too much difference and difficulty. She knew he was frustrated, but not because he talked about it. She knew because that night and the next few nights, Oz tirelessly chirped pulses on the phone so he could listen to prerecorded messages from faraway places. Oz let the recording of a woman's voice—it was always women—efficiently but politely say something in a foreign language. Then a beep to signal an error and the voice started over again, saying exactly the same thing in exactly the same way. He listened to the repetition for a while and then he connected to another defunct line in another country. Again he listened as a prerecorded female voice repeated its polite lines over and over.

Jelly's main interest in phone phreaking was to talk to people far away. Not recordings or pulses. Other people out there. It was a modern mystery: the connection with strangers on the phone. Not crank calls, but reaching into a network of other people and finding the ones you liked. Like writing a message in a bottle, a faith that even if no one wants to connect with you here in your immediate life, out there—the big Out There—someone is just waiting to hear from you.

For a time, Jelly had attended graduate school in communications with a concentration in film. But after she became partially blind, she had to drop out. Jelly got only a small monthly disability payment from the state, and as her sight improved, she looked for a job. Since she was good at talking, she had easily found work at a call center, first doing customer service and then moving into sales, which made more money. Everyone there hated making calls, hated the customers. Jelly hated it too, but she was excellent at it. Every day she got a stack of cards with her "turf": names and contact history. Each time she had to force herself to hold up her magnifier, take one of the cards, and begin. Usually she sold vacation time-shares for a place in North Carolina.

David Johnson. (973) 623-1816.

Sometimes the cards had financial data and a history of previous sales on them, either with this product or a related one. Rarely was it a totally cold call.

Jelly had the script and had been trained in the techniques. KISS—keep it short and simple. Use their name. Get them to agree to something small, and then work to a bigger yes. Ask questions—if they answer a question, they are committing to you. But she understood the gist and did her own variation on the techniques. She often went off script and long.

"David, forget my Outer Banks Escape Offer for a moment. Tell me what would be your ideal vacation if you were entirely free to do what you wanted? Not the kids, not your wife. You," Jelly said.

David Johnson—of Maplewood, New Jersey, previous purchaser of a deluxe gym membership that was canceled after six months, thirty-eight years old, fifteen-year member of IBEW, income in the lower-middle bracket—said nothing.

Jelly waited. She heard David make a wordless humph sound through air hummed out his nose that meant it was too ridiculous to consider such a thing. But then, into the waiting air, he spoke.

"I would like to fish, somewhere with no phone, no TV, and no family. Just me and the water," he said. "Somewhere different from here, quiet with no traffic. Maybe a cold beer afterward, and some fried fish, a cabin."

Jelly pictured what he said, and imagined David, handsome and tired, with his fishing pole. It helped if she imagined them as handsome. David had black hair and wore a flannel shirt. If you touched his flannel-covered arm, you could feel the hardness of his muscles through the fabric. Soft flannel, hard muscle.

"No neighbors," David said. "No work, no talking. None. Not even the radio."

"Yes," she said, in her low, slow voice. She had learned to take a deep breath and relax her throat before a call. This was her phone register, hummed and liquid and soft.

"No phones!" he said, laughing.

Jelly returned a bright laugh sound into the phone receiver. "Silence?" she said.

"Maybe I would play my guitar. I like to sit around and play, but I never have time for it. But somehow I have time to watch two hours of TV after dinner, right? I don't know why I don't play more. I am beat after work, and anything but TV feels tiring. I guess that's it." Dark-haired David in a sad room lit only by the flickering light of the TV.

"You want someplace simple and quiet, away from work and obligations. No pressure, no shopping centers or traffic jams. Somewhere you have time to relax, but also do something you love and are good at, like play your guitar and fish," she said.

"Yeah," he said.

"Sometimes doing something you love is the most restorative thing. TV seems to relax you, but it is the relaxation of being drugged. It deadens you, and you want something deeper and more satisfying."

"It hypnotizes you. I don't even care what I watch. We watch—me and my wife—Johnny Carson and the news and before that whatever nine o'clock drama is on. They are all the same, really. I just hate those comedy shows the kids watch. I can hear the canned laughs in steady bursts, drives me nuts. God, I hate it. Like nothing is worse than hearing laughing when something isn't funny. And I wonder what it does to them, day after day, watching that garbage. All of us, hypnotized by lousy television. I tell you." David in the doorway of the sad room. Watching his kids watch TV. Their faces impassive as staccatos of laughter erupt from the TV speaker.

Something would happen between them, a transaction. It didn't matter if the time-share was not a cabin by a lake but a condo by the beach. It would suffice with the right emphasis. You don't need to answer their answers so much as repeat the answers back to them. To be heard is a gift you can give them, and after, they will then do what you suggest. Don't let them defer to a later time. Use a personal story to humanize yourself and relate to them. ("My own time at Outer Banks Escape is spent walking by the water early in the morning. I hear waves instead of traffic. The rhythm of the waves has been shown to mimic the rhythm of the heart, did you know that?" Jelly said.

"I do think I heard that somewhere."

"Yes. It soothes us the way we were soothed before we were born. But I also love to walk to the bay side and the docks, where people take out small boats and fish. Or fish from the dock.")

Always get the credit card numbers. The advantage was all hers—she did it dozens of times a week, while the people she called were not sales experts at all. They were just predictably human. It made her vaguely sick. What she liked was the connection she felt with them—and that's what it was, a genuine connection between two strangers when they buy something. They trust you: it moves from transactional to faith. She liked that, and she knew that on the phone she was irresistible. She didn't even mind making things up (her own experience at Outer Banks Escape, for example, was limited to emotive elaboration of the photos on the brochure). Making things up was okay because it was all about feelings, real feelings and real longing. How they came about, fantasy or not, didn't matter to her. What she hated was that it was all for money. She hated that it all got reduced to numbers in the end, quantified. She had a quota, and she found this humiliating and stressful. Then one day she began to call strangers for fun, not money, from the call center. It felt a little rebellious, and it also felt good.

The first time she allowed herself a nonsales call was with Tim Estes. Tim was forty and lived in Mamaroneck, New York. Divorced father of three in the upper middle-income bracket. A handwritten notation on the card indicated that he had a gatekeeper—a housekeeper or girlfriend who kept deflecting calls. This was not promising.

In any case, she called and to her delight Estes himself answered the phone.

"Hello," he said

"May I speak to Tim Estes?"

"This is Tim." There was something sad in the tone of his voice that made Jelly not want to sell him something. But what then was the purpose of her call?

"Hello, this is Nicole Lamphor." Jelly hated the name "Amy," and her phreak nickname, "Jelly," was too weird and, well, private. She used "Nicole" for sales and now this, whatever *this* was.

"Do I know you?" he said. She paused and smiled into the phone. Jelly knew that he could feel her smile through the phone—it changed her breathing and then the sound of her voice.

She just said—quietly, slowly—the truth. "I don't think so, but it is the strangest thing. You sound very familiar to me. Where did you grow up?"

A pause. "In Albany," he said. "Just outside Albany. In a boring suburb called Guilderland. But I guess all suburbs are boring, right? It's their point, really."

"That's funny. I'm from an upstate suburb too," she said, "but not that one. I grew up in a suburb of Syracuse called Solvay." All true.

"And was it boring?" Tim said, a little tease in his voice.

"More awful than boring. It was built to make soda ash out of the local salt beds. I never understood what soda ash was, but growing up there everyone knew the mining had leaked toxic chemicals into the groundwater and the lake. We used to say the kids from Solvay never got lost because they glowed in the dark."

He laughed. "Well, Guilderland's main feature was easy access to arterials. Nothing going on, but you could get the hell out of there in any direction. And most everyone does. Leave, that is."

"Everyone also tries to leave Solvay because there are no good jobs anymore. Depressed economically and poisoned environmentally, instead of merely depressed like most of central New York."

"Okay, you win, but the name's nice. Sol-vay."

"It sounds French," Jelly said. "Isn't it cruel to give cold, toxic cities in New York exotic-sounding names? Like Rome, Syracuse, Troy, Solvay?"

"Cruel, yes. But Solvay also sounds like solvent, so apt enough, right?"

"I never thought of that. Oh, gross," she said, laughing.

She heard Tim laugh. The sound of the laughter released them and made them laugh harder. They talked for twenty minutes more, and when she got off the phone, she promised to call him again soon. He never asked why she had called and she never told him. It was her first "pure" call experience. It was its own reason and there was no "why."

Jelly loved it: a man giving in to her, falling deliciously in with her. The feeling buzzed through her the rest of the day. Like the sex scenes she used to daydream about, the talk on the phone made her feel a tiny bit radiant and high. The feeling continued when she got home to Oz, and she found she didn't resent his not talking to her as much. She couldn't talk to him about it anyway. The past few months a pattern had emerged between them. She wanted to hear someone's voice besides her own when she got home. Oz was not willing to say more than a short closed answer to her questions about his day, or about the world (so much to be discussed: Nixon, the women's strike, the war, the Beatles breaking up—although Oz didn't care for the Beatles, but still). She wouldn't mind if he shared an idea, or even a joke. So most nights after dinner she dialed into the open-sleeve phone line to listen to the unmoderated free talk. No sales, no money, just people telling stories, talking over each other, talking politics. She called in even though it irritated Oz. He would always leave the apartment for a couple of hours. She couldn't help it—she really needed it. But on the day she had talked to Tim, she didn't feel the need to patch into the open sleeve. But Oz went out anyway; it had become his evening habit.

Tim was the first one, and she moved on to others. There was a life expectancy, or a limit to these connections. Soon, very soon in some cases, he would try to see her in person. Or ask for a photograph. This took all the mystery out of it for Jelly, and she would say she would arrange a meeting or send a photo, and then never call again. She started over with someone new. Each time she did this, she became a little more agile at deflecting, a little better at postponing the inevitable escalation. They were at her mercy: she had done this over and over, while it was all new to them, just like the sales calls.

After a few months, Jelly found that almost half her time at the call center was devoted to nonsales calls. Her commissions went down, which she couldn't afford. But it was now a part of her, a part of how she saw herself. Stopping would be too hard. She cut back; she limited herself to one pure call a day.

She thought it would be good for them, for Oz and Jelly, because she no longer needed the conversation with the phone phreaks in the evenings. Her need for conversation sated, she could stop driving Oz from her house. She even told him she had lost interest in the open sleeve, but to her surprise, Oz still continued to leave the apartment most nights for several hours. Was he with someone else? He vaguely described meetings and a singing group he liked to attend, but he never invited her.

Soon Jelly began going to the movies when Oz went out. She hadn't told Oz, but her sight was steadily improving. She could see things more clearly on the giant screen. Sometimes she saw white spots or streaks that obscured the image. But she could see the image, if not the details, and she could hear everything. She was so grateful that she could see movies again. When she was growing up, she would spend all her baby-sitting money on movies, usually devoting all of a Saturday to watching one film after another. When she got sick, she thought she had lost the movies forever. But now she went nearly every night. Sometimes she saw the same film two days in a row. This went on for weeks.

The only time Oz and Jelly spent together was in bed. The sex was still there if she was awake when he got home, but often she fell asleep, and they started to have sex less often. Her orgasms were constant for them when they did have sex, but that meant less than she would have guessed. All the parts between them were becoming less and less. She knew, although she didn't let herself really think about it, that things would end soon. She would try it out on herself over coffee, after she woke next to sleeping Oz and she had worked hard to not wake him. You don't wake him because it is considerate. No. You don't wake him because you don't want him. Don't want to do what you should, wake him with a touch and a kiss—but then she would shake her head and not think about it. Yes, it felt as though things would end soon, but it also felt as if they might go on like this forever.

Then one Saturday afternoon, right after the wall clock chimed three, Oz made Jelly sit on the couch next to the phone. Oz suggested that they both connect with the open sleeve: Jelly on one line, Oz on the other.

"There is a special phone happening in the next few minutes." Jelly made the free call to information, and when the operator disconnected, Jelly stayed on the open, free line. She used her blue box to make the tones that got her connected to the open sleeve. Oz was already patched in and then there were others.

"Hey, Oz, I'm here," said one voice. "Slap Dog in Memphis."

"Me too, as promised. Motor Mouth in Detroit. What's up?"

"Thanks for coming," Oz said. "This is a gathering, all. We are going on a phone phreak adventure. Get comfortable, as this will last a while." More people called in. Jelly soon figured out that without her being aware of it, Oz had connected to the open sleeve number every day for the past few weeks and told everyone to phone in at this time for a special happening.

At 3:30, Oz began to speak. She could hear the delight in his voice. Oz sounded happy, and she realized she hadn't heard him sound that way in a long time.

"Okay, let's begin. Welcome Ma Bell and local phone companies everywhere. You aren't onto us yet, but we will give you plenty of time. Everyone quiet!" Then Oz whistled some digits and soon they were all on the line with a man at the American Embassy in Egypt.

"Hi! This is DJ Oz calling from my radio show on WSYR in Syracuse, New York. Can we interview you about the work you do there? Just some basic questions." He then asked him to hold on as he connected to another person. Some people at some places said yes, and then Oz asked them to stay on the line too. Then he called another embassy and did the same thing. He was gathering a crowd on the open sleeve, and he was blatantly courting trouble by involving government agencies. Some of the phreaks bailed when they realized what he was doing, but a lot stayed on for the prank's full elaboration.

"I am Professor Oz in Syracuse, New York. This is my talk show with embassies around the world. Please stay on the line."

After he called a number of American embassies across the world, he then called foreign embassies in Washington. Even Jelly knew that government agencies—certainly embassies—were dangerous places to call using hijacked lines. Any calls to these places were monitored by security. No one knew how much could be traced or was traced, whether it was the phone company or the FBI, but surely this would be noticed. Jelly felt adrenaline raise a wave in her stomach. She could hear her heart pumping faster. She was part of it too, and it would not end well. She pulled the phone away from her face and took a breath. Then she slammed the receiver down on the cradle. Oz laughed.

"We're losing some folks, some phreaks, and some embassies. And here we are just about to hit the payoff, the punch line. Quiet, please!" Then Jelly heard Oz sharply chirp into the background hum. He held the phone receiver slightly away from his ear.

"White House switchboard," Jelly heard a woman say. "With whom should I connect you?"

"This is Citizen Oz in Syracuse for President Nixon," Oz said. "This is a live interview."

"I am sorry, the president is not available at this time. I can take a message and give it to his office."

"We want to know what is going on in Cambodia, can the president talk to us? Exactly what are we doing there?"

Apparently at this point people hung up or began speaking, because Jelly heard a lot of voices on the phone.

"Shhh!" Oz said in a loud stage whisper. "This is on the down low with See-No-Thing, Hear-Every-Thing Blind Oz. What about Kent State? What about the B-52 bombing runs? Can we ask the president about his secret war? His crypto-presidential activities? I mean the activities on the sub rosa, the ex officio, the whispered back channels."

Again Oz turned the phone receiver away from his ear and Jelly heard a roar of voices. Oz laughed at the chaos—the babble—on the line, and then he gently placed the phone on the cradle, disconnecting.

"I can't believe you did that," Jelly said. In a few minutes the phone rang. Oz let the rings vibrate into the room. He didn't pick up. He let it ring until it stopped. Then it started up again. Jelly went to bed and put the pillow over her head. On-and-off rings into the night. Although lately Jelly fell asleep before Oz went to bed, tonight she was still awake when he came in. She heard him moving around the room, undressing, and she slowed her breathing and pretended to be asleep. In the middle of the night, half-asleep, they sometimes fucked. But whether he thought her asleep or not, Oz didn't reach for her, and soon Jelly heard the sounds of sleep breathing from Oz's side of the bed. She rolled over on her back. She was fully awake. To her surprise, she felt tears dripping into the corners of her eyes. And once she felt the tears, she let more come, the saltiness in the corners of her mouth, the clutch at the back of her throat. She stayed quiet and she cried.

It took a few days, but eventually the FBI came and questioned Oz. He was charged with malicious mischief and had to spend the night in jail. Jelly was not charged, but she gave up her blue box and swore never to phreak again, which she didn't. The incident was reported widely in the press, and in interviews Oz stated that he just wanted to get a job with the phone company. That was why he did it. Jelly figured that the phone company was not keen on rejecting a blind youth in such a public way, because indeed they did hire Oz to help with line security and system weaknesses, something he understood better than anyone. Two months later, Oz moved out of their apartment and she let him go without an argument.

Jelly knew that she had lost Oz long before the phreak debacle. In the painful last weeks of living together, deep into the limp nights of being in the same bed without having sex or touching at all, she sometimes thought about it, traced the tendrils of misery all the way back to the first hints of problems. But in the morning, when she would be momentarily happy before she remembered the state of things, Jelly blamed everything on that phone incident, the way we like to pinpoint things in one moment, one increment of time, the way it happens in certain movies or stories. But some part of her knew that wasn't the truth. One day, years later, she would even remember that she had been doing her own secret thing elsewhere for months, so how could she blame Oz?

JELLY AND JACK

The phone rang very early one morning. Jelly woke in her bed, the room dark. She had fallen asleep talking to Jack, and the phone was on its cradle on the nightstand. She reached out from under the covers and picked up the phone. She held it to her ear and half asleep she whispered, "Hello?"

"Nico," Jack said in a low voice.

"Are you okay?" she asked, and her voice sounded girlish and sleepy.

"Yes," he said. "Are you asleep?" Jelly pulled the covers over her head and held the phone to her ear as she closed her eyes.

"A little," she said, and she made a long exhale into the mattress by the receiver.

Years ago when Jelly was in college, she had rented her first apartment, just off campus. She was excited about having her own space and her own phone. One night the phone woke her. She was still partially asleep when a man's voice said, "Hi," as if he knew her.

"Hi," she said.

"It's me," he said. "Did I wake you?"

"No," she said.

"You sound sleepy."

"I am a little sleepy," she said.

"It's good," he said. And then she heard something in his voice. "So good," he whispered. "And you like it, don't you?"

"Who is this?" she said, now awake and angry. And he moaned a little into the phone. She heard it, paused for just a moment and slammed the phone onto the cradle. Who was it? But it wasn't anyone she knew. He just randomly called her, a crank call. He called women in the phone book, probably, and got them to talk to him by acting intimate, by whispering to them while they were disoriented from being woken in the middle of the night. What upset Jelly the most was how he sounded, gentle and easy. She replayed the voice in her head, and it wasn't a deviant voice. It was sexy. He never called again, although she almost wished he had. It was the first time she realized the phone could be like that, a weapon of intimacy.

Jelly closed her eyes and said his name into the receiver, "Jack." She lay on her stomach with the phone next to her. "I'm in bed." And she listened to him breathe.

SOLAX STUDIOS

Meadow had moved back upstate full-time after an aborted attempt at attending NYU in the fall. Carrie wasn't able to make frequent excursions to Gloversville to visit Meadow. It was Carrie's sophomore year, and school kept her very busy. She had also met someone, Will, and Meadow gathered that she needed to spend a lot of time cooking and playing house with him. By June, Meadow had a full agenda of projects she wanted to execute. Carrie couldn't stay the whole summer, but she did come up for most of June and July as promised.

First they made reenactments of silent films lost or destroyed. They focused on the lost Alice Guy-Blaché films because she was a woman and didn't get enough credit as one of film's early greats. Meadow didn't have to talk Carrie into it; she was up for whatever Meadow had in mind. They shot black-and-white silent film, and Meadow felt such relief in not having to think about sound for a while. The silent, colorless world: at least two variables eliminated, some constraints. They used a vintage wind-up Bell & Howell 16 mm Filmo camera, "just like the one Jean Rouch used to make *Moi, un noir.*" The camera shot for twenty seconds and then needed to be cranked again. They would make black-and-white silent vignettes, like pieces of a dream.

For inspiration Meadow insisted they watch *Barry Lyndon*, Kubrick's film about eighteenth-century Europe. It is a film of poses and artifice, each scene composed as clearly as a painting, each actor stiff and unmoving in giant wig and elaborate costume. Meadow remembered how Carrie and she hated the film when they saw it on video at Meadow's house the summer of eleventh grade, a long Kubrick summer where they watched his films in a binge and then watched their favorites over and over (*Paths of Glory*, *2001: A Space Odyssey*, *Dr. Strangelove*). *Barry Lyndon* had seemed a laughable misfire for the first fifteen minutes and then turgid and boring after that.

But recently Meadow read that the disdained *Barry Lyndon* was playing for a short run with a new 70 mm print. She took the four-and-a-half-hour bus ride and snuck into the city, not telling anyone. She went straight to the beautiful Paris Theatre on West Fifty-eighth Street and made it just in time for the 3:30 show. Again the resistance in the first fifteen minutes, but already she felt herself change in relation to it. The baroque music, the minimal dialogue: it worked like a silent film. And it was almost a film of no movement from the actors or settings, a film about stillness. All the movement was from the camera, which languidly tracked in or out of the heavily sumptuous tableaux. Meadow felt it most in the remarkable scene in which Barry first kisses his future wife, Lady Lyndon. The music: the second movement of Schubert's Piano Trio in E-flat Major, with pulsing piano that gets complicated and intensified by a violin melody and then switches so the violins are pulsing and rhythmic and the piano plays the melody. The actors: Lady Lyndon walking in her huge silk dress to the edge of the terrace and turning to the moonlight. She stares at the sky, her face covered in powder, beautiful and unmoving. Barry moves slowly in the background until he is at the door to the terrace. Kubrick shows them in a medium-distance shot. Slowly—so slowly, wind-up-toy slowly—Barry walks toward her. They are separate but pulling toward each other, as in the music we hear, as if one is the piano and the other is the strings. And as the watcher of the film waits, the length of time—the duration, the time endured—works on you and changes you. It could take an hour and you would watch. It mesmerizes you. The music resolves as the characters finally kiss—the uncanny slowness lets him make a minuet of a kiss, as stylized as the wigs and the clothes. What an arresting, striking thing. Next Meadow watched the cold pale thighs of Lady Lyndon seated in a bath, catatonic with sadness, her white face like Ophelia in that Rossetti painting. The actress barely moves as the camera pulls farther and farther away. Meadow felt pinned to her chair, every part of her body alive to this film. She stayed for the second showing, almost seven total hours of sad, immobile faces burdened by beauty and decoration and decadence, trapped by their own lack of expression. Meadow felt the tears stream down her face and she didn't wipe them away. How could she have missed the beauty of this film? She despised her younger, callow self and worried about what else she had missed or misunderstood.

After the second showing, Meadow thought about it but didn't call Carrie, didn't want to talk to anyone. She took the midnight bus back upstate, in and out of sleep on the way. Now she wanted to share *Barry Lyndon* with Carrie, had been waiting to share it, and had rented a print for them to watch. She wanted their silent films to use music the way this film did, to entrance the audience. And their films wouldn't have the usual typical silent-film look of flickering light and too few frames per second speeding up the action. They would have a *Barry Lyndon*–like devotion to slow, slow time, a languid moving into a painting-like scene, but in twenty-second pieces. So they set up scenes as almost unmoving compositions: a girl at a table with a young man. A boy feeding a kitten. A girl in bed waking. Everything long and slow, but with odd jump cuts every twenty seconds that returned you to the exact same scene. A jump cut out of technical necessity, the camera's limits, but somehow that worked and made all the difference. It was odd: kinetic and static at the same time. Carrie played pieces of music as they worked (just as Sergio Leone used to so that his shoot-outs felt like ballets), the actors expressing the music in odd ways in their bodies. Carrie used only music of the lost-films era or earlier: she found a gramophone and a stack of 78s at a local antiques store. So they invented films out of titles and technical restraints and found records. Made one, made another, then another. All of them acting and operating the camera, taking turns. They double-exposed the film and made slow-moving ghosts of themselves. They used a filter to render everything a pale lavender. There was a feeling that something good could be happening, a sense of deep possibility among them. This was happiness.

Later, when editing these pieces together alone late at night and adding Carrie's music, Meadow could feel how good they were becoming, how she made something good into something truly special, and this also was real happiness.

In the last two weeks of Carrie's visit, Meadow insisted on working on other reenactments, not of lost silent films but of iconic classic films. They would pick a scene from a famous American Western, and they would redo it as precisely as they could with Meadow or Carrie playing the hero. John Wayne's part or Alan Ladd's or Gary Cooper's. All they needed was some Western gear, then they watched the scenes Meadow had decided on, over and over. It was fun: as Meadow redid the scenes, she figured out how they worked. As she acted, she felt the power of the men in her. The mysterious male of the West. It was so simple, and, well, so easy. She also suspected it was more interesting in idea than execution, like many of her ideas. Meadow knew she had a weakness for perfect geometries of concepts, theories, and images. She could feel how it lacked the happenstance magic of the silent films they made, the way the limits of the form had inspired them to do unexpected things.

By the time Carrie left in August, Meadow had raw footage and months of editing ahead of her.

"This is my favorite part," she said. Carrie hugged her.

"I can't wait to see how they look," Carrie said.

"You can stay and help me, you know," Meadow said.

"School, I have school," she said. "And Will."

"Yeah, I know."

In the end, the Alice Guy-Blaché reenactments were indeed wonderful: beautiful, old in feeling rather than in cliché representations of "old." The films had some relationship to Guy-Blaché's titles, but they also had evidence of Meadow and Carrie's noticing everywhere. Kubrick and the found music and a summer in Gloversville. Reimaginings rather than reenactments, they had found a way to collaborate with the history of cinema.

The Western reenactments, however, were as bad as Meadow feared: silly, obvious, and smug. The idea never went anywhere unexpected. Meadow had hoped that you would move to a different place once you got the initial joke. But it didn't happen. She couldn't make it interesting in editing, because the concept was to replicate the editing of the original films. Formally it felt too schematic and dull, and she couldn't think of it as anything but an exercise. Meadow grew frustrated with all of it. She quit doing anything movie-related for three weeks. She slept late and then lay on the couch and read the paper. So bored was Meadow that she had sex with Deke three times a day.

"What's wrong?" Deke asked. She shrugged him off. At the end of the three weeks, she woke up and went for a long run. She ran through Gloversville until the main street suddenly gave way to farmland. She could see the long view of the horizon where the peaks of the Adirondacks were visible. She could breathe, and she could shake off all the sitting in the dark looking at shadows. Stupid, boring shadows. She ran faster until she had to stop, breathless. She bent over and waited to catch her breath. A wave started in her stomach. Her mouth moistened and she felt that she might vomit.

It sickened her. Some of her ideas would fail no matter how hard she worked. She couldn't always figure it out ahead of time. She could fail.

CARRIE GETS A GIFT

Will's band was the second to last to go on. It would be midnight before the set started. Carrie waited, sipping a beer at the bar, trying to bide her time.

"This is Carrie. Carrie, this is Mike," said Will. All night he had introduced her to his music friends. She had been with Will for months, and still there were new friends to meet. They were at a place called Enid's in Greenpoint, and everyone knew Will. They looked at her closely, not unkindly, as though they thought it was great that Will had found someone. Will was six years older than Carrie, and he hadn't had a serious girlfriend since a big breakup three years ago. Despite being in a band, he was not rock-star handsome. He was a little heavy, and he was losing his hair. Carrie didn't find him attractive at first, but he quickly grew on her. He was very funny, and, most appealingly, he was attracted to her, every inch of her. The more she knew Will, the sexier he became.

They had met when she was the crew for a short film made by her college classmate Lindsay. They all worked crew on one another's projects. Will was a friend of Lindsay's, and she had recruited him to act. He was really good, playing a kind of savvy loser, a role Will was born to play. Carrie and Will talked about music. Or rather he mentioned his band rather proudly, and Carrie told him she preferred opera and musicals. He invited her to a gig, and she surprised herself by showing up and even dancing a little. She bought all three of the band's albums (released on a local indie label, but released), and she listened carefully to each one. Will was an accomplished songwriter, witty and poetic. But the thing she loved best about Will, what really struck her, was his lack of indifference. So many guys she met were cool and, well, uninterested. She always felt she had to hide her enthusiasm. Carrie just fell in love with people, that was her way. She knew it frightened men. Will: not frightened. Will met her enthusiasm and exceeded it. For instance, he collected vintage ephemera, and he would write her long notes in black ink on old ads or toy packaging that ironically played off whatever he wrote in his note. She soon had a collection of love notes, and all together they looked of a piece, like an art project.

Carrie drank her beer and congratulated herself on her own instincts. She never understood the appeal of unrequited love. It was much healthier to love someone who loved you back. She liked being attended to. He called her every day. He met her after class and walked her home. He bought her dinner (albeit at a cheap Polish diner, but still). And after they spent a few weeks together, they both declared themselves in love. Loving Will made Carrie feel happy. Now she didn't have to worry or guess. She had Will.

The band finally went on at 12:45. Carrie rallied herself, and Will dedicated a song to her. They went back to his place, a one-bedroom railroad walk-up. In the winter, it was either freezing or way overheated from the clanking steam heat. When she complained, Will sang, "Oh my California baby," which was part of a song he had written for her. But the apartment—god. It had mice and was very dark. There were gates on the five windows: three in the bedroom and two small ones in the kitchen that went to the fire escape. It was spacious, but the space was awkward. The middle "living room" section was full of band gear. She thought it funny that they both had so much gear; so much stuff was needed.

Will made her a late meal of a hamburger with a glass of red wine. He handed her a wrapped box.

"What's this?" Carrie said, the first bite of food waking her and making her suddenly hungry.

"A birthday present," he said.

"My birthday is two months from now."

"A Saturday night present, then."

She unwrapped the small felt box. Inside was a clear plastic heart on a chain. The heart had bent gold wire embedded in it that spelled the word *Sweetheart.*

"Oh," she said.

"Do you know what it is?" Will asked.

"It looks antique," she said.

"It's a piece of sweetheart jewelry from World War II. The Lucite heart is made from the windshield of a fighter plane. Handmade. Some soldier made it for his girl back home so she would remember him. Like trench art and love tokens."

Carrie put it on. "I love it."

Will smiled. "I will get you more."

"Thank you," she said, and leaned over to kiss him.

In the morning she picked up the heart from the side table and watched it spin on its chain. She pulled the chain over her head and felt it bump against her breasts as she moved. When she got back to her apartment, she hung it over her desk so she would see it every day as a reminder of how strong love and longing could be. Someone made this by hand for his love as he waited for whatever fate held for him. He was far away but their love would endure.

People need forget-me-nots and mementos so they remember they are loved.

But the opposite idea was true too. That all love ends. Why was Will able to buy this cherished object, this marker of some long-past connection between two people, in an antiques store? At some point there had to be an ending, a death or a breakup, and it got tossed in a box to be given away or sold.

PORTRAIT OF DEKE

Meadow's desire to make a film returned to her as she and Deke sat up one night. They'd had a couple of drinks, and Deke was smoking a cigarette. Young Deke was such a beauty that sometimes it was hard to hear what he said because his prettiness upstaged him. But talk he did: one of Deke's characteristics was to be quiet and retiring during the sober light of day and to transform, Mr. Hyde–like, in the night. Meadow liked him this way: unspooling and unable to hold back as he told her everything about his young life. He smoked and drank and added another clause to a long endless string. Deke had a voice she liked to listen to, a face she liked to watch. After an hour of watching and listening (in-and-out listening, looking really), Meadow started to film him. Just picked up her camera and shot a three-minute silent film of him as he talked.

"And then I go— Wait, are you filming me?" Deke said.

"Yeah," Meadow said.

"How do I look?" he asked.

"As you no doubt know, no face was ever better built for a viewfinder than yours," she said, and Deke laughed.

"So I go, are you going to pierce it? And he goes, it only hurts for a second, but there will be a lot of blood—"

Deke moved his face a lot when he spoke, eyebrows furrowed, lips twisted. His drunkenness was making him silly, and with his large eyes he looked like an animated creature, a cartoon. Not the beauty she expected. She put her camera down.

"Why did you stop?" he said, looking at her, the animation now toward a frown.

Meadow held up another pack of film.

"Oh lord," he said.

"And no sound," she said.

"This will never do," he said, his eyes rolling and his voice in some theatrical zone between joking and serious. He was imitating someone without knowing it. An imitation of some fake gay man in a bad movie. So an imitation of an imitation. Meadow loaded the camera and aimed it at him and when she began to film, he got back into telling his story. He had waited for her camera. The fakey theatrical element was still there, but it almost always is when you shoot someone in three-minute segments. It isn't long enough to shake off the fake, but it is long enough to do something to the person being filmed. Depending on the person, of course.

In high school when Meadow got her first real movie camera, she wanted to make films like Andy Warhol's screen tests. She set up a tripod in front of a sheet in her garage. She lit it with three stark, hard lights so there were no shadows to hide in. Unlike Warhol's, her tests would have color and sound. Still only fifty feet of film, or three minutes. It was a kid's project, simple and derivative. Film various people doing nothing. Use the same background and precise setup each time. The person on a stool, the camera four feet away on a tripod. The exact same harsh lighting. Then press record and film them for three minutes. Meadow thought her big variation on Warhol—aside from the addition of sound and color—was that she wouldn't slow the film down to four minutes the way Warhol did. She would show her faces in real time. It seemed a little like cheating to her to slow the film down, as if the audience must endure something the subject and the filmmaker did not. She wanted to experience time, and the discomfort of that duration would be the same for everyone. Three minutes felt long indeed, and she imagined that some people would get very uncomfortable. Being filmed doing nothing required composure that not everyone had. Which is why she was interested in the first place.

Meadow knew what it felt like because she filmed herself first. She stared into the lens of the camera and did not move. She resisted the urge to entertain the camera, to do something. She would be a statue, like Gerard Malanga's Warhol screen test, not a collection of twitchy fake emoting like Dennis Hopper's screen test. She refused.

She knew her screen test concept was a little too obvious, even for a high school kid, but it didn't go as she had expected in a number of ways.

First she filmed Carrie. Carrie smiled and talked to her the whole time *(Is it on? Should I look into the camera? It's funny, when I was a little kid I used to hate it when my mom would make a movie of me. Whatever I was doing I would stop as soon as I saw the camera . . .).* Meadow did not respond but watched her closely, arms crossed, face neutral. It wasn't a dialogue. This didn't faze Carrie. Right away she relaxed into stories of her mother sneaking up on her. *(I could feel the camera on me like a rash. I just knew I was being filmed . . .)*

"Okay, that's it. Film is done," Meadow said.

"Three minutes up already?" Carrie said. "I can go longer if you want."

"Fuck you," Meadow said. Carrie laughed.

But other people were not as comfortable as Carrie or as stubborn as Meadow. Meadow's mother, for instance, sat with a rigid smile on her face. Impossible to sustain, it melted away and she grew older in seconds. Her father fidgeted and did not hide his irritation *(this stool is uncomfortable, you know)*. But he tried to be a good sport and gamely stuck it out.

Meadow asked a few friends from school to do it, and to her surprise everyone she asked said yes. Many of the girls moved their heads as if they were in front of a mirror. The three-quarter turn of the face and the look back. The slide of hair in front of the eyes. It was a photo shoot, and they had practiced for the gaze of a camera since they were eight. Some of the boys she asked were the same way: actory, striking various poses. One sang a song a cappella. Then it started to happen. Kids she didn't even know asked to be filmed. Everyone wanted a screen test. She shot two a day after school for weeks. She thought the volunteers were self-selected extroverts, so she sought out kids beyond the film and drama people: the punk rock kids, the skateboarders, the math nerds. Everyone said yes. Even one of the basketball players told her he wanted to be filmed.

She also noticed that although many people readily agreed to be filmed or volunteered themselves, some of the subjects didn't enjoy the actual filming as much as they expected. A number of them started out playing up to the camera and then appeared a little bored as they waited out the clock. They didn't seem to experience the filming as something challenging the way Meadow did. It was more of a nuisance. A very small group hated it, and of these, one became very upset by the filming. Lisa Helprin had bad skin, but she was still fairly pretty. Her long hair fell in her face, and she kept playing with it as Meadow filmed. She looked down, and then she looked up at the camera with a wince. She looked at Meadow, but Meadow was behind the camera staring back, unmoving. Lisa's eyes darted down again and then back up at Meadow. Lisa started to bite her lip. Her eye twitched. What was she thinking about? One minute was up, and Lisa looked a little sweaty. She breathed out loudly, almost a sigh, and put her hand on her head as she heavily breathed in.

Lisa looked up again, now a little annoyed, almost angry. Meadow stared back. Lisa mesmerized her; Meadow could watch her all day. Then Meadow saw Lisa's eyes redden and start to tear up. She finally jumped up and ran out of the frame.

"Sorry," she shouted as she stumbled out the door, but Meadow didn't look up from the stool where Lisa had sat. Then the roll ran out. Three minutes. Lisa Helprin's would be the best screen test by far.

Two other subjects also walked off before the three minutes were up. Some others stayed but looked deeply uncomfortable for the last minute. Uneasy, nervous laughs. One person turned his back to the camera. He was so hostile that she half-expected him to smash the camera to the ground like Frank Sinatra. Meadow began to feel that her camera was a magic machine that made people reveal themselves whether they liked it or not. Some people could resist and control it, while others quickly unraveled. She suspected that if she had longer than three minutes, and if the subjects didn't know how long the shoot would last, she could undo anyone.

After she had thirty-two screen tests, she spliced them together in four twenty-four-minute reels, eight screen tests per reel. Then she showed them in one of the mini-auditoriums at school for her eleventh-grade end-of-the-year project. It never occurred to Meadow that anyone who agreed to be filmed would feel any differently after the experience of being filmed, even the people who left. Everyone who came to the screening claimed to love it, but many people left after the first reel was done. Many more left after the second. And by the last reel, the audience that remained were mostly teachers and some of the subjects who were still waiting to see their screen tests.

In the end, Meadow thought it was more interesting to make than to watch. And she decided her whole senior project would investigate the subject of watching the screen. What makes something compelling to her? If it is only narrative, then repetition should make it boring, right? Once the narrative is known, it has to grow less interesting. So slowly she came up with her own test. She had the idea of watching her favorite film over and over, night and day. She knew that Godard learned about film by watching Bresson's *Pickpocket* ten times in a row, over and over. And Orson Welles learned everything by watching John Ford's *Stagecoach* twenty times in a row. She needed to do something like that, for she was convinced that endurance tests revealed that there is no such thing as "familiar." The longer you looked at a person or a thing you knew, the stranger it became. Now Meadow saw a chance for another kind of endurance test.

Meadow's proposition to Deke (but she wasn't really proposing, she was telling) was simple. She would set her camera on the tripod and film him all night long. She had read about Shirley Clarke's *Portrait of Jason* although she had never seen it. Clarke made the film in one twelve-hour block, letting Jason talk with occasional questions thrown at him. She later edited it down to 102 minutes. Meadow wanted to make a film that allowed enough continuous time for the subject—no matter how comfortable—to come undone. Then they would keep going and see what happened next. Clarke used continuous sound but the visuals of the film went black periodically when she had to change rolls of film. Meadow decided she would go to the city and borrow Carrie's Betacam video camera so she would have two. She would film on video so she could shoot thirty minutes without having to change the tape. She would set up two tripods next to each other. When one was almost done, she would press record on the other. This way, she could shoot continuously all night long. All she would do was edit the pieces together, and every thirty minutes there would be a slight jump, a few seconds lost, a marginally different angle as she went from one camera's tape to the other's. She would go all night and show it as an eight-hour video. She would not direct Deke, but she wouldn't pretend she wasn't there either. She would hand him a drink or even sit with her back to the camera in the foreground. She wanted it to be a long night with Deke. And she wanted to see what it would do to Deke. And to her.

"Yes," said Deke. "Let's do it."

PORTRAIT OF DEKE

480 minutes, Betacam video

TIME STAMP: 00:00

A young man sits on a couch. He is smiling. He wears a sharkskin mustard yellow suit jacket with skinny lapels over a white t-shirt. His chin-length black hair is combed neatly behind his ears.

DEKE

Is it on? Good.

He pours from a bottle of whiskey into a highball glass filled with ice. The rings he wears on his middle fingers clink against the glass. He lifts the glass and sips. He lifts a cigarette with his other hand, takes a drag, and leans back against the couch.

DEKE

Where should I begin? Wouldn't it be funny if I just ran out of things to say the minute you pressed record. Ha, ha. No chance.

MEADOW

Maybe you should say who you are.

DEKE

You know who I am. I am Deke Wicket. Let's start at the start. I was born in Johnstown, New York, in 1969, which makes me seventeen. I was born at home with a midwife, with, whatever, hot water and sheets, my parents moved up here to be natural people and go back to the land and get away from all the materialism and bullshit of the cities and the suburbs, so no hospitals or antiseptics for them! I was raised a dirty hippie kid in the middle of redneck country, like that was a great fucking plan, right? *(Takes another sip of whiskey, lights another cigarette.)* Want to know how I was potty trained? Yes? *(The back of Meadow's head nods. Deke laughs.)* Oh, for fuck's sake, you are nodding and not speaking? Okay, I can see how this is going to go. I am on my own. But it has always been that way. I used to sit in the tub and make up monologues. I liked the sound of my voice bouncing off the tub and the tiles. That's what this feels like. I just feel comfortable talking, it calms me down. Like opening a faucet and pouring all the me out. I talked to myself my whole life, and it doesn't matter who is listening or if anyone is listening. I can listen to myself. Like Deke, wow, I hear you, man.

MEADOW

You are your own echo chamber. That must make you feel very self-sufficient. Or self-contained.

DEKE

She speaks! It sounds crazy when you say it like that. That I talk to myself or to anyone who will listen. That I need to spew and spew. But I always think that if I talk enough, people will see me finally. Like I want you to see me. *(He stops and looks at Meadow in the foreground. The camera only shows the back of her head.)*

MEADOW

Of course I see you. And filming you is how I see. An outpouring of self. I find it touching that you trust the world so much. But I should let you finish your story. Your life story, right? We were at potty training?

DEKE

So potty training was just me naked. No diapers involved. I walked around with nothing on. When I started to get into a crouch to shit, they would pull me over and sit me on the toilet. Needless to say, this resulted in some accidents. And it involved various people looking at my naked ass all the time. But it finally worked. I am proud to say that I am fully toilet trained. *(Grins, puts an arm across his waist, and bows his head.)*

TIME STAMP: 01:37

Deke is now leaning back on the couch with his arms crossed in front of his chest. The whiskey bottle on the side table is a quarter empty. His hair is in his face.

DEKE

So I stopped taking the bus. I walked on a back street, I found an out-of-the-way long cut, I snuck between houses, whatever. But still the fucker found me. Mitchell Hammond, that prick. Actually, you know that shit shack off of Winston Street near the library, the gray house with the falling-down porch and roof covered in moss and the decrepit-looking dog chained to it who barks like a madman all the time? Just like a postcard of freakin' backwater architecture, a testament to the prosperity and opportunity of this town, this fucking place?

MEADOW

Yeah.

DEKE

He lives there with his mom. Mitchell. He would push me, rather than punch me. Just pushing. He would push me until I fell on the ground. And then he would hold me down, pin my shoulders with his knees. And then let fly a long dangle of spit in my face. Or rub dirt on my face. It was always my face. He would call me faggot or girl and then put a hand on my chin and push me until I couldn't breathe. But I never fucking cried. And by this time, by fourteen or so, my dad was long gone, back to the city. Ned came into my life. *(Deke raised his eyebrows and gave a blurry grin.)* My evil stepfather, except not actual "step." He hates me.

TIME STAMP: 2:47

Deke has removed his jacket and now wears only the t-shirt and black jeans. His legs are open; he leans forward, elbows on his knees as he speaks.

DEKE

I do fuck all the girls I can. It is *(he gestures with his hand picking fruit off a tree and laughs)* super easy, always has been. It sounds so conceited but it is just I think that I am a certain kind of pretty and not scary. So skinny and feminine, the girls always want to play with me. Plus I am not picky—I just wanted to fuck everyone. I want to fuck everyone. I don't care. Ugly girls, fat girls, stupid girls. A couple of moms. One teacher. Anyone. I will screw anyone. No offense. *(He winks.)*

MEADOW

I'm not sure I buy it.

Deke shrugs. He picks up a cigarette and slumps back holding it. He is so thin that his stomach looks almost concave.

DEKE

I feel shitty about it. It got worse, like a kind of obsession. The worst was tenth grade. I don't know why I did it. I went to my neighbor's house once. Oh yeah, it is usually only once, you know? So it feels pretty gross after. I went to Mrs. Lamford's house because I was sick of school and sick of my stepfather. I knew she was home, and I knew Mr. Lamford was at work. But this was not erotic or a fantasy I had had. She was just a messy forty-year-old woman. She watched TV in sweats and had frizzy bleached hair hanging in her face. She didn't smell great or taste great. But I looked at her and felt this hot surge of need. You know I just invited myself in, and when she got me a glass of water I took her hand and held it. Then I put it on my cock. What can I say.

MEADOW

It is that easy for you. I almost believe it.

DEKE

Sure. But that was just her. Different girls make me do different things, different ways in. I just get a feeling for it, and I want it so bad that it happens. And then, whatever, it goes away after I have done it a few times or less than that. It is nothing to me after, it is like the cigarette I just smoked. I just want another one, and then I forget the one I just smoked. I'm a chain-smoker, chain-fucker, chain-drinker. I am covered in chains. *(Deke starts to laugh and cough. Then he starts to sing.)* Whoa, whoa, these chains of love gotta hold on me, yeah. Chains, chains of love. *(He stops singing.)* Chains of love for you, Meadow—

MEADOW

Tell me about the time—or times—you slept with men. Or your stepfather, or something.

DEKE

I like fucking you, talking to you, being with you. *(Deke starts to get a catch in his voice. He sniffs, looks into the face of Meadow in the foreground.)* I want to do it over and over. There is only one other girl I felt that way about. In love or whatever. But it is more than ever with you; I get a feeling around you that makes me wanna lay down and do whatever you say.

MEADOW

(Quietly.) Then tell me all of it. The part you don't usually talk about. The part you don't even whisper to yourself, not in your tub monologues, not in your drunken presentations you rehearse for me.

DEKE

What? I have already told you about being shoved in the dirt. What do you want? I told you I fucked my ugly neighbor.

MEADOW

You are comfortable with that story, your being bullied. Your helpless desire for women. Your compulsion for sex. But isn't that just a part of it?

She pauses. He looks at her; then looks off to the side, as though he is absorbed in thought. He doesn't speak.

MEADOW

What I think, Deke, is that every victim has a moment of trying out being a bully. You have done some things that you don't like to talk about. Things that make this story more complicated. Some messy ends you can't make work for poor pretty Deke, all the boys beat him and all the girls love him. All this seduction and fakery.

DEKE

Am I supposed to talk or are you?

Deke shakes his head. Meadow hands him the bottle of Canadian Club. He grabs a handful of ice out of the bucket. He is muttering as he pours the drink, his gestures loose and slightly sloppy.

DEKE

I am not fake—

MEADOW

What? You are muttering.

DEKE

I am not fake! And fuck this. *(He waves his hand at her and the camera.)*

MEADOW

No. You promised to go all night long. That's the deal.

DEKE

You are not letting me. You—

MEADOW

Tell me something, Deke. I will stop goading, I will stop talking, but you need to stop all this pretty wound stuff. As if the worst thing you have done is sleep with a middle-aged woman, you fucking saint. Our Misunderstood Man of the Mohawk Valley, a Lily-draped martyr.

Deke takes another sip and looks at her. Then he looks at the camera. He slowly stubs out a cigarette.

DEKE

You want me to be lousy. Okay. Let's talk about Mel. Mel is not his name, because I don't fucking know his name. He is just a desperate old dude, a gross, fat, ugly ordinary guy. And I have fucked a few men. It isn't my thing, but I had the chance and at a certain point the wind could make me hard. So the novelty or whatever, curiosity. There were a few boys I enjoyed fucking so that isn't what this was about. I was not feeling great, like getting pushed on the ground most days and pushed around at home most nights. I was fifteen. And it was so regular that he was beating on me—Mitchell, my tormentor—that I felt his body was more real than mine. It was a creepy feeling, to grow used to his shoving. I almost didn't care. But I did, it is just further in, it is there coiling and festering. A need to hurt someone grew in me and it lay right by the desire and the sex. The pleasure, even. So fucking Mel, just a helpless loser. I found him in a bar in Fonda. I was playing pool in a t-shirt, and I had my eyeliner on. I knew I could get beat up, and I didn't care. I was reckless. I felt so beat on that I was indestructible, 'cause that's how it works. You are looking for pain, and it sends weird things out to the world. Someone is always up for that. I thought that is what would happen. I would get beaten or even killed by some biker or redneck gay basher.

He has stopped looking at Meadow, who is unmoving in the foreground. He looks at his drink, and then he looks into the camera. He is locked there, talking deliberately, like he wants to appear sober. His eyes are not amused or animated, just big and steady, looking in, and Deke now appears much older.

DEKE

But here comes fucking Mel, on his own destructive goddamned trajectory, like right into my out-of-control orbit. He picks me up, and like an idiot I let him. We go to his car, and I let him suck me for a bit. He looks so sweaty and ugly, which, I mean we all do when we are desperate and looked at with no feeling, I know that. Desire makes us ugly unless the other person is lost to it too, but I wasn't. I felt so disgusted by Mel. His sucking and his gripping of my thighs. He is in the well of the fucking car, like an animal. He would do anything. Oh god, the poor fucking guy. Oh god. His poor stupid face, like I think about him sometimes and I fucking hit my head to make it go away, I am so ashamed. I just wish I hadn't ever been like the way I was. I hate myself for this, and I don't even feel like me in this moment. It is like watching a movie. But it is me, I feel this disgust, and then I feel like I want to hit him. I have never ever hit anyone. But here is my chance, like the moment I get on top of this feeling. Not in the dirt, not with some hungry girl or delicate person, but with a big soft ugly man, like a slug he looked to me, like someone weak. So I pull him off me. I open the door and pull him outside the car. God. Really fast. I feel this adrenaline in my body. And I start to hit him. Punch him. First in the stomach and then in the chest. I punch his nose and there is a crack. It hurts my hand, but I feel no pain. I am only a surge of hate and power. Like a monster, like a real monster.

Deke is crying, and his nose starts to run. He picks up the bottom of his t-shirt and uses it to wipe his face.

DEKE

Of course he doesn't fight back, that isn't his deal tonight. He does say "No, no. Stop." It isn't like he wants me to, make no mistake. No. He gives up and curls into a ball. Arms over his head and face. I kick him in the ribs, hard. I do. And then it is like I wake up. I see him again, this fucking mess. I just run. Just as fast as I can I run out of there. I run out of town and up the hill. Like miles. And so probably someone found him in the parking lot and called 911. Or maybe he took his broken nose and bruised ribs and just crawled to his car and drove home, ashamed, like I know how he feels, like when I am left in the dust. But not really, right? I don't know. I leave him bleeding and fucked up, way worse than anyone ever did to me . . .

Deke stops and brings his hands to his face. He covers his eyes. And then he sobs, a stifled, strangled sob. His mouth contorts as he sobs again. His nose is running and he sniffs. Uses his shirt to wipe his face again.

DEKE

I don't know why I did that. Well, I do know why. But god, I wish I never did that. You can never forget that you are this person ever again. And it is you, so you know I can see how someone becomes that kind of person. A bad person. It isn't hard to be that. It should be fucking harder.

He stops talking and looks at the ground.

TIME STAMP: 6:58

Deke is leaning back on the couch and staring straight ahead and almost dozing. His hair is disheveled. His t-shirt is off. He is drinking out of a mug.

He starts to hum. It is almost a monotone hum like static on a TV, but then he starts to smile and it turns melodic. Finally he smiles widely and begins to sing a song. He sings a few lines and then stops. He eyes the camera and then shrugs and looks away. He yawns and stretches.

DEKE

Okay. It's morning.

MEADOW

Another bathroom break?

DEKE

I am going to eat some eggs and go to sleep.

MEADOW

So we are done?

DEKE

Yes, we are done.

Meadow turns around and we see her face for the first time as she turns off the camera. The spinning numbers of the time stamp remain as the screen goes black, then the video stops.

SHOW YOUR WORK

It was brutal to watch Deke's raw footage. Meadow knew there were a lot of ways to proceed. She could do as she planned and cut the pieces together and make it an eight-hour installation piece of real time, a long day's journey into night. She could cut off the beginning and just make a two-hour film of the meaty pay dirt at the end. She could edit until it showed a ninety-minute highlight reel of his undoing. She could cut out all her questions, so it read like a monologue confession, which would make him seem even more unhinged. She could do many things. She could even record Deke on voice-over commenting on what he was doing in the film the way Jean Rouch did in his anthrographic films. But instead she did a variation on Rouch. She did what the Maysles brothers did to Mick Jagger in *Gimme Shelter.* She filmed sober Deke looking at rushes of what they had filmed on the video editing monitor. She filmed him looking at himself break down and confess to beating up this person. He pressed rewind and carefully watched it again. She queried him from behind the camera.

"What do you think?" she asked.

"I am very drunk," he said.

"Yeah," she said. She zoomed into Deke's face as he watched Deke on the TV. He lights a cigarette, and we hear him crying on camera.

He watches as the video keeps going and he is calmly sitting on the couch. The video goes to static. He stares at the monitor.

"I love it," he said.

"Really?"

"Yeah. But you should edit it. No one will watch an eight-hour film."

"So."

"We want people to watch it. You do, Meadow."

This was how the film ended, with Deke talking about editing the film. *Portrait of Deke*, the first of Meadow's films to go out into the world. She had the video transferred to film and, through connections Carrie had made at NYU, she entered it in three documentary festivals. It won a jury prize, and it received glowing reviews in small but significant places. She was now a real filmmaker.

Deke went along to some of the screenings. And although there was no sudden break, no breakup, Meadow traveled a lot and they eventually, gradually stopped sleeping with each other. By the end of 1988, Deke moved in with new friends in the East Village to try acting or some kind of performance work. Although Meadow was often down in New York and staying at Carrie's only minutes away, Meadow rarely saw Deke. They were no longer lovers and they were no longer friends either.

There were other changes—consequences—that came out of making *Portrait of Deke*:

1) Meadow used her video camera. She liked that it was just her on her own. No sound person and natural light. Later she would get a pro Mini DV camera and she could carry it in her shoulder bag.
2) She understood that there is the film, the idea of it, before you make it. Then there is the film during the making of it, the

filming and then the editing. But even when the film is done, it still changes. There is the film right after you have finished, then the film after you have shown it for months, and then there is the film after a year, or five years. Each time it feels different to her. Each time it is different to her. But why would this surprise her? When she watched *Barry Lyndon* at seventeen it was terrible. But at nineteen it was beautiful. That is the thing about films. They don't change. You change. The immutability of the film (or a book or a painting or a piece of music) is something to measure yourself against. That is one of the things a great work of art does. It stays there waiting for you to come back to it, and it shows you who you are now, each time a little different. But when it is your own film, it isn't immutable. It feels part of you, and so seems to change with you. The filming, the editing, the showing: all of it looks different to her.

At the very first screening in front of an audience, Meadow almost had to leave. It was strange to see herself there in the film. Talking and exposing a personal element of her life. Who loved her and whom she loved. What she did to him in the film, or let him do to himself. Her goading and her relentlessness and the insistence on an all-night shoot. It was a kind of ambush, no matter how consensual, no matter how willing. It unsettled her to see it there. She realized that Deke was confessing to a crime that could have actual consequences for him. It never occurred to her until that moment. And that you can't trust people to know their own interests, because even with the film right in front of them, they can't see themselves. But why shouldn't she believe him when he says he loves it? (Then there was the fact that they ended things between them with the film, even if it wasn't obvious at the time. Years later she would see that very few relationships of any kind could survive the intensity and complication and power differential of filming a person as themselves.)

3) Most of the reviewers and juries remarked on the power of the film, the truth of it, the raw emotion.
4) She was very good at this kind of filmmaking and she liked doing it.
5) Nonactors—the unrehearsed, revealed, willing subject—captivated her. If this entailed a certain amount of distress, so be it. Something is there, but filming it, the act, transforms it somehow. The raw human drama—that's what she wanted. She found the complex inquiry of documentary—not making up the narrative, but discovering it as you went along—was more exciting to her than filming actors in a fictional narrative. Or filming trains.

JELLY AFTER OZ

A few years after Jelly and Oz broke up, Jelly came home from the call center and saw that she had a message. One of her friends from college, Lizzie, had moved to Los Angeles to become an actress. She called Jelly once every couple of weeks, and they would talk for an hour or so. It was Jelly's big indulgence. Lizzie didn't work much as an actress, and she worked part-time as a housecleaner. She was always broke, so Jelly called Lizzie back and the call would go to Jelly's bill.

When Jelly called, Lizzie was very excited.

"Guess what?" Lizzie said.

"What?"

"I was cleaning this gorgeous—I mean unbelievable—house on Mulholland. Me and three other girls."

"Marlon Brando's house?" Jelly said.

"No, nobody's house, but listen."

"What?" Jelly was washing dishes as she spoke, gripping the phone between shoulder and ear. She ran the water low so she could hear.

"I was in the office off the bedroom dusting, and I notice that this guy has a big Rolodex with a lot of handwritten numbers on it."

"So," Jelly said. "I thought you were going to say you found a drawer of whips or something."

"They all have that drawer, believe me, but I started to flip through the Rolodex, and you won't believe the numbers—"

"Who?"

"Jack Nicholson. Warren Beatty. Robert Evans."

Jelly took vegetables out of the crisper drawer and rinsed them in the colander in the sink.

"I see the circles he runs in," Jelly said. "What is his name?"

"I don't know. No one you would know. Wait, it is on the schedule."

Jelly moved the phone to the other shoulder and the other ear, and she began to arrange the vegetables on the cutting board.

"His name is David Weintraub."

"He is a producer, a very important producer," Jelly said.

"How do you know that?"

"How do you not know that? I read credits," Jelly said. Jelly had been so thrilled when she recovered enough sight to see the words clearly again, she now stayed and read every name of the credits.

"Plus you see more movies than anyone."

Jelly cut the onion in narrow slices. The fumes wafted up and she sniffed.

"Should I call one? What would I say, though," Lizzie said. "Give me a job?" She giggled. "You can't call people that famous anyway. They will just hang up on you, or their assistant will answer, I guess."

Jelly stopped cutting and ran the water, rinsing her fingers. She stopped and sat down.

"You know what?"

"What?" Lizzie said.

"Next time you go to this guy's house, or any really fancy house, write down some of the numbers for me. The names and numbers."

"All right," Lizzie said.

"But not the really famous ones, the huge names. The other names, the names you don't know."

"You are weird, Amy."

Once Lizzie gave her some numbers, Jelly began to do a little research. She went to the university library and looked up the names. She began to read the trade papers. When she felt that she had sufficient background information, she started to make calls. It was just for fun, and for a few years she only did it occasionally. But as she talked to more men and learned more background and connecting details each time, she began to feel that she was a part of this wondrous world. She began to believe that the distance between her life and their lives was not so big after all. The greatest moment came when she called a sound engineer and he said to her, "Nicole? *The* Nicole? I heard something about you."

JELLY AND JACK

"Good morning," he said. His voice was croaky, as if he hadn't spoken today.

"Good morning! How are you feeling?"

There was a long pause. Jelly pulled a velvet pillow onto her lap. She rested her elbows on it, the phone carriage on the pillow between her arms, the receiver held lightly by her ear. The room was bright. It was mid-morning. She was still in her silk pajamas. Her kimono robe opened to the morning air. The sun was strong and warmed her face as she spoke. She heard Jack light a cigarette. She resisted the urge to fill in, jump in, talk. She waited for him to speak.

"What if I said something crazy?"

Jelly waited some more. But she could feel what was coming. It always came.

"What if I bought you a ticket and you got on a plane to come see me?"

She laughed. Not a mocking laugh but a fluttery, delighted laugh. It was a delicate situation. She could feel his want. All down the wires the want traveled. In his scratchy morning voice, his cigarette voice, his sentence didn't sound like a question until it went up a half register on the word *me*. It was touching.

Still she didn't speak. This was the moment she was longing for but also dreading. It always fell apart after this.

"I mean it. I have been thinking. I think—well, not thinking. That is the wrong word. Feeling. I have these feelings for you. I want to be with you."

"I have feelings for you too," she said. She did. She loved Jack.

"I'm in love with you," he said.

"Yes," she said. As they spoke, she could feel her heart beating in her chest. She was not calm; her body was going faster and faster.

"Is that crazy? Never meeting in person, feeling this way?"

After she got off the phone, Jelly began to cry. She let herself feel loved, in love, the incredible feeling of connection, however fleeting. No chance for them, not after what she had done. She had no choice. She only wanted their perfect connection to last longer. It seemed harmless.

The first time Jelly had come to such a pass was with another man she called, Mark Jenks. He was a mildly successful film director. Things had gone on for months; things had gone as far as they could (nothing stays in one place, people need more), and one day he asked her what she looked like. She had described herself accurately but not too specifically: long blond hair, fair skin, large brown eyes. Those true facts would fit into a fantasy of her. She knew because she had the same fantasy of how she looked. But after a few weeks of that, there came the request for a photograph. She took some photos of her beautiful friend Lynn. She had met Lynn through the Center. She was the mother of one of the low-vision kids Jelly worked with. Lynn was lovely to look at: a slender girl with delicate-but-significant curves. She was not that bright and had a flat, central New York trailer accent, but she also had the most appealing combination of almost too pouty lips, heavy-lidded eyes, and an innocent spray of freckles across her tiny nose. Lynn invited her to the beach with her son, Ty. Ty was six, and Jelly met with Ty once a week to help him adjust to his fading eyes. Although she had regained nearly all of her own sight since Oz, she still had to use extremely thick glasses, she was tunnel-visioned and had great difficulty in low-contrast situations. Like Ty, she didn't fully belong in either world, sighted or blind. She was like a character in a myth, doomed to wander between two places. Belonging nowhere. That's the word, *belong*. How much she would like to be with someone, and *be long*—not finite, not ending—with someone.

At the beach that day, Lynn looked even more beautiful than usual. She wore very little makeup. She had a tan and wore a white macramé bikini. She looked happy, relaxed. Jelly took three photos of her. Just held up her cheap camera and clicked. One showed Lynn looking away, thoughtful. One was blurred. The third showed her smiling into the camera. Lynn looked sexy but not mean. A happy, open, sweet-looking girl. Jelly knew as she took the photos what she would do with them. She dropped the film at the Kodak stand to be developed. She made sure she kept the negatives in a safe place.

The photos bought her some time with Mark, but they also escalated things. She knew there was no coming back from the lie. She tried to enjoy the moment, the delicious male desire directed at her. She often imagined herself looking like Lynn and being worshipped by Mark.

Jelly never thought, even in her fantasies, of Mark loving Jelly the way Jelly looked. She was always Jelly but not Jelly, even as she lay in her bed with the lights out after Mark had whispered his love for her and she had replaced the phone on the cradle. She closed her eyes and leaned back into her pillow. Her hand found the top elastic of her panties. The curly hair and then the tiny wet bump. She took her time, and she thought of Mark meeting her at last. With all the possibilities of the world at her beckon, she did not imagine Mark loving Jelly, squishy middle-aged Jelly. She was herself but in Lynn's body. She imagined Mark undressing her and touching her perfect pink-tipped breasts as they spilled out of her bra, her smooth thighs under her skirt, her supple-but-taut midsection, her round high ass. In all of Jelly's fantasies she looked exactly like Lynn, not even a better version of Jelly. She watched her fantasy as if it were a movie; she could see the man—Mark—undress the perfect girl, and Jelly could feel him lose his breath. He cannot believe how exquisite she is. And after Jelly came, she didn't think too much about it. Was it unusual to exclude your own body from your fantasy? Why not imagine he loves you as you are, if anything is possible? Because (and she knew this absolutely without ever saying it to herself) her desire winds around her perfection in the eyes of the man. The fantasy—and her arousal—was about her perfect body. That's what excited her. And how a man like Mark—a man who already loved her in theory—would worship her in that body. It was impossible to fulfill, and she was never dumb enough to believe that Mark could love her as she actually was.

After Mark, she used the photos with two other men. Things always proceeded in one direction, and she ended things when they escalated to an unavoidable meeting.

But what about Jack? She didn't want to send him those photos. Some part of her thought that maybe Jack would love her no matter what. She thought about sending a neck-up flattering photo of herself, just to see what happened. The second time he asked her for a photo, she addressed the envelope and started to cry as she put the photos of Lynn inside and sealed it. She realized she was ending any future between them. But she had to. Before he wanted her photo, before he wanted her to visit him, he asked her the question they all had asked at some point. But it was an artful, gentle version with Jack: "You sound so young when you laugh. How old are you?"

She laughed again. Jelly knew how to avoid answering questions. But you couldn't laugh off questions forever. She didn't want to lie to Jack, which was something she'd just realized. But all of his circling around eventually came to the point. *What do you look like?* It wasn't that she didn't expect it or that she didn't understand it, it was just so hopeless to always wind up against it. And how could she answer it? After she hung up the phone, she sat on the couch for a long time, staring into the faint dusk light.

What do I look like? If you look or if I look? It is different, right? There is no precision in my looking. It is all heat and blurred edges. Abstractions shaped by emotion—that is looking. But he wants an answer.

What do I look like? I look like a jelly doughnut.

Jelly got up and looked in the mirror. What to do if what you look like is not who you are? If it doesn't match?

I am not this, this woman. And I am not Lynn-in-the-photograph. Jack must know, Jack knows who I am. I am a window. I am a wish. I am a whisper. I am a jelly doughnut.

I am beautiful when my hair brushes my shoulders, when the sun makes me close my eyes, when my voice vibrates in my throat. When I am on the telephone, I am beautiful.

How would it go? Jelly knew, just as she knew so many things without ever experiencing them. The knowing seemed to come from her senses, her fingertips and her skin. She knew that if she met Jack, he would be disappointed even if she were beautiful in the common sense of "beautiful." *Common* is an interesting word. It could be comforting when you mean what we all have in common. But it also means ordinary; it means something we have all seen many times and can find easily. So a common sense of beauty is agreed upon by all but also dull in a way. Still his disappointment would come out of something human and inescapable: the failure of the actual to meet the contours of the imaginary. As he listened to the words he heard come across the line and into his ear, he imagined the mouth saying them. Even more so, as he spoke into the receiver, he imagined a face listening, and an expression on that face. Maybe it was made of an actress on the TV from the night before plus a barely remembered photo of his mother when she was very young and a girl with long hair and bare tan legs that he glimpsed at the beach. But there was no talking without imagining. And once imagining preceded the actual, there was no escaping disappointment, was there?

What about Jelly? Would Jelly feel disappointment with Jack, when he showed up sweaty, old, smelling of breath mints and cigarettes? It never occurred to her to think this way. She would be so focused on him that her own feelings wouldn't matter. She would feel disappointed if he felt disappointed. She would hear it in his voice, and she would feel herself lose everything, all the perfect, exquisite moments that she had made with him.

"I want to see you," Jack had said. "I need to see you."

"I know. I know. Okay," Jelly said. "I will send you some pictures."

Of course she was right to send Lynn's photos; she needed to make things last just a little longer. But she cried, because for a minute it might have gone a different way.

JELLY

The alarm went off, and Jelly stared into the murky early morning light. It was the day she was supposed to get on the plane to California, a 9:00 a.m. flight. She hadn't packed, but she thought about it. She really did. Last night he laughed on the phone, excited, and she would never have let him go this far if she was sure she wasn't going to go. Last night, after a glass of wine, she laughed too and imagined being with him at last. But as they said good night and hung up, she knew.

She hit the button on the alarm, pulled the comforter up over her head, and heaved a long breath into the dark, warm air.

CARRIE HAS A WEDDING

Meadow came an hour late to Carrie and Will's rehearsal dinner. As toasts were being made, she slipped quietly into the empty seat next to Carrie with a smile. Later, Will made a face when Carrie explained traffic, parking, picking up the dress. (Meadow wore a silk suit to the rehearsal dinner but had agreed to wear a dress to the wedding. Meadow never wore dresses, but she would do it for Carrie.)

"At least she showed up," he said.

"Of course she showed up," Carrie said, slightly annoyed. She knew he was only being protective of her, but she couldn't help feeling protective of Meadow.

"And she didn't make it to your screening even though you gave her a month's notice."

Carrie's thesis project—a short called *Girl School*—had been selected for a film festival as part of the shorts program, but Meadow was not able to attend. The night before, she left a message on Carrie's answering machine. Will rolled his eyes as they listened to Meadow apologize, but Carrie knew that he read Meadow wrong, that Meadow was in deep in her upstate world. Editing. Or researching and filming. Meadow disappeared into a frenzy of work. "You went to her screening," Will said, and although that was true, Carrie felt she should have visited Meadow more often; she hadn't managed to in a long time. How long since they had seen each other? A year? No, nine months. But now Meadow had come down for Carrie's wedding; she was the maid of honor and, although she showed up late to the rehearsal dinner, she appeared perfectly on time to the wedding, with her angular sidekick Kyle holding an arm around her waist as though he might lose her in the crowd. Early in the evening, Carrie whispered to Will that she wondered how long Kyle would stay in the picture. Surely he would soon exceed Meadow's usual short expiration date? Will snorted in agreement, and she immediately regretted saying what she said. She actually liked Kyle. And Meadow. So why? Often her comments were harsher than she intended, meaner. And she wished she could unsay them.

Although neither she nor Will were Polish, they had their reception in a Polish wedding emporium in Greenpoint, Brooklyn, where they received a discount for getting married during Lent (when no Polish couples wanted to have a wedding). They did everything themselves, getting some of their friends to donate help instead of giving gifts: flowers, invitations, photography. Even so, it all cost more than Carrie had hoped. She resolved to enjoy herself and the tacky perfection of the mirrored wallpaper stippled with gold and the giant bride and groom thrones strewn with dingy net and worn white ribbons. Each table had bottles of Polish vodka on it, and when they first saw the bottles, Carrie joked to Meadow that it would be a drunken marathon like the Polish wedding in *The Deer Hunter*.

"Russian. Russian wedding," Meadow said.

"As long as no one lifts me in a chair," Carrie said.

"The close-up of the wine spilling on the white dress was not exactly an example of subtle foreshadowing," Meadow said.

"I liked it."

Meadow shrugged. "I liked it too," she said. "And it captured the desperate hope of a wedding, how underlined in futility it is."

"Said the maid of honor to the bride," Carrie said.

"C'mon. I don't mean you and Will. You and Will are great."

Meadow was Carrie's entire wedding party, and Carrie had requested she wear some kind of blue dress. Meadow wore a long vintage blue sleeveless silk slip-style dress with a black evening jacket that made her look even taller and leaner than usual. Carrie wore a mutton-sleeved size-ten wedding gown that she had starved herself to fit into, and secretly she worried that Meadow's thin body would make her look fat, but then she willed herself not to think such things.

After the wedding and the dinner and the cake, after the first dance and the thrown garter, things began to wind down and the band played the kitschy pop songs Will had requested for the end of the reception. Will danced flamboyantly with Carrie, then Will danced with Meadow, and Carrie danced with Kyle, who spun her around with mock seriousness. Kyle's appeal became more apparent to her as the night went on. But the last two songs Carrie danced with Meadow as the boys sat on the sidelines drinking together. At eleven the band—also friends of the groom—had to go to another gig and the allotted five hours at the emporium were done. The wedding was over, and Carrie thought it was both too long and too short for her. After months of planning, it seemed like some difficulty overcome and accomplished, and she was relieved it was over. Which also made it seem like the lamest party ever, stingy rather than carefree. But that is what they could afford, five hours (with her mother and father helping, and Will's parents, but no one could pay much). They still ended up exceeding their planned budget and spending most of their savings.

Earlier in the evening, at the start of the reception, Meadow had handed Carrie an envelope from Meadow's father. Meadow's parents couldn't attend the wedding, but they sent a check for five thousand dollars to help with Carrie and Will's costs. Carrie started to cry, but Meadow ordered her to stop or her makeup would run. Carrie sat in her throne next to Will, drinking champagne, and felt very lucky.

After the reception was over, Carrie said goodbye to Meadow and her lovely boy, and she grabbed Will's hand. They took a cab back to their apartment with all their gifts. Carrie couldn't wait to get out of her dress, out of her shoes, out of the control-top hose. Barefoot in her silk slip, she went into the kitchen and grabbed the phone. She ordered a pizza for delivery.

"I'm starving," she said.

"What about all the food at the wedding?" Will said. "All those pierogi and the suckling pig."

"I couldn't eat! I was too excited and my dress was too tight," Carrie said.

"Me too," Will said. "My dress was too tight." And he slapped his belly as he undid his belt.

"Will you still love me after I eat too much pizza?"

"Yes."

"If I become fat?" Carrie asked as she put her arms around him. He put his hands on her hips.

"Of course."

"If I become enormously fat?"

"Yes, but is that part of the plan?"

Carrie laughed and shrugged. She leaned down and pulled a bottle of rosé champagne from the refrigerator and handed it to Will. He began to peel at the foil capsule and then began tugging hard on the cork. Carrie took it from him and placed a kitchen towel over the top and gently twisted the cork until it came loose with a low pop.

She handed him the open bottle and picked up the glasses. "I can't believe Meadow's father gave us so much money," Carrie said.

"He has a lot of money to give," Will said.

"Of course. But it was so generous of them."

"Meadow must have a big trust fund—"

"So generous," Carrie said, and held up her glass.

Will poured the champagne fast and the glasses overflowed a little. Carrie said, "Whoa!" and tried to catch the overflow with her tongue and started laughing. They sat on the floor, looking at the gifts and cards. They ate half a pizza and drank most of the champagne. All at once, Carrie felt completely exhausted. They went to bed the way they usually did, and they didn't have wedding-night sex. Just before Carrie fell asleep, she worried that one day she would look back at not having wedding-night sex as a bad omen, like that drop of blood on the wedding dress in *The Deer Hunter.* She thought, briefly, I have to tell Meadow that, about the omen. Then she fell into a deep, dreamless sleep.

CINEMA TRUTH

After the success of *Portrait of Deke*, Meadow applied for various grants, "borrowed" money from her father to pay some expenses, and cobbled together enough money to make two new movies, *Kent State: Recovered* and *Play Truman*. Around the same time she tried to make a third film, which she abandoned in the early stages.

Kent State: Recovered (1992)

A few years earlier, during Meadow's first spring in Gloversville, she had read in the paper about the fifteenth anniversary of the Kent State shootings. She had cut the article out and put it on her studio wall. It fascinated her ever since. What a thing, students shot at by the National Guard, students killed and then that photograph of the dead student and the girl on one knee beside him. Young people now didn't think or talk about it, but Meadow had kept thinking about it. There wasn't film, though, of the shootings. Unlike other famous acts of violence, this one did not have an amateur with a handheld to give us a grainy glimpse to watch over and over. Still, Meadow had some ideas. Maybe there was a way.

First she had the idea to track down the girl in the photograph—Mary Ann Vecchio. Meadow could easily imagine her as a compelling subject. Here was one moment in her life, a moment of anguish, and then it comes to define her life. She is kneeling in the quad by a dead college student, crying out to the world. She is a runaway, a flower child in pursuit of a college boy she liked, Jeffrey Miller. Her face has anguish, yes, but also, with her arms outstretched, an expression of disbelief, almost a plea. Mary Ann can't believe this happened, students shot for protesting, right in front of her, in the United States. This was supposed to happen in other countries and on TV. We were supposed to watch and say *tsk tsk*, should we help these poor people? Instead the whole world watched us. Everyone felt that way, and so the photograph became a pieta for American purity. But the next morning she is just a girl again. She is fourteen, and this will be the thing people note about her for the rest of her life. Not because she was there, but because she was photographed. The photo will win a Pulitzer Prize. Because of the photograph, Jeffrey Miller is the most famous of the four dead students at Kent State. The photo is carried in papers around the world. Governor Claude Kirk of Florida will label the girl a Communist sympathizer. She is pictured on her knees, in her genuine anguish, on t-shirts. Her parents will sue people for a share of the proceeds. She will try to move on, but the photo will affect her life for years to come. Not to her face, but at the edges of her. When she leaves her kid's PTA meeting, a parent will lean over to another parent and whisper, "You know who she is, don't you?"

The parent shakes her head.

"She is the girl in the photograph at Kent State. The girl on her knees, the crying girl."

"Really?"

"Yes. Crazy, huh?" And they will smile in awe: a piece of history right in their lives with them. Maybe eventually Mary Ann will decide not to tell anyone about the photograph. She will keep it a secret from the people in her life. She is not ashamed, but she doesn't want it to be so important, so defining. She wants room for other ideas about her, other selves. She remembers the day vividly, though. She loved the boy who was killed. You don't forget seeing someone shot right in front of you, and then die as you kneel over him. They are there, protesting the invasion of Cambodia, doing what they think is right, and then, instead of going off to smoke a joint and make out in his dorm room, Jeffrey is bleeding on the pavement, a facedown deadness all over him. The event—not the photo of the event—did change who she was, did mark her for years to come.

Meadow wanted to track down and interview the girl in the famous photograph, but she discovered that it already had been done. Some TV show had the idea—the obvious, ordinary idea—to get the girl and the photographer together for a reunion.

Meadow decided to interview other people about the day. She wanted students, but she also wanted the National Guardsmen—the young men the same age as the students—who fired into the crowd.

Meadow would interview everyone in a plain room, a static space. She hated documentaries that showed people in their living rooms. Your thoughts became about interior design and psychology. She wanted eyes on faces, and she wanted a deliberate frame. A sameness, a feeling of isolation. After shooting some interviews, she realized that Deke was unusual; looking directly into the lens of a camera felt unnatural to some people. They needed a face. If she stood next to the camera, they seemed to look shiftily off to the side. Her solution came from *Tokyo Story*, the Yasujirō Ozu film she had watched at the Nuart. Ozu used a "tatami shot" in which he filmed his actors from a low angle, looking up from a fixed camera. She tried it, and she stood behind and slightly above the camera as she listened to the interviewees. This gave the approximate illusion of a direct gaze, although the seated people often appeared to look into a space just above camera, which made everyone look thoughtful rather than shifty.

Meadow used a tiny crew, including Kyle, who had begun as her assistant and then almost immediately became her boyfriend. He was a student in the film program at Columbia, and Meadow thought he was brilliant. He looked like a younger, Bengali version of Deke: black hair worn long, lean-muscled and small of stature, sharp angles to cheeks and jaw. When Kyle smiled or laughed, Meadow always felt distracted by his sudden flash of white straight teeth and she wanted to make him laugh even more.

She took her tiny crew to various locales after she phoned and wrote to witnesses and participants. That was what she called them, participants. She had to admit she was drawn to the National Guardsmen—young men on the wrong side of history even before that day. When a group of soldiers fire, everyone in the group must feel guilty yet no one is responsible. That is the point, clearly, of firing as a group. She wondered how that wore as the years went by. She wanted to prick them a little in a room and film them spilling their secrets out. She imagined it might be good for them, cathartic. She started in the Gloversville library with the microfiche, getting the names of the people there. The student witnesses were quoted in the papers.

"Can I film you telling your experience of that day?" and sometimes they said yes. Other times she would have to gently persuade them. As she expected, the National Guard people were the most reluctant. They were the shooters, after all.

"I just want to hear all sides of the story. How it felt to be so frightened. The danger, the rocks thrown."

"But I don't feel that way. I can't believe we shot. There was an order to fire, or at least we thought there was. We all did it, but I can't believe it. Those dead kids," he said. He was spilling already. This was no good. She wanted that on film, not on the phone.

"Okay, so let me film you and you can tell me, okay?" she said, holding him off. "Just tell me the story so we know some National Guardsmen feel pain about it. Regret." And she knew he would. He would be glad to because there is a particular joy in telling the darkest truth about what you did. In letting yourself say out loud, "I did this terrible thing." It is out of you and in the world. We are all desperate to get it out of us instead of waiting for it to be discovered. The waiting contaminates a life, wakes a man in the middle of the night. Meadow knew everyone had in them this compulsion to confess, was born with it: guilt and the need to tell all. She shot hours of footage. She let people digress, tell their life stories, even sit speechless for minutes. She was shooting blind, discovering things as she went along.

But unlike the filming of Deke, there was sometimes something inert about these people talking to the camera. Some people's faces, no matter what they are saying, are inert. Maybe it was the tone of voice? They often had a rehearsed feel, as though they had practiced in the shower for this very moment. They had been asked these questions many times before. They'd had years to make a narrative of what happened. What could she do to make it feel less distant? She went through archived footage for things to show during some of the stories and in between some of the talking. Meadow considered reenactments. Brief moments from the past, a cinematic séance conjured by speech. She did not want the feeling of cheesy tabloid docudramas, the "dramatic reenactments" of Paul Revere's ride that she remembered from educational TV. And if she just showed photographs as people spoke, zooming in and out, she thought it would look like third-grade film strips. But she kind of liked film strips and the way they made you dwell on a photo until it almost moved. There were plenty of photographs from before and after and during. She could, maybe, animate the photos somehow. She could use stop-action animation to take elements in the photos and alter them slightly until people in the photographs seemed to move. It was enactment, and it was not real. It was a manipulation. She fudged it further by taking a camera on campus and meticulously re-creating—in grainy Super 8, amateur film—the feeling of campus that day. Meadow even used actors, but only very briefly and only in flickers. An arm moving, a person kneeling to shoot in a uniform. It wasn't, of course, re-creating that day in 1970. The "real" feeling came from using film that reminded us of that day. So her reenactments used the materials—the look—of the collective memory. The photographs had long overwritten the feeling of 1970 in people's minds. It was what you saw looking at photos in *Life* magazine. She had the grainy Super 8 blown up to 16 mm. She took close-ups of maps of the campus, of rifles being fired in a kind of dreamily lit studio space, as if the film were showing the consciousness of each speaker as he spoke. And, in very short glimpses, she used the manipulated photo animations. When she edited it all together, it added great drama and reality to what was being said by the participants. It came to life.

Then something emerged that she didn't expect. People on both sides—the students (now in their thirties) and the Guardsmen (also in their thirties) mentioned a supposed agent provocateur. She remembered the article on her bulletin board and its description of this figure. There was one sentence about a student radical "some people suggested" worked for the FBI. They quoted a person who thought this man fired a shot at the National Guard, the one that made them turn, kneel, and shoot at the students. She discovered that there was a growing conspiracy at the center of some of the stories of that day.

A saboteur, a boogeyman. Who was this provocateur, this fellow accused of causing all this violence? Maybe he was the responsible one. Not the students, clearly. But maybe it isn't entirely the fault of the Guardsmen either.

"I saw him there, he had a gun. Right after the shooting, he said he had to shoot, had no choice," said a Kent professor who had come out on the quad after the shots were fired. "He was arrested after, and I heard they released him. That he was working for the FBI."

"What did he do?"

"He fired the shot that provoked the National Guard," he said.

"You saw him?"

"No. But other people did."

"You think the FBI infiltrated the Kent student protests?"

"Of course they had undercover people in there. The agents are always the ones urging everyone to violence and mayhem. They wanted to discredit the student activists."

"But all they did was make the students into victims."

The professor shrugged and smiled. "I didn't say it was smart or effective. It was the FBI."

But some of the members of the Guard also believed it.

"If you listen to the tape, the audiotape, you can hear a lone shot before we kneel and shoot." It was true. There was no video, but an audiotape existed, made by a student doing a project in which he kept a tape recorder on his dorm room windowsill. It was very staticky—the audio version of grainy—full of pops and cracks. Meadow included it in the film, played it while showing a black screen. She put titles on the black screen to point to sounds. Somebody is talking and words appear in large typed letters as you hear them: *You* and *after they come* and *taken* and *tell them* and then when you hear the supposed shot, *(gunshot)*, a pause of blank screen, *(running)*, then a word that sounds faintly like *ready*. Then *(garbled)*, seconds go by on blank screen, then *(shots, screams)*.

It is true that the isolation of sounds on a blank screen can deceive, that anything isolated in a sense-depriving way can feel odd or wrong no matter the content. And suggesting what a sound is makes you hear that sound. Meadow knew that. She also knew that once the provocateur was mentioned, she would bring him up to each person she interviewed. She would sometimes put her question about him in the film. Other times she would discuss it with the person before the filming—*you know what, several people have said this*. And the person would get around to mentioning it when she filmed the person talking. But she already had fake film mixed with real film. Her film was a stylized, constructed thing, a version of reality. Not a pure, untainted object. You cut, you put this next to that, you edit this out, you ask, you enact, you show an image. It was a fictiony thing: a fictional thing comprised of pieces of real life. A hybrid, a combine. Only one line of events actually happened, but it was obscured by memory and time and wishful confabulations. She wanted to convey that.

Slowly the film bent toward a conspiracy, with one person after another circling back to the saboteur, essentially blaming him as ultimately responsible. The Guard turned for a reason, and maybe this was it. The belief was that most of the violence on the student left was instigated by fellows like him. And truly, there was a guy lurking around Kent State who appeared to be protected by the FBI. He was always at meetings, always taking photographs. He was off in obvious ways. People felt that he was some kind of narc. And the Guardsmen were sure someone fired at them—they wouldn't be ordered to shoot actual bullets because of a few rocks. Although the rocks hurt—a number of Guardsmen claimed to have sustained injuries from rocks. And from chunks of cement and gas canisters. ("A rock could kill a person, you know. We were the same age as the students, but we didn't go to college. We were enlisted or drafted, lucky to be stateside in the Guard. Lucky!")

Eventually Meadow understood where the film should go. She had been filming for a year already. It took another year to locate and talk to him. He was easy enough to convince to speak once she found him in a Boston suburb. He had always lived with a hum of doubt under him. "I will talk to you." He was pained—no one got more contempt in this world than the turncoat. Misguided true believers? Fine. But the deceiver, the liar, the betrayer? Everyone was united in their hate for Marvin Joseph.

Marvin lived in a small brick split-level house on a suburban street lined with old oak trees. She would film Marvin, and Marvin alone, in his living room, where his ordinariness was palpable. People would expect a fully satisfying narrative, a bad guy. But she would give them the unknowable, the meaningless. The mistake.

"Is this okay?" he said. He was wearing a dress shirt under a wide-lapelled blazer. He was chubby and wore outdated aviator frames that made him look, with his tight shirt, a bit like a porn producer. This was not right. Meadow found him a looser shirt, a more conservative blazer. She didn't suggest he shave his sideburns, but she asked him to take off his glasses. So the lights won't reflect so much, she told him. She expected him to be squirmy and deny everything, not convincing, but his apparent powerlessness would mark him as a scapegoat for the regrets and wishes of the others. No matter what he said. But instead he gave a speech, something entirely born for the camera. And in minutes he had rewritten his life.

"Here is why I wanted to talk to you," he said. He leaned in, looked directly into the camera.

"I didn't fire a shot at the Guards," he said. "But I did work for the FBI." He had never publicly copped to being an informant before. Meadow felt a tingle on the surface of her skin. She looked at him and didn't say a word. Let him. As he spoke, his face grew animated and his features became more defined. "I was a photographer. I was not a radical, not a student. I liked to photograph them at protests. They looked interesting; they were so passionate. Occasionally scary. Often beautiful—they were all young and beautiful." He paused, as if he were remembering.

"I was known as someone who took pictures, and the FBI asked me for some of my photos. It is true. I complied; I don't deny it. I was scared of the FBI, everyone was. I let them have my photographs. I took money for the photos, it is true." Marvin looked down for a moment. He took a deep breath. "I already had the rap of being an informant. I was older, I was awkward. I didn't know how to dress like the cool kids. My hair is curly and doesn't look good long, really. So I was already an outsider. And I tried to impress a girl once by saying the FBI bought my photos." He laughed bitterly. "I was a little naive about it. Not political at all, which condemned me in any case. I did not win the love of this girl, and from then on I was marked as an agent provocateur. I didn't even know what that was." He shook his head. And then came the astonishing part. Big cinematic tears started to flow. Not the sobby, messy kind, but elegant tracks of teardrops on cheeks: a clearly visible indication of emotion.

"I was on the quad that day, more or less shunned as always. Everyone knew there would be a confrontation, and I was a stringer for some papers. That is how I made a living. I would photograph the protests. And that is all I planned to do." He stopped and wiped his eyes with a handkerchief. "I did have a gun, it is true. But that is because I'd had death threats. I had already been beaten up once. I didn't even think it was loaded. I just kept it in case I got jumped, so I could scare people off."

Marvin paused, and then in a breaking but emphatic voice, he spoke. "I never fired a shot that day. I swear that I did not." He stopped. "For years now people have been hounding me. I used to get calls in the middle of the night from people telling me that I killed four kids. The police arrested me that day because some of the students attacked me and I pulled out the gun to scare them. But the police report shows that no bullets were fired from my gun. I know people think the report was all fixed by the FBI. What answer can I have to endless paranoia? There is no answer." He shrugged, and looked down.

"Look, I admit I was an awkward, stupid jerk. That I should have disappeared after everyone made it clear they didn't want me around. I don't blame them! I didn't think of it this way at the time, but the FBI ruined people's lives. I am sorry I gave them photos. And I am truly sorry for what happened that day, which I witnessed and will never forget. Our kids murdered by our other kids. For no good reason."

Marvin's speech, true or not, was the most vital moment in the film. Meadow framed it, set it up, gave Marvin the last word. Because his was the best.

In the first cut of her film, the professor looked like something out of *The Crucible* and Marvin looked like a victim. Meadow edited it again to make it more complex—she placed a convincing and weeping and nearly contrite Guardsman at the very end, after Marvin. Meadow thought that it was okay, this interaction with real lives. Look, look. It's okay. She was raising questions, and if they made people uncomfortable, all the better.

She filmed one more scene. Her cameraman filmed Meadow editing with her photogenic assistant, Kyle. The camera showed Meadow and Kyle watching a playback: the professor clip followed by the Marvin bit.

Meadow says, "Marvin's so convincing but it isn't just about Marvin. Can you call up the Guardsman who admits guilt?" Kyle nods. "Let's slip him in at the end. Make him the last word to complicate Marvin's story a little."

"What about one of the survivor students?" Kyle says.

"Naw. We all know how we feel about them."

"What?"

"Bad. We feel bad about the students. They feel bad. It is too easy. The Guardsman? Marvin? We feel bad in a more interesting way. Let's end with them."

Then the film shows a repetition of the crying Guardsman, and then the film ends. Meadow knew this was a fake ending, but it was a fake ending that admitted its fakeness instead of hiding it. Then she thought it too jarring to have herself only at the end. She and Kyle went back and inserted film and audio of her throughout. Her questions. The back of her head as she worked to animate still photos. Her filming new footage on the quad. She showed some of the strings, but not all of them, of course—it was still a highly constructed thing. An essay more than a neutral rendering. It had a point of view. A film is an idea about the world. Meadow thought of it like that, but she also knew that people can know something and visual images will override anything they know. Cinema truth is deceptive that way. It can tell you something but show you something very different. And you can bet you will walk away believing in what you saw. She thought she should make this problem an explicit part of her film. The way to manage a problem is not to solve it, which is impossible, but make the problem the material of the film.

After a few weeks, she had Kyle go back and cut out all the scenes of her. The fake footage watching her watch her own movie was too similar to her strategy on the Deke film. All that self-reflexivity seemed narcissistic to her and, well, too obvious. After all, the title said "A Film by Meadow Mori" right on it. Of course it was cut a certain way, constructed by her. Of course it had fraught objectivity; it was constructed of first-person points of view.

Kent State: Recovered took four years to research, shoot, edit, and promote. When it finally was shown, she waited for people to say it was manipulative and false. Objections. But that's not what happened. Maybe it had something to do with the timing: the film was first shown in September, right after President Bush launched the initial stages of Desert Storm. War was on everyone's mind, and *Kent State: Recovered* struck a nerve with some critics. It won several prizes, and in the winter, after everyone watched the clinical footage of the Desert Storm air strikes, the film was nominated for an Academy Award for Best Feature Documentary. Carrie was the first one to call.

"I can't believe it!" Carrie screamed into the phone. Meadow laughed. "I mean, I can believe it because you're a total genius, but I mean I can't believe that the world finally caught on. Oh, Jesus, you know what I mean." Carrie screamed again. "Tell me everything," she said.

"Some interviews and write-ups. Runs scheduled in LA, New York, and San Francisco."

"That's great!" she said.

"Yeah," Meadow said. "How's your movie going?" Carrie's student short, *Girl School*, won enough prizes that Carrie was able to find backing from a small independent production company to make a feature-length film based on it. She had asked Meadow to work on *Girl School*, but Meadow said she was too busy. The truth was that

Meadow thought it was a little silly, and the way Carrie planned to film and edit it was too conventional and boring to her.

"Great," Carrie said. "We start shooting in three weeks."

Meadow took Kyle to the awards as her date, and they had fun because they were pretty certain they would lose (although Meadow had a breathless moment when the nominees were being read). In the last few weeks, some people in the Academy and in various established critical circles objected to the fictional footage and animations used in the film. It wasn't a "true" documentary. It didn't matter; she was now making films that people would watch. No longer just a kid fooling around. Not everything changed for Meadow, not the way she thought it might. The problems of making films were still there; it didn't make her any better. But now she had this thing, this credential, and it helped her get money, get access, get trust.

Aborted Desoto Film Project

While working on *Kent*, she remembered an underground filmmaker she had first heard about in high school, Bobby Desoto. He made some amazing short films in 1970 and 1971, but he was mostly famous for vanishing after a protest bombing he was involved with in 1972. Meadow attempted to locate him. She spent some time in California, where he grew up, and then later in the Northwest. But she couldn't get anyone to talk to her. Not his family and not his friends. It was a dead end, and she gave up on it. However it wasn't a total waste of time: she ended up using clips from his films in *Kent State: Recovered.*

Play Truman (1993)

Meadow made *Play Truman* quickly. It was a short speculative film essay about the dropping of the second atomic bomb. Historical footage of Truman and Nagasaki were intercut with an actor in a room, which was Meadow herself in a suit as Truman. She read from Truman's journal. As Meadow went into Truman's biography, she showed archival film clips of regular people in their homes, rare films made in the early part of the century with very early hobby cameras, which she hoped conveyed a sense of the American middle-class security that Truman came from. She intercut these with home films of 1940s ordinary Japanese people—not exactly home films, but they appeared that way: a woman in a garden, children playing. She used intertitles and tinted some of the images to make them individual but also of a piece. As she showed these images, she read from Truman's journal to show how he made the case to himself that the continued fire-bombing of cities was worse than dropping an atom bomb. She let her Truman make his case, but the dropping of the second bomb gave the lie to most of the reasons. Still she caught, somehow, the way this unimaginable and world-changing power fell into Truman's hands, a man who didn't even know the bomb existed before his predecessor died. She felt his raw humanness melt away as he decided who would live and who would die. It made her shudder, pretending to be Truman. The film was her hybrid projection, a leap from her earlier reenactments to something else. And no one knew what to make of it. It was fantasia more than documentary, and it hardly got shown, won no prizes. It was clearly not what people wanted from her after her Kent State film, which made her feel pleased in a complicated way.

After the success of *Kent State: Recovered*, the failed Desoto project, and the perverse satisfactions of *Play Truman*, Meadow decided to take some time to consider what her new project might be. She flew home to LA for the first extended visit with her parents in years.

Meadow slept in her old room, and she walked through her old life as if she had never left. She wanted to, somehow. She let herself regress a little: watching videos and movies on TV, smoking on the patio in the cool desert night, drinking expensive white wine with her mother, and even going shopping. She spent hours at the flea market looking at old things. She picked up broken vintage electronics, sorted through boxes of ephemera, bought a number of obsolete devices. Whatever caught her eye and interested her. She put the things she bought in her bedroom and arranged them on a low shelf. She flipped through a box of old postcards and read the notes from long-dead people. She spent days like this.

Coming home and staying home was unsettling. It was impossible not to feel like a ghost visiting her old life, because everything in her house and the city seemed the same except for her. She was different, and Los Angeles made Meadow lonely for her grown-up self. All her friends were in New York.

"Meadow!" Carrie said.

"How are you?" Meadow spoke into the handset of her beige plastic cordless phone. She was stretched on the bed and starting a second glass of her mother's white burgundy.

"It is so nuts right now. We are doing all the postproduction stuff. I can't believe it is really happening."

"Oh. Good," Meadow said. "I am at my parents' house doing nothing."

"Why are you staying, then?" Carrie said. "Come back to New York."

"I will. Soon. I just need to regroup, I think. Watch a bunch of movies and think."

"What's that you say? Watch a bunch of movies, you, really?" Carrie said. She laughed. "I wish I could be there. Even if you make me watch some real-time antinarrative film essay about Portuguese fishermen—"

"Actually I was thinking all screwball comedies. *Bringing Up Baby*, *Twentieth Century*, *His Girl Friday*—"

"Very tempting!" Carrie said.

"Why don't you come here?" Meadow said. "We can watch whatever you want. A Peter Sellers festival. Woody Allen films. I'm up for it."

"Meadow, I'd love to, but I can't right now. I am working."

"All right, all right," Meadow said.

"Are you okay? Are you working on something new?" Carrie said.

"I'm fine. But I have to go."

"Well, I am glad you called. We seriously need to hang out when you get back."

"Yeah. And I really want to see that Portuguese fishermen movie."

Carrie laughed. "*The Way of the Fish*, you mean?"

"No, I think it's called *Scales: Eyes.*"

"*Man with a Fish.*"

"*Triumph of the Fish.*"

"*Le Sang des Poissons*," Carrie said. "No, wait. *F Is for Fish.*"

"You laugh," Meadow said, "but I would love to see any of those films."

As soon as she heard Carrie disconnect, she pressed the glowing call button, waited for the dial tone, and punched in Kyle's number. She offered to pay for his ticket, and her parents let Kyle stay in her room with her. For three days after he arrived they mostly concentrated on having sex during the day while her parents were out. She enjoyed having Kyle on her bed, in her room, surrounded by her books and posters from high school. By the afternoon of the third day, even that grew tiresome.

Meadow got up and pulled on a tiny t-shirt and some panties. She rummaged in her bag for her cigarettes, then sat in a chair by the window. She folded her long legs under her, opened the window, and lit up the cigarette.

Kyle stared at her from the bed.

"What?" she said.

"You realize this is like a full-on suite, right?" he said. Meadow burst out laughing. "It is. You have a luxurious starlet bathroom and then you have a huge bedroom and then you have like an anteroom. A suite."

Meadow shrugged and blew smoke toward the open window.

"You act like you are from the ghettos of Bombay," she said.

Kyle yelped out a laugh.

"I am sure," Meadow continued, "that in the privileged cul-de-sacs of Westchester, a dedicated bathroom is not unheard of."

"Racist," Kyle said, smiling. "And it would be a ghetto in Dhaka, not Bombay!"

"But Westchester, in any case," she said.

"This is a different level of wealth."

Meadow looked around, imagined the house from the eyes of someone else. It was opulent, partly because her mother had larded the place up with sumptuous, decadent decor: velvet pillows, silky carpets, chandeliers.

"I'm going to make bacon and eggs now," Meadow said.

Later she took a long run through the hills of Bel-Air, followed by a swim in the pool with the view. Then her parents came home, and as usual, there were guests over for dinner. At first Meadow thought this was for her benefit, or that her parents were showing her off to their friends. But then she realized that this was what they had been doing since she left: entertaining. On the previous evenings, Meadow and Kyle drank too much wine and slipped away after the main course was over to watch movies in her room.

But tonight Meadow lingered because one of her father's guests mentioned a mysterious woman, "Nicole," who used to call men in Hollywood.

"It wasn't just me. She called a number of men in the industry. We all used to talk about her," said Jeremy, a screenwriter who was also her father's client and friend.

"I think I remember hearing about her," her father said. "She seduced men on the phone, right?"

"But no phone sex," Jeremy said. "That was the thing. It was very personal and even erotic, but it wasn't explicit. I mean, that's what I heard. I only talked to her twice. I didn't see the appeal, and I guess she felt the same way because she never called me again. But some people became obsessed with her."

"Did she call you?" her mother said to her father. Her father shook his head.

"I believe she only called 'creative' types," he said. "The snob." They all laughed.

"Wait, wait. So she would cold-call these men?" Meadow said.

"Yes, but not really. She knew your friends. She knew everyone, somehow. She had a lot of confidence, and she was persuasive without it ever feeling that way. Jack Cusano was one of the guys."

"Hey, do you remember Jack Cusano? We had him over a couple of times. The Robert DeMarco guy," her father said.

"Of course I remember him. He was very cool. He told me all about working with DeMarco. And we talked about John Cassavetes, about our love for *Love Streams*. So Jack Cusano spoke to her?" Meadow said.

"I heard that he was really into her. For a couple of years," Jeremy said.

"That's surprising. He doesn't seem like the type," her father said.

"Did anyone ever meet her in person?" Meadow said.

"No. People tried, and she would stop calling them. And then she stopped altogether. She just disappeared a few years ago," he said.

"I wonder why," she said.

There was a pause at the table. Everyone looked at Meadow.

"Uh-oh," her father said, smiling.

"What?" she said. "It's interesting."

Meadow hung up the phone after "Nicole" had finally agreed to meet with her. Their talk made Meadow feel a bit uneasy. It was undeniable that Nicole was reluctant; yet she sounded almost happy to hear from Meadow. She was impressed that Meadow had tracked her down. One of the men, Jack Cusano, had given her Nicole's phone number. She took it as a sign of fate that it was a Syracuse area code, just a couple of hours from her place in Gloversville. The number didn't work, but the phone company (once Meadow explained to them it was an urgent family matter, she was looking for her sister) was able to look up the name of the woman who had the number in the past. With the real name, Amy Anne Thomas, and the city, Syracuse, it was simply a matter of looking in the phone book.

"Hello?"

"Hello. Is this Nicole?" At the last second, Meadow decided to use Amy's phone name, just to see how she would respond. There was a pause.

"Yes, I am Nicole."

The minute Meadow heard the woman's voice, she knew she had to make the film. It was a very appealing voice. And the perverse idea of doing a film about the power of a voice excited her. Meadow could feel herself drawn in right away. Meadow tried to persuade Nicole to let her interview her for a film. She listened to Meadow and then politely refused.

"I think you are a fascinating person—you captivated all these big power guys in Hollywood. And then dropped out of it altogether. You are a legend."

"That's very flattering, but I am not that fascinating in real life. I think."

"I doubt that. I really do. You are mysterious, and no one can resist that."

"Mystery only lasts until I am exposed. I don't want to be exposed, and I don't want to be filmed," she said. "I mean, you can see that was the point of using the phone, right?"

Meadow laughed. This woman was smart.

"Of course," Meadow said. "Maybe no filming. Maybe we can just do voice recording then? Hmmm. Even film your apartment, your world, but not you? It's such a good story. And you deserve credit for doing a brilliant deconstruction of male desire, a brilliant confidence game, a great hoax."

"I don't think of it that way, a hoax."

"Maybe that is too hard a word, too public. How would you describe it?"

Meadow proceeded slowly. They agreed to speak again in a few days. Meadow didn't push her. She talked about her previous films and sent Nicole her videos. She had credibility and would only make something interesting and sympathetic. She flattered the woman but meant what she said.

"I get you," Meadow told her. "We are alike. You know how to read people. You are an inventor, a story conjurer." She reassured her that the process was collaborative. Meadow also said (which Meadow of course didn't mean as a threat but as a statement of fact),

"I respect your feelings. It's fine if you don't want to do it. I can make a film about it without interviewing you." Nicole didn't seem to mind Meadow's interest, in fact she liked to talk on the phone with her about it, but she would not say yes to the film or even to meeting in person. Meadow's instinct told her that Nicole didn't have a lot going on in her life. She knew that there was a good chance if she spent some time with this woman in Syracuse, if she expressed a profound interest in her and her life, she would come around. But Nicole kept saying no. Then the key came: Meadow mentioned that Jack Cusano had agreed to be interviewed.

"You spoke with Jack?"

"Yes, a few times."

And then Nicole told Meadow she would meet with Meadow in person, if not yet go on camera.

CHILDREN OF THE DISAPPEARED

When she had finished *Inward Operator*, Meadow felt uncomfortable with the outcome: it wasn't that things had gone badly for her subjects, but more that she had orchestrated so much of it. She worried that it was too contrived, too forced, too cheesily consequential. So she quickly started something new. In her next film, she wanted to be invisible and not make anything happen.

Meadow and Kyle plunged into researching and planning a new film. They worked from the apartment she had rented in Washington Heights. It was a large and very affordable place, with two bedrooms, a living room, and a dining room. She could see the George Washington Bridge from her living room window if she stuck her head out and looked to the far left. The reason it was so cheap was that it took a long ride on the A train to get anywhere, and the neighborhood was devoid of other people like her, which was fine with Meadow. It didn't feel like Manhattan at all, it felt like an outer borough with young Dominicans and old Italians. Plus the striving middle-class families that needed more space but refused to leave the city for New Jersey or the suburbs. Meadow felt she had privacy, as though she were in New York and not in New York. She could even park her car on the street and heading upstate was easy: over the bridge and onto the turnpike and 87. She could be in Gloversville in three hours.

She read the tabloid papers looking for things that interested her, and one day she read about the children of the *desaparecidos*, the people who were disappeared during the Argentine junta's Dirty War. Meadow was hungry for real stakes beyond trivial American concerns. She didn't want to have to gin up any drama; she wanted to make a film about life and death, lies and deception. She wrote down the names of the young people interviewed in the article, the ones who discovered that they had been adopted by the very people who had executed their parents. Several of them were attending boarding school in the United States, and she contacted them. All were trying to come to terms with what they had learned about their parents, understanding it but not quite believing it. One girl, Maria Suárez, was willing to be interviewed. She wanted to defend her "father" although Meadow knew a paternity test said he was not her father, and the records showed she was part of the mass abduction of babies. Meadow filmed her as she went about her life, in class, in the dorms, and out with friends. She sometimes talked about her father and his work against the subversives, but Meadow didn't push it. As she was doing laundry and eating, Meadow stayed with her. She wanted her to forget there was a camera. Meadow did this for a few weeks until the girl trusted her. Then Meadow sat her in a room and gently asked her to speak about the paternity test and what it meant. The girl conceded that her father had done something terrible, and he had lied to her her entire life. She said, tearfully, that you can't undo a life all at once, and that it was also true that he loved her. Her helplessness and confusion made for a vivid piece of film, her emotional dilemma poignant. After filming her and watching the video, Meadow realized what she was really interested in. Not the poor children, the victims. She wanted the parents. The perpetrators. She had to talk to the parents.

Her father bought her a plane ticket to Argentina and a Mini DV camera she would use by herself (no crew). She filmed the parents in their homes. No interviews, she assured them. Just the house and the stuff and the faces. She showed up each day and quietly filmed everything. But they knew why she was there, why she was interested. So sometimes they did talk, they alluded, they justified themselves to her. Meadow discovered that she didn't need to ask questions. The camera on a person was itself an interrogation. She stayed with them, and they grew more comfortable. They wanted her to understand. She accrued hours of footage. It was creepily banal, the kids in New York and the "parents" in Argentina talking about ordinary things: the daily routine, plans for holidays, memories of family vacations. Or not talking. Maria's false father, Colonel Raúl Suárez, who was rumored to have been involved in the infamous "death flights," showed Meadow his woodworking studio. He was making a bookshelf. He appeared to be an affable, harmless fifty-year-old father and husband. As he worked, he would sometimes speak in slow, careful Spanish, which Meadow mostly understood. He told stupid jokes. He recited poetry. And he talked about how to make perfect dovetail joints. She indulged him, appeared to find him fascinating, and eventually, after many hours of this, he talked about the war years. Obliquely: "that time" and "those people." Pronouns not names. His sound reasons. His long-cultivated justification. His unimpeachable actions and his unstained conscience. He was free to speak, as the Ley de Punto Final had cleared all but the top junta actors from prosecution. Then came an almost confession, right into the camera: he was proud that the junta had cleared the country of insurgents, and the children of those people got a second chance, a chance to be raised by patriots. Suárez was so calm about it all, and he believed in his own righteousness. She found no gap in his story, no niggle of regret or guilt. He said he was a loving father. He looked the part, acted it, believed it. He could point to the good he had done. Meadow found it riveting: what machines of comforting delusions we humans are. Our language, our words, our ever treading minds and interior thoughts, all of these to make an architecture of lies that even we almost believe. No wonder the world is such a mean place, each of us judging one another without seeing our own terrible cruelties.

Back in New York, Kyle and Meadow watched the footage, and Meadow felt a bit sickened by it. Her movie, *Children of the Disappeared*, was coming together in a most peculiar way. Not didactically essayed. She inflected nothing, judged nothing. The problem, she felt, was that documentary filmmakers could watch their subjects the way an American watched the distant world's traumas on television. Watching but not engaging. Very happy with the distance between, very happy with the power and privilege of not getting too involved. Content with pointing out the horrors of people so far from each of us.

To overcome this problem, she thought she should be unobtrusive and flat, not pointed, no obvious juxtapositions of Dirty War statistics with bland home life. No easy ironies so we can hate the perpetrators from a great distance. She did this not because she had been given the trust of these monstrous people, these cold-blooded murderers and kidnappers. But because she wanted the human everydayness, their non-monstrousness to come through. She wanted the contradiction, the tension, to be clear: they participated in a horrible regime and they loved their stolen children. This made her feel very uncomfortable, which she thought was the right feeling. She let Kyle do a lot of the work as she started to feel numb toward the film. Inured to all of it. She hadn't felt that way making a film before.

One afternoon she slipped off to Union Square. She walked to the Village East Cinema by herself, and she bought a ticket to see *Girl School*, Carrie's feature film. It had been out for weeks and Meadow hadn't seen it yet. She was catching the second show of the day on a

Monday. Only a few people were in the audience, but she gathered that the film was doing very well. The "funniest film of the summer" was what the *Times* said. Or at least that was what was quoted on the poster outside.

She wasn't in the right state of mind to see Carrie's light comedy. She could feel her resistance, and she could see the setup for each joke, each pratfall, coming before it happened. It was, on its own terms, well done. Its ambition—to make a raunchy school comedy about women—was fully realized.

Meadow couldn't wait until it finished and she slipped out before the end. She walked down the street and came to a stop. She turned back toward the theater. What was wrong with her? Why was she like this, so ungenerous? On a different day—or maybe a different time in her life—she would have laughed and gotten lost in the fun of Carrie's film. Carrie's perfect, playful comedy. Meadow stood there, unmoving, and lifted her glasses to wipe her eyes. Her stingy tears. What kind of person had she become, and why couldn't she be better?

CARRIE GOES TO THE MOVIES

There were reasons, very reasonable reasons, they had not been as close. Meadow was hard to connect with on the phone, Meadow was cold sometimes, you had to be right in front of Meadow for her to engage with you. Some people were like that, but it just felt sad to realize that you hadn't been in touch with your best friend, and in fact Carrie had closer friends if you looked at her current life. Carrie had heard nothing about Meadow's new film until she got the invitation to the screening of *Inward Operator*. Carrie should have called more, but it was hard to keep up with anyone. She barely remembered to talk to Will on some days. Twelve-hour days in production. Nearly the same in postproduction. She now had a chance to make a big studio film with a real budget and well-known actors. She had been very busy, but she was determined to make it to Meadow's screening and she did.

It was being shown as part of documentary film festival at the Walter Reade. The place was packed, and she didn't see Meadow. Carrie sat in the dark, and she wondered if Meadow had seen her film, *Girl School*. She worried that Meadow had seen the film and didn't like it, and that's why she hadn't talked to her about it. After all, it wasn't Meadow's kind of movie. But Carrie decided that Meadow was simply too busy to go see it, and eventually she would watch it and say something. The *Inward Operator* promotional sheet had some quotes from Meadow:

> *I had a formal problem right from the start. How to make a nonvisual story visual? I tried to find a way to make hearing—not seeing—the dominant sense of the film. To make the viewer listen, somehow. But by the end of the film, the power of the visual again overtakes us. The ending silent very long take of Nicole, for instance. This is Cesare Zavattini's idea of remaining in a scene for the longest and truest duration*

Carrie put it down without finishing. God! Meadow could be so pretentious sometimes. Carrie felt bad as soon as she thought that. And it wasn't even accurate, was it? Meadow was not *pretending*, that wasn't the right word. She was self-conscious and ambitious; she took herself very seriously and sometimes Carrie found it exhausting. Shouldn't the work speak for itself? And yet there were lots of great filmmakers with manifestos. Essays and polemics. Why not Meadow? Why was Carrie so harsh on her?

The lights dimmed. So many times, in the dark waiting, and then the feeling when the music and the credits come up. This film, Meadow's film, stayed dark after it began. A woman's voice only, a beautiful woman's voice and a black screen. *My name is Amy, but I am also known as Jelly and Nicole.*

The voice continues to tell her story and the screen stays dark. Carrie thought it looked very close, maybe too close, to the black-screen section of Meadow's Kent State film. Why make a film if you are not using a visual? Why would Meadow want to cut off the most important sense element of cinema? But of course a black screen is a visual, isn't it? As the woman's voice explains phone phreaking, Meadow adds things: graphics of old phones and a series of tonal sounds. "I loved the phone. I mean, I could be myself on the phone, the self I really was, or ought to have been. I never thought of it as lying. Oz wanted the tones, the machine. I was always happy to reach an inward operator." Then it returns to a black screen.

"What is that?" Meadow's voice.

"People who can connect you to wherever you want to go; they are deep in the machine and essentially superoperators. I wanted to reach them because they were voices, humans, somewhere in the big wide world. Remember I was nearly sightless at the time. They talked to me from somewhere. I could be anyone and they could be anyone. A voice on the phone.

"After Oz and I broke up, after I was finished with phreaking, I moved into this small apartment by myself, where I have lived ever since 1973."

Meadow kept withholding the image of the woman in the movie, "Nicole," and yet Carrie still found it gripping. An occasional illuminated word from Nicole's monologue interrupts the black screen and then fades like a firework, leaving a faint trail of itself. She talks about her life, her childhood, and how she lost her sight for a time. Still the film doesn't show Nicole. A cityscape in black and white, Syracuse, presumably, with all its faded November bleakness.

"After the breakup, I recovered most of my sight, which was great. My pastime has always been watching movies. Even when I was mostly blind, I would try to watch movies—that's how much I loved them."

Now the film screen contains another film screen, like a movie theater, but the image is blurry, just moving shapes and colors.

"I listened and watched the blurs. Sometimes it felt like a hallucination, trying to fill in what I couldn't see."

A bright circle obscures the center of the same blurry image.

"Maybe it is like how the brain fills in our imperceptible blind spot, the part of all our eyes that actually has no photoreceptors. I looked at certain parts of the screen and imagined what else was there. It tricks you into thinking you see more than you do."

The blurry film is slowed down until the images become stills and frame lines appear. Meadow's voice speaks over the images. "All films are a kind of hallucination—the way we see twenty-four static images a second as movement. The speed tricks the eye, and the eye fills in what is missing. The form constant delusion." The images speed up and slowly come into focus. They are from Francis Coppola's film *The Conversation.* Gene Hackman is destroying his apartment, looking for a microphone. Nicole's voice is heard as Hackman methodically peels his wallpaper down.

"After Oz left, I went to the Cineplex all the time. I went through the *TV Guide* and I circled films I had to watch. I would stay up all night sometimes." Now the images are of another film, black and white, what is it? Agnès Varda's *Cléo from 5 to 7.* "My other pastime was to call men and have conversations with them. More than a pastime. My vocation was calling men. You know that word, *vocation*, means a calling? Calling was my calling."

"Strangers?"

"Yes, I had learned cold-calling from my sales job, but I did this for no real reason. Not money, anyway." Her voice trails off. A close-up of stacks of cards by a phone. Then a close shot of a woman's hand dialing, a little animation of phone lines across America. "One day an opportunity came up for me to combine my pastimes."

Meadow's camera moves slowly toward an artfully lit Rolodex. No shots of this woman. Soon, Carrie thought, she will have to show her.

The film cuts to the talking heads of the men. Three middle-aged guys, all successful in the entertainment business. All talking about this girl who called them, Nicole. Each one describes his phone connection in sequence, showing how Nicole used a kind of formula on the men. Through the manipulating of the men and the repetition of her technique, Nicole starts to emerge as a con artist.

The three of them talk about wondering what she looked like, even though they sensed an issue there. A black screen returns but with an intertitle: *After weeks of being interviewed off camera, Nicole finally agreed to be filmed.* Then a cut to the first full view of Nicole. She walks down the street with a small dog on a leash. She looks older than her voice and has a lumpy white body that wears its years heavily. Her blouse is a little too tight, with slight gaps where her body strains between the buttons. Watching Nicole walk made Carrie feel weary. She could see where this was going. A clean cut to Nicole on her couch in a blue kimono, a more flattering view. She isn't ugly at all, Carrie thought, and Meadow has lit her nicely. Her blond hair frames her face in fragile wisps, but the hair is styled, smooth. Her made-up face is round and clear, her eyes and her mouth are pretty in a puffy, tender way. She is a somewhat attractive, large-bodied fiftyish woman. But she is far from beautiful. As she talks, she becomes more lovely, her voice smooth and just on the edge of throaty. She laughs, and it is a delicate, soulful-sounding laugh.

"Jack was different for me, the last person I had a call"—she paused, looked around for a word, smiled—"thing with."

Meadow's voice from off camera. "What happened, why was Jack different?"

Another long pause. It was great the way Meadow let people pause, let them say nothing. And that she included her question in the film. Carrie hated when the pauses got cut out. "I really fell in love with Jack"—an L cut to Jack in his kitchen while Nicole talks—"and I think he fell in love with me. I mean, I know he did." He is making some coffee with a French press. While he waits for the coffee, he lights a cigarette. The sound is now no longer Nicole's voice. It is Jack lighting up. And having a coughing fit. He is also older, easily sixty. He has a full head of gray hair and wears a black sweater. He looks attractive in a dissipated way. Lots of wrinkles from smoking, a jawline weakened by age. He laughs at his coughing fit, then he talks about Nicole. He says it was a long time ago, but you can see he is still upset as he describes his attachment to her. He says he persuaded her to meet him. Meadow cuts to Nicole, who talks about how she sent a photo of her friend, which meant she could never meet Jack.

"Why didn't you send a picture of yourself?"

"Look at me," she said. "Do I look like anyone's fantasy?"

"Why a fantasy?"

"Because that is what I enjoyed, imagining myself like that. It is for me as much as them."

"But they don't know that." Another pause. She looks wavy, and her face colors. She looks a little emotional. *Shamed.* That's the word. Carrie didn't want Meadow to keep at Nicole.

"It was different with Jack. I let myself be myself more and more with him. Under different circumstances, we were very compatible."

Now it is Jack's turn: Meadow shows him in Malibu, walking on the beach. It interested Carrie, where the film was going, however obvious its point; how enslaved we are by our bodies, our selves concealed. How much are we our bodies? And why is it so different for women? Why is Nicole's tumid, faded person so much less appealing than worn, old Jack? And it isn't just success or money. It is men and women. Carrie felt a heat rise in her face.

Carrie was watching Meadow's film, but she was also thinking about her own life, her own disappointing body. She was barely thirty-two, and already she could read it in the faces of the interesting men she met. She would be having a great conversation with another filmmaker. Someone her age, someone with a comparable amount of success. Not even actors, for god's sake. Just male equivalents of her, people behind the camera and not built for glamour. And she would feel a rapport. Then they would say, I want you to meet my wife. Or, here is my girlfriend. And out she would come, so young and perfect. Breathtakingly attractive. Not stupid by any means. Full of admiration and adoration. Why should these men get it all? It was such a cliché. And what did Carrie get? A tired, frustrated husband she had no idea how to please anymore. Things were going so well for her, and yet she knew she was slowly losing him. Carrie's eyes blurred.

Next, the film settles into a straight monologue from Jack that doesn't get intercut with Nicole. Meadow's presence is felt even though she doesn't say anything; she is who he is talking to. The camera is Meadow, and the waiting is the question. One of Meadow's favorite techniques.

Jack tells the story of being stood up by Nicole. He sits on his white couch. His legs are crossed and he lights a cigarette. "I'm over it now, but for years I tried to figure it out. I am not a player, you know? Not like a lot of men I know. I'm divorced, I work a lot. It's an old story. Nicole listened to me, and I think I made her feel good. I liked that I could. I'm a little cynical and rough around the edges, but there was something about her voice on the phone. She didn't interrupt me. She told me about her life, and I told her about mine. I wanted to meet her. Actually, I wanted to be with her. Change my life, whatever it took. I never felt that way before."

A pause and Jack's eyes look to the side, then back to the camera.

"I thought she was a student at Syracuse University, interested in the film industry. I think I thought she grew up here—she seemed to know everyone. I don't know—there wasn't a lot of backstory with details. She elided details; we talked about movies and music. Our childhoods. She was very intelligent and kind." He shrugs. "Okay, kind until the end when she stood me up and disappeared."

Jack lights a cigarette, sighs, and exhales. "I wanted to meet her in person. She seemed to want to meet me. She sent me these photos of herself." Now Meadow finally cuts away and old snapshots fill the screen: a beautiful woman in a bathing suit, clearly not Nicole, not even young Nicole.

Meadow's voice says, "Were you pleased with the way she looks in the photos?"

"I was, but I wasn't surprised. I could tell from how she sounded on the phone that she was an exceptional girl. I mean, she was very young for me, I know it would make me seem like a cliché, but I didn't care what anyone thought. I loved her. I thought, maybe this is an old photo, but she said no, it was recent. Why would I disbelieve it?" He puts out his cigarette. "It isn't much of a story from here on out."

Jack is smiling, but you can hear the edge creeping into the tone of his voice.

"I bought her a first-class plane ticket—and I am a pretty frugal guy, so I had never done anything like that. I was really infatuated with Nicole. Wanted her to feel loved when she got on the plane. It was all set. I spoke to her the night before, nothing odd about it, no cryptic hints. I drove to LAX, with fucking flowers in my hand and a sign, just as we had discussed. I planned a dinner at my house; I was never happier than when I bought the food for that dinner. Lots of women walked right past me. None of them looked like Nicole. None of them looked at my sign. I stood there, stupidly, ridiculously for an hour. I asked if everyone was off the plane. They were. I asked if Nicole Lamphor was on the plane. She was a no-show. I tried calling her from a pay phone. No answer. No answering machine. It rang and rang."

"What did you think happened?"

"At first I worried that maybe there was an accident."

Following Jack is Nicole's version of the same story, also a monologue. She tells her side of it. "I made the plan thinking I would go. I wanted to go. I had fantasized about him, about that house by the beach. Of making dinner together and sleeping in the same bed and not being so alone. Of sex and affection. Of belonging. But I couldn't do it. I even took the bus to the airport. When the bus pulled up, I didn't move. I stayed there until the bus headed back out, away from the airport." Nicole wipes her eyes with her hand. "I couldn't face him. I couldn't face it."

"What?"

"That I lied and he wouldn't understand. That I was unlovable, deep down. It was not a nice thing. It was mean what I did. I stopped calling and I stopped returning his calls. I just cut it off."

She pauses.

"I had nothing to say. I let it go too far. Of all the men I called on the phone, he was the only one I ever considered meeting. But they all ended the same way: me cutting them off."

The next section, somewhat predictably, consists of Meadow arranging for them to meet.

"What if I told you she would be willing to meet you in person, now?"

Jack shakes his head. He turns away from the camera. He puts his hand in front of his eyes. He collects himself. Shakes his head. Then he looks at the camera/Meadow.

"I miss her so much. Still. It is pathetic."

"That isn't her in those photos."

Jack nods, resigned. "Yeah. Of course not."

"You still want to meet her?"

"I do."

Nicole is getting ready. Carrie was already cringing. Why would Meadow do this to these people? Why would they go along with it?

Meadow shows Jack waiting at a diner table. There is no sound from the scene, only music: low, steady, minimalist pulses. Nicole walks in. Her face already looks broken. She is trembling as she approaches the table. The camera moves into a medium shot as they meet, and the ominous pulsing gets louder. Clearly it is a disaster. Jack's face when he sees Nicole; then Nicole's face when she sees Jack. They sit at the table. He is speaking but still the only sound is the loud, oppressive music.

The next scene has the sound of Jack talking over images of Nicole at home by herself, looking particularly solitary as she feeds her dog and then sits on her couch.

"She lied to me, and she manipulated me," he says as the camera stays on her. "I never cared what she looked like." A cut back to him, smoking. "I didn't realize it until she was in front of me, but it was all a lie. Not just what she looked like or her age. I am glad I finally met her, because now I can see it was all a trick. I can't have feelings for her if there is no her. How can I know if any of it—of her—was real? I trusted her." He is very upset. Then back to Nicole, looking awkward on her couch. Her face looks so blank, she is obviously waiting for the filming to start. Meadow has started filming Nicole without her realizing it. Carrie knew that everyone looked peculiar if filmed before the person thinks the camera is turned on. Using it was a bit manipulative. Carrie watched Nicole sitting there as Jack's voice says, "Why did she do it to me?"

The camera stays on blank, unaware Nicole, for an uncomfortable thirty seconds. Finally Nicole's voice. "I did it for love."

The film ends.

JELLY

Jelly took the bus to New York City and then took another bus to her aunt's house in New Jersey. The next morning she went back to the city and made her way to the theater in lower Manhattan where *Inward Operator* was playing. Jelly had ignored Meadow's invitations to press events or screenings. But Jelly did, finally, want to see the film.

She sat in the dark and looked at the huge screen with her huge face. And Jack.

She watched Jack's face when he first saw her. Meadow hadn't recorded the sound in the conversation. It didn't matter to Meadow what was said, but it mattered to Jelly. Jack said that he was glad to see her, to actually meet her, but he couldn't get over how much she had lied to him. Worst of all was how she dropped him, cut him off. "I thought," he said, "that you loved me." Jelly didn't know what to say. In the film, Jelly stares down at her hands.

But now Jelly watched his face on the screen, looked for the disappointment and revulsion and all the things she feared. What she saw on Jack's face was none of those things. She had missed it in the moment because she was so overwhelmed. It flashes across his face, a very specific expression. He is hurt. Stricken. As if someone has slapped him. And then it is all gone. The cynical old man takes over, and he appears cold and annoyed. Finally she looks up at him. What can't be heard in the film is that she had then whispered, "I'm sorry."

All her life, Jelly loved and needed the calming dark of a movie theater. The way the shadows on the screen would make her forget she had a body, forget she was in a place. The way the movie light and sound swallowed her and let her lose herself. But not this time. To see herself, her tiny life blown up and public, ruined everything for her.

Jelly's face got hot and her breath stuck in her throat. Her eyes flooded and the images blurred. She closed her eyes and pressed her fists to her forehead until the knuckles made her head ache. She heard herself make a moan sound with exhaled air. She was not mad at Jack, but at herself and that woman Meadow. Why did she ever have to meet Jack? Why did she let Meadow talk her into it? She knew how to talk people into things, and yet she couldn't defend herself.

She opened her eyes and watched as long as she could, and then she abruptly stood up. She sidestepped, stumbling along the empty seats, until she reached the aisle. She looked away from the screen into the dark corner of the theater. She blinked, spotted the glowing light of the exit door, and headed toward it.

PART THREE

WOMEN AND FILM

Home/Explore film and TV/Reviews and Recommendations/Articles

"HOW I BEGAN" INSTALLMENT #36: CARRIE WEXLER

Prefatory note, 1/15/15: I have been reluctant to contribute to the Women and Film Series, even though I think it is a great resource for filmmakers. Of course no one can describe the single right trajectory for how to be an artist, but she can describe the history of her own project: who inspired her and what helped her (and what hurt her). My reluctance to do this myself was simply personal—I didn't want to make something private public; I didn't want people speculating and commenting. But the irony is that silence does not, in fact, protect you. People will publicly say what they think of you, will speculate and judge. I don't mean to complain about it—it is part of what it means to have an audience, isn't it? I don't want to be defensive. I want to express my gratitude for all that I have. C. Wexler

My early films came out of attending NYU's Tisch film school and the contacts I made there. I have benefited from the generosity of my professors, who are accomplished filmmakers, and for this I am eternally grateful. But all of that is known and well established. I want to tell a different origin story today, because I am convinced that your sensibility is formed at a much earlier stage. What comes later is a matter of determination and luck, but the details are prosaic and practical. The earlier sensibility is what makes you particular (and ambitious, I think).

I grew up in Los Angeles in the '70s and '80s. I had a loving but chaotic childhood with a confusing amount of privilege and hardship. My parents divorced when I was eight, and we never had actual money. Nevertheless, we often lived as if we did. My father—who died several years ago—went through various forms of bankruptcy during my childhood, and my mother had a steady but low-paying job as an English and drama teacher, which required her to stay after school most days for rehearsals and theater club. I was an only child, so I spent many afternoons in the house alone. This was nothing unusual in the '70s—everyone seemed to have divorced parents and working moms, and people thought nothing of letting kids be on their own for the hours after school until dinner. It was lonely but also full of freedom, which I largely used for watching TV and eating. Most days I watched TV for at least six hours. And this was in the bad old days, when television was truly awful: *The Love Boat*, *Charlie's Angels*, *The Bionic Woman*, *Good Times*, *The Jeffersons*, *Donny and Marie*. On the weekends it was Saturday-morning cartoons that were even worse: except for the bright spots of Warner Brothers, most of the animation was two-cell and rudimentary. It was *Spider-Man* and *Super Friends* and *Josie and the Pussycats.* I watched this stuff for years, and most of it I watched over and over. What we used to call, with an air of weary resignation, "reruns." The only way I can explain just how much TV shaped my childhood is to give you a description of one of my days, which was also typical for me. A Tuesday, for example, when I was twelve, went like this:

Get home and throw giant book bag on the kitchen table. Pour large glass of Tab and also consume a Cambridge or SlimFast powdered mix or whatever else we were "doing" this month (my mother and I were often on a fad diet—it was something we did together). Turn on TV. Wait—that was first, TV on with the volume way up so I could hear it in the kitchen as I mixed my snack. I watched old syndicated reruns after school. (Usually I watched *The Odd Couple* and *Emergency!*, but sometimes it was *The Mod Squad* or *The Partridge Family*.) At around five, I would pull out my homework as I continued to watch. At six I would stop because 1) my mom came home, 2) the news was on. I would go to my room, put on a record, and do more homework sitting on the floor. I might play with my dad's video camera, or dance or even do some halfhearted sit-ups. Then dinner in front of the TV while Mom and I moved into Tuesday prime time: *Happy Days*, *Laverne & Shirley*. The world in half-hour increments and punctuated by an endless stream of repeated commercials. At nine o'clock it was more "adult" time, and I often read a book while looking up and following *Three's Company* and *Taxi*. Here is the thing about this that amazes me: I did read and do my homework during this TV watching. Maybe because the shows were not demanding or engaging I could concentrate on what I was doing? The other thing that seems important to note is that I knew how bad, as in quality, a lot of this stuff was. I knew *Three's Company* was stupid and not funny. I did not laugh with the fake laughter on the soundtrack. I watched a lot of situation comedies, but I don't think I laughed much at all. I enjoyed watching it just the same. It was comforting, the TV itself, its familiar sound and its images. It made the house feel lively and comfortable. It was how I connected to the world outside my home. In those days everyone watched the same shows on the same days, so you could talk with your friends about what was on *One Day at a Time* or *M*A*S*H*. It was a continuous thread. So my generation (I was not unique!) was raised on some terrible TV, but with bright spots. Here is how I look at it now: the shitty stuff made you really appreciate the good things. When something good or interesting was on, it was like the world lit up with possibility, and then you trudged through the crap until you found the next good thing. I loved the reruns of *I Love Lucy* and *The Dick Van Dyke Show*. To this day just the sound of those theme songs makes me happy in a small but deeply embedded way, almost a visceral response. I watched those shows, and I would laugh, and the sound would surprise me and sound so different from the constant laughter on the TV speaker. It made me stop, self-conscious for a second, my own real laughter coming out of my mouth with the dusty haze of sun coming in streams through the drapes in the midst of my afternoon solitude. It is the only time I felt lonely, when I wished I had a little brother to catch the eye of and see if he was laughing too. There is some weird dynamic that happens when people laugh—like a usually suppressed secret about the silliness of the world is being blurted out, and you need someone to share it with you. You need someone to hear your laughter for it to work right. (Maybe that is why insanity seems to be exemplified by people laughing maniacally at their own private jokes.) But I was very drawn to things that really made me laugh. On the weekends I stayed up past 11:30 to watch *Saturday Night Live*—that was a big bright spot for me. I loved the adult jokes, the ones about sex or drugs that I didn't really get, but I wanted to get. I would laugh along because I could feel the joke in my body, in the performers' bodies, and in the sound of real live laughter. That was my modus in those days: laugh at the funny jokes even when you don't get them. It is like a wish about your future. Part of the joy was staying up late, after my mom went to bed, for *Saturday Night* and, on Fridays, the *Midnight Special.* I had the *TV Guide*, and I circled all the shows I had to see. Who was on Dinah Shore or Mike Douglas, for instance. I circled movies I wanted to see too, but I wasn't as into films at that point. I wish I could say I was devoted to film noir or that I stayed up until 2:00 a.m. to glimpse *Johnny Guitar* like some people, but I didn't have much interest in old films then. I liked regular movies. I would circle *The Parent Trap* with Hayley Mills, or later watch edited-for-TV versions of dramas like *The Turning Point*,

Julia, or *An Unmarried Woman.* I loved musicals—the classic MGM ones from the '50s but even the lousy later ones from the '60s. I loved the idea of feeling so strongly about something you would break out into a song and dance. But mostly my sensibility was being formed by all the bad TV that washed over me and created a constant hum of cliché and contrivance, ideas I could see even as a kid as shopworn and formulaic. But instead of this making my taste hackish, I think it made me hunger all the more for something different. It made me imagine what might be good or even better. What struck me through the noise of ads, processed TV, and dull fake laughter, what I hungered for, was something that surprised and delighted me. I was raised on a constant stream of uninspired images, but I was primed for something more than the dumb double entendres of Mr. Roper or the "awww" platitudes of *One Day at a Time.* And into this hunger came my first piece of luck at exactly the right time for me: when I was in ninth grade, I took an English class that included a lot of unusual films.

One thing my mother's teaching afforded us was free tuition at Wake School in Santa Monica—which is an arts-focused private high school. In those days it was a no-frills enterprise, simply an alley with prefab box classrooms on each side. But it had—and still has—extraordinary teachers. Attending Wake helped make me a filmmaker in a number of ways. [*Editor's note: Carrie Wexler has endowed fellowships for young women of limited means at a number of elite high schools across the country.*] I had the great fortune to take a class from Jay Hosney, the (now-retired) legendary English and communications teacher. He never patronized us, and he taught challenging and important films. He showed us great silent films like *Sunrise* by Murnau and *Joan of Arc* by Dreyer. He showed us iconic American films of the '40s and '50s, not just film noir and Westerns, but the perverse women's films of Douglas Sirk, which I loved because they seemed to both celebrate and subvert—in vibrant Technicolor—the consumer culture I recognized. He also had us watch European films like *Persona*, *Bicycle Thieves*, *8½*, *Jules and Jim*. Of course we saw *Breathless*, but also Godard's *Week End*, and let me tell you how much the world opens up to you when you "get" a cinematic joke that Godard has told. There is a moment in *Week End* in which the girl, Mireille Darc, stops at a car wreck and pulls designer jeans off a dead body. Laughing at this—as a young girl in Southern California—changed me. We were not Godard's famous "children of Marx and Coca-Cola," we were more like the children of TV and Tab, but in some of us grew a profound hunger for a funny and provocative joke, a want from the depths of our processed American childhoods. Finding humor in Godard worked for me like reading *Mad* magazine or watching the conceptual jokes of *Monty Python*, or collecting the satirized ads of Wacky Packages: a cynical, knowing joke was an inoculation against all the crap we still consumed, what we swam through every day. We reminded ourselves that it was bad and we knew it was bad, even as we were saturated in it. We forged a kind of default irony as a way of making meaning and authenticity. This sensibility is a hallmark of people of my generation, and Jay Hosney's film classes gave me a way of looking at it all, an approach. Culture, then, became mine for the taking. I cannot explain what a gift it was to learn that at a young age. You waste no time feeling intimidated. You are in the know in a most empowering way. That is why comedies are so important to me: they are both in the culture and pointing at the culture. Mainstream and subversive, at least ideally. So school made a huge difference to me. But the other leg of my apprenticeship came from a friendship. My closest (if not best) friend in those years and for many years into my adulthood was Meadow Mori.

I met Meadow at Wake School when we were both in eighth grade.

When I saw her the first time, I thought she was older than I was: she wore stovepipe tight black jeans, black motorcycle boots, and a ribbed black turtleneck. She was slim and flat-chested, her brown hair cut in an asymmetrical bob, and she wore no makeup except dark red lipstick. She had a large, straight nose that gave her a defiant, anti-pretty edge. The look was a kind of '60s beatnik variation of punk, which was a tremendous amount of glamour for a thirteen-year-old. At the time I was still feathering my blond hair and wearing badly applied blue eyeliner. I bought too-tight jeans at Fred Segal and had them altered to cut close at my ankles (we all did), but I was too chubby to look good in them and I wore oversized men's shirts to cover the bulge at my waist. Which probably made me look even fatter. I was uncomfortable and awkward in my body, and what impressed me most about Meadow was how confidently she inhabited herself. She glided into a room and every eye turned to her and she seemed unfazed by the attention. She fascinated me; I had one of those adolescent girl crushes on her, half admiration and half envy. I would have admired her from afar for years, but I had the dumb luck to be assigned a seat next to her in Jay Hosney's ninth-grade honors English class. That first day, I was thrilled to see her up close in all her detail. She had ditched the black and now wore a white sleeveless shell shirt and white tailored capri pants tucked into flat-heeled ankle boots. She had applied a perfect cat eye with liquid eyeliner, and her lipstick was very pale. A sleek sex kitten, but modified by her muscled arms and her slightly butch attitude. I could not help sneaking glances to my left as she sat there. She smelled of cigarettes! So exciting. She caught me staring and I started to giggle, which is what I did—and still do—when I am nervous.

"What?" Meadow said, but with more weariness than irritation. I was laugh-snorting, could barely speak. I caught my breath.

"Nothing," I said. "I like your outfit."

"Yeah?" she said.

"I'm really into retro-slut," I said, and barked out a dumb laugh. She rolled her eyes, but I could see she was laughing.

"You are, huh?" Meadow looked me over in my oversized man shirt and my jeans so tight that when I bent my legs at the knee, skin pinched into the folds of the fabric. "What look are you going for?"

"Fat and poor," I said. She gave out a guffaw at that, a sound that betrayed her surface cool. We had that in common: loud, awkward, unladylike laughs. She smiled broadly and her wide mouth softened her hard edge. She was—and is—a seductive person.

That day, when class was over, she invited me to her place after school. Of course I said yes, what would I miss? My TV and my Slim Fast? But first she suggested we ditch last period. We walked to Lucy's, the cheap taco stand behind the alley, and ate greasy quesadillas wrapped in foil. We decided to walk over to the Santa Monica Pier to get coffees, and then I watched her roll and smoke a cigarette. I remember watching her smoke and knowing somehow that my adult life was beginning and she would be the key to it. I truly could not have been more impressed.

We ate ice creams to get rid of the cigarette breath and made it back to campus in time for her mother to pick us up in her big green Mercedes. The car had a burled wood and tan interior with a creamy leather smell: so different from my mother's old Honda Civic's reek of french fries and stale candy corn.

Her house in Bel-Air was extremely lavish compared to our little rented house in Santa Monica, but I was used to that. Everyone at Wake School had money except for me and a few other scholarship kids. Her wealth was merely typical in that world. But what did strike me was her collection of books and records. She was, it turned out, brilliant on top of stylish and beautiful. I have to admit that I thought for a second that it wasn't quite fair. Meadow had everything. But I stopped myself and just thought, *She wants to be friends with me*, which felt very good. We sat on the floor of her room and listened to *Talking Heads: 77*, which I also owned. We all bought that record. In those days, whether it was jeans or records, the whole class acted in unison: the same records in every collection with a few variations. But here is where Meadow began to change me. Instead of watching TV, she suggested we make a movie. She had a Super 8 camera and actual black-and-white film, which was rare. She wanted us to film each other in the canyon behind the house. And we did, first Meadow directing me as I walked through the shrub and rocks.

"You have lost something," she said. "Something important."

I walked, looking. I imagined I was lost in the canyon, looking for a way out.

"Move over to your left, where that stream of light is." I moved. "Beautiful! Wow," she said. "Just walk slowly, and think of the saddest thing you can." I now imagined my dog, Sylvester, who had died the year before. Thinking of him could bring me to tears in seconds. "Great," Meadow whispered, and then I felt it. When things get intense, it always happened. I felt the genuine tears flood my eyes, and then I turned my body into a giant wet noodle, and did a huge forward pratfall, flipping over and letting the weight of my ass send me over again, exaggerating my tumble until I heard Meadow laughing. I heard the laugh and continued to tumble, adding cartoony sound effects as I rolled painfully over the rocks. I would do anything to get people to laugh at me. And tripping, falling, at pretty much any moment, never failed.

Then it was my turn and I was at a bit of a loss. I thought about what I wanted to see. I told her to nonchalantly walk up to the edge of the pool and drop in, fully clothed and with no expression on her face.

"Really?" she said.

"That's what I got," I said. "Falls. Unexpected falls. That's pretty much it." Meadow laughed, but then she did the slowest and most serious deadpan walk to the edge of the pool. I filmed her, and she stood there in her white clothes, feet together on the lip of the pool. She was very still and expressionless. Then she began to sway. Gently at first, and then more widely but still expressionless until she keeled over like a felled tree into the water. I think I loved Meadow from that moment on.

After we had filmed for a couple of hours, Meadow promised to get the film developed so we could edit it the next week. "I don't know how to edit," I said.

"I will show you," she said. "And you will show me what you know." I had never worked with someone before. It was a revelation: I could share my peculiar view of the world with other people.

"I have made some videos," I told her.

"Yeah?" she said, and put a stuffed olive in her mouth. We had unloaded from the refrigerator a bounty of fancy appetizers in plastic catering containers.

"My dad bought me a video camera for Christmas last year," I said. "Yeah. So I made this goofy series of videos."

"Like what?" Meadow said, really looking interested.

I started giggling.

"What?"

"It is very silly. I film my cat, Denton, doing his Denton stuff like chasing a string, looking out the window, walking—and I narrate his interior monologue." This was how I spent my lonely weekends, aside from watching TV. I made these silly videos and I watched them.

"Really?" she said.

"It started like that. But then it got more elaborate. I put the camera on a tripod, point it at him, and then I read Sartre and Camus while he looks meaningfully out the window." Meadow made an "ahh" sound and tilted her head. "It works even better if I read it in French. Denton speaks perfect French."

"Of course he does."

"Other times I film him but I play a song on my stereo, mostly musicals or opera. He stalks a moth or nothing really and we hear a song from *Carmen*. He likes songs from *South Pacific* too." I took a big gulp of Tab. "I call it *Denton's Diaries*."

"You are very funny," Meadow said, like being funny was a diagnosis. "How many of these diaries exist?"

"Probably twenty? I watch them and that's about it."

"No editing and one shot, huh?"

I shrugged. "I just film it, stop if I need to switch angles. It's just for a goof."

"It isn't really making a film until you edit. Otherwise it is like filming a skit."

"Funny you should say that. I also used to make fake commercials."

"With the video camera?"

"Yeah. I made a bunch of these. Directed by and starring me. With occasional guest turns from Denton. At first I tried to do take-offs, like puns or *Cracked* magazine stuff. But then I realized that just exactly redoing the commercials with my found props and my pets was funnier. The more precisely I imitated and recited the words as they were, the funnier the videos turned out."

"Interesting. I have to think about why that might be. It is odd what is funny, right?"

"Yeah, it really is."

"So you like making things," she said.

"Do you want me to show you sometime?" I said, swallowing my third perfect ball of mozzarella wrapped in red pepper.

"I don't even need to see them. I know they are great," she said and barked out a loud laugh.

We continued to eat in the kitchen, by ourselves, Meadow's parents nowhere in sight. They had apparently gone out to dinner. I suppose that as different as we were, we shared an affinity for solitude, for making private worlds within the real world. All I know is that I was very comfortable with her and in her house. My mother picked me up shortly after, and on the ride home, I could not stop talking about Meadow.

When the developed film came back from the lab a week later, we watched our "raw" footage on Meadow's projector. First my prat flip, then Meadow's deadfall.

"It is funnier when you do it," I said.

"Why do you think so?" she asked, looking puzzled.

"Because no one expects the glamorous skinny chick to do something goofy. But the chubby girl has to do something funny. I mean, why else are we looking at her, you know? If you are expecting it, not as funny."

"I don't know if that is true. You tell someone something is a comedy so they know it is okay to laugh. They expect it to be funny, and it is," she said. I thought about that. Nodded.

"But yours is still funnier," I said.

"You mean yours. I was only the actor; it was your film." She was right, it was my film—the idea, the phrase, hadn't ever occurred to me before. She taught me how to edit my film.

Our life together had begun.

* * *

Most days we hung out after school, almost entirely at Meadow's house. Sometimes we made films, but more often we watched films. Meadow was already movie obsessed: we went to the revival art house theater, the Nuart, and watched whatever films they were showing. We went to Westwood Village and spent entire Saturdays seeing movies, going from one movie theater to another, watching everything that came out: blockbusters, teen films, war films, comedies. And as Hosney's class opened a world of great older films to us, we also began to watch more obscure movies on video at Meadow's house. Foreign films, black-and-white American films, silent films, documentaries, everything. And we watched what we loved over and over. What we discovered was that the more you saw of something good, the better it became. Being comprehensive also was important. When Meadow was on a James Cagney kick, we watched *The Roaring Twenties*, *The Public Enemy*, *Angels with Dirty Faces*, *White Heat*. Dialogue memorized, scenes recalled: we became our own insular world of reference and repetition. If you didn't know the films, you didn't know us.

We were best friends the way girls can sometimes be at that age. We wrote notes to each other. After we went to our respective homes, we would call each other on the phone and do our homework together. We made occasional movies as well, with Meadow's Super 8 camera and then her 16 mm camera and with my video camera. We made epics and shorts and parodies. Then, at last, came Meadow's sixteenth birthday, and her parents gave her a car. We were free to do as we pleased: drive to the beach, drive to the movies, and sometimes just drive.

We were different, even then. Meadow was very serious about seeing what she wanted to see, and she was always more obsessive than I was. I remember a Saturday in junior year. I wanted to see *Fast Times at Ridgemont High*. Again. (We had seen it the previous weekend.) She wanted to see something at the Nuart. *My Little Loves* by Jean Eustache.

"It is only playing one night," she said. It mattered, in those days. Sometimes you had only one chance to see a film. A lot of films were not available on video yet. The night before, she had taken me to another film by the same director, *The Mother and the Whore*. In French with subtitles. Full of dialogue and long static shots in low-light black and white, which made it feel like a documentary, like a cinema verité film. Three and a half hours of Jean-Pierre Léaud chain-smoking with manic desperation. It felt very cool to me to see a French film about sexual despair when I had yet to have had any sex at all. In the end, I was glad I had seen it, but I was not eager for more.

Meadow was determined, and tonight was a chance to see Eustache's only other film "on the big screen," which was like the final verdict.

"Oh my god, but it is Saturday," I said. She shrugged. "Can't we be dumb tonight? I think Jean Eustache is a genius, but do we have to see genius films all the time?"

"Not all the time," she said. "Just tonight."

"I just want to get stoned and see something," I said. "Something with jokes."

We went to *My Little Loves*, which was, as it turned out, great. And it was in color and shorter than his other film. Then we got stoned, blowing smoke out the window of her room, and watched *Monty Python*. That was our compromise. Usually I did what Meadow liked and I was better for it, I think. She wanted to challenge the very idea of what films were or could be. She was always questioning everything. She wanted to challenge herself and the audience. But I was different, kind of lazy maybe. Flabby in every way. It only emerged slowly, and in contrast to Meadow, what I wanted from movies. I didn't want to change everything. I didn't want to challenge in dramatic formal ways. I watched a bad sitcom, and I thought, what would make this good? What would make this really funny? I saw a comedy that I liked, and I imagined what my version of that would be. A silly teenage comedy with girls as the main characters instead of boys. From a girl's point of view, but just as raunchy and silly. That seemed radical to me. That's what I wanted to make. I wanted seduction, not challenge. Or maybe I wanted to smuggle the challenge in a little, not subvert the whole form. Meadow and I were very different, but it was Meadow who made me see that I could—and should—make films. She did it, so I did it. And if we disagreed, had different ideas about the kinds of films worth making, it made us both all the better. I wouldn't have become a filmmaker, I think, if it wasn't for Hosney's class and Meadow's friendship. If it wasn't for them, I would have become a Tarzana housewife who cracks a lot of silly jokes after a few glasses of white wine on girls' night out. Nothing wrong with that, really, that's my audience, my people. But now they have something to watch at the movies. Meadow put me in that direction, there is no doubt about it, and that brought me to the Tisch School and all that followed. I still think about what Meadow would think of every film I make and it pulls me to take more risks, find the edge of my jokes. It is part of how I view the world, no matter what.

Now I suppose it is time for some revelations about Meadow Mori, which I think should be obvious to everyone, and not revelations at all. Meadow's "affair" with Orson Welles: she loves his movies and loves him. Did she live with him for a year or even meet him? No, she did not. If you read her essay carefully, the clues are all there, at least for Welles nerds. (Wrong house, wrong date of death, *Stagecoach* not *City Lights*, etc.) Meadow was creating what she called a fabule, a wish-story about herself, half dream and half fact. I know Meadow, and I alone seem able to read her perfectly. Meadow is playful, and she tells her own truth in her own way—you just have to yield to her version of the world to see how it all fits together, surrender to her possibilities. In a sense, she is the lover of Welles. Welles the great confidence artist, the prevaricator, the big fake who tells you he is manipulating you and that makes the magic all the more magical. Sleight of hand, she is all of that. She would say film is an art form built on an illusion. Static images shown quickly create the illusion of movement. All of it is a magic trick to Meadow, and that is part of what makes it so miraculous and beautiful: it isn't real life. She didn't ever meet Welles, but she loved him, the idea of him, completely. When she graduated from high school, she moved to New York to go to college just like I did. She deferred a year, rented a huge studio in a discarded and unused factory in Gloversville to make movies on her own, and when she finally tried to attend the next fall she didn't last long in the program—she wanted to invent her own way. She—and we—created a kind of film camp in the summer of my freshman year. She got the idea from Nicholas Ray's film commune in Binghamton, New York. [*Ed's note: Nicholas Ray made a documentary with his students called* We Can't Go Home Again, *which you can find* ***here*** *and streaming on Netflix.*] That was our only collaboration after high school.

As for this rumor that Meadow and I had a falling-out, we did not. The truth is much less dramatic. We slowly grew apart over the years, but she is still my oldest friend.

Finally, why did she quit making films? I don't really know. Meadow stopped making films for her own private reasons. She had an accident in 1999 that I think had something to do with it. She stepped back, and now she prefers to teach film at a college in Albany and live a very modest life. I respect her choices. But I miss her work and I miss her.

I will close with what Meadow once told me about being an artist. It is partly a confidence game. And partly magic. But to make something you also need to be a gleaner. What is a gleaner? Well, it is a nice word for a thief, except you take what no one wants. Not just unusual ideas or things. You look closely at the familiar to discover what everyone else overlooks or ignores or discards.

—Carrie Wexler 1/15/15

Carrie Wexler was born in Los Angeles in 1966. She has directed six feature films including Girl School *(1997);* WACs *(2001);* Lindy's Last Chance *(2003);* Making It *(2008);* We Are the Ones Our Parents Warned Us About *(2011);* A Baby! *(2014). Her films have won great acclaim, including a Writers Guild of America award for Best Original Screenplay and two Golden Globe nominations for Best Motion Picture (Musical or Comedy).*

Related links

Carrie Wexler, **A Conversation with Mira Shirlihan: Number 8**
Meadow Mori, **How I Began: Installment Number 32, 2014**
Meadow Mori interview, **Sound on Sound, June 1999**

comments are closed

CARRIE TELLS THE TRUTH

Everything Carrie said publicly in her essay about Meadow was true, but she also knew much more about Meadow's breakdown than she said. Was that the right word for it? She would never say that to anyone else, but that was it, a breakdown. And it didn't start with the accident, it started with Sarah Mills and the film they tried to make about her back in 2001. Meadow came up with the idea as a way to exonerate her (exonerate Sarah, and in a weird way, exonerate Meadow). But it didn't work out that way. Carrie had called Meadow after a very hard article was published in *New York* magazine. It was titled "Handmaiden to Monsters." It was about *Children of the Disappeared.* Meadow was interviewed, but her discussion of her own film was offset by comments from Argentinean survivors—most of whom hadn't seen the film but had heard about it. Meadow's subtle, uncomfortable film was "a defense of genocide." Why didn't she include footage of the survivors, the few who escaped death in the cleansings? Or the families holding up pictures of the disappeared? Their agony was left out of this "bizarre" film. "I am interested in the perpetrators, not the victims. I want the audience to see the perpetrators as complex humans, to see that we are not all that different from the perpetrators. Not to let them off the hook, but to put us all on the hook." But under her photo (black and white, Meadow's long legs in jeans, her motorcycle boots on the table in the foreground making her look insolent and almost blasé at her "film factory" upstate) the caption read, "I am interested in the perpetrators, not the victims." It was a creepy article that seemed to admire and revile Meadow for exactly the wrong reasons: here is this hot, privileged, brilliant woman, and don't we sort of hate her and enjoy hearing people say she's bad? The message being, who does this woman think she is? After Carrie read it, she called and left messages for Meadow at her apartment in Washington Heights and in Gloversville. "Hey, I need to see you soon. Did I mention I am pregnant? Call me back." Finally Meadow called her back and they agreed to meet at a restaurant near Carrie in Brooklyn.

Carrie watched the door for Meadow. She probably had trouble parking, or did she say she was taking the train? Carrie shook her head at herself: she might be doomed to a hormonally induced dementia for the duration of her pregnancy. She had read a shocking number of books about it even though she knew that she tended to be highly suggestible. But she couldn't resist, and when she read about "milk brain" causing women to lose ten IQ points, she felt a logy veil of space-out descend on her. This even though milk brain was a product of nursing ("milk") and not part of the actual pregnancy. For whatever reason, imagined or biological, Carrie not only felt out of it and forgetful, she had a placid affect: she didn't really care. She laughed into the empty seat and touched her swelling belly. She liked feeling slow and heavy, embodied. A world unto herself, and barely anything else mattered.

Carrie jumped. Meadow had bent over her and kissed her cheek.

"Hey!" Carrie said. Meadow smelled of mints and cigarettes. Carrie watched her sit on the bench on the other side of the thick-hewn butcher-block table and take off her hat and sunglasses.

Meadow's black hair was long and sleekly straight. At thirty-five she was already getting some gray strands along her face, which Carrie felt proud to think looked quite fetching. Carrie always gave herself a pat on the back when she found a sign of aging in a woman genuinely attractive, as in, *She has wrinkles around her eyes when she smiles, but they look pretty cool. They really actually do, at least on her.* But then it usually turned inward and backward to Carrie, as in, *But I hate the first tiny hints of a weakening jawline, no one looks good with it, and I catch it in photos now, my wavy jaw especially on the left, just like my mother, and there is nothing to be done, really.*

"You look great," Meadow said with a narrow smile.

"You haven't even looked at me, you phony bastard," Carrie said and shook her head. Meadow smiled more broadly now. Carrie got up and turned sideways. Meadow looked her up and down.

"You do look very healthy and glowing and so on," Meadow said. Carrie nodded at her. "Quieter too, huh? Peaceful? Content?"

Carrie snorted. "Yes, and smugly self-satisfied. Open doors for me, give me the right of way. I am my own reason, people. Because I am manufacturing a person in my freaking body, what are *you* up to?" Carrie said.

"Seriously, though, the maternal vibe is off the charts."

The waitress came by. Meadow ordered a glass of wine and Carrie ordered a cranberry juice and club soda. The waitress brought the drinks and a basket of bread. Carrie took a piece and buttered it. She missed having wine, a little, but she liked that she could eat with near impunity, which she hadn't let herself do since she was maybe six years old.

"How's Will doing?" Meadow asked.

"Will is good," Carrie said. "Did I tell you he applied to a bunch of creative-writing MFA programs?"

"I think so. I didn't realize he wanted to write fiction. Or is it poetry?"

Will had been having a hard time. When he turned forty, he decided a change was needed. He was tired of rallying his bandmates and sick of working as a waiter in a neighborhood restaurant. He was always a good songwriter, and then he started writing short stories as well. One day he came home very excited and told her what he had finally realized about himself. He believed it was a great idea for him to attend a fiction program. Somewhere funded so he could be paid to write for a few years. Carrie honestly found his stories wild and quite funny, and she supported the plan. But secretly she was hoping he wouldn't get in—she didn't want to move to Iowa City or Charlottesville or Syracuse. God, no. In fact she couldn't. They would have to be apart for three years. So deep down she rooted against him getting in, which was selfish and awful of her. He applied to all the top MFA programs, and in the end he was rejected by all of them although he was wait-listed at Michigan and at UVA. There was a time, not that long ago, when she would have gladly confessed all this to Meadow. But things were different now. She felt protective of her life with Will and maybe she didn't want Meadow to know that she felt the way she did.

"Fiction. His stories are excellent," Carrie said. "Funny and dark, with lots of language jokes."

"Like puns?" Meadow said with a rueful lift of an eyebrow.

"No, not fucking puns!"

Meadow smiled.

"Like Mad Libs," Carrie said, and this made Meadow laugh hard enough to choke a little on her wine. "No, you know, like making fun of jargon, crashing various language systems together for absurd effect, or exaggerating them, like New Age motivational speakers or corporate execs. Like that."

Meadow nodded and looked at her food. She wasn't eating much, more pushing the food around the plate. She caught the waiter's eye and ordered another glass of wine.

"Anyway, he didn't get in anywhere. Those idiots. So he will be Mr. Mom for a while."

"Lucky Will."

"Yeah."

Meadow drank her wine and looked around the room.

"So how are your folks?" Carrie said.

"Great. They said they saw you at your screening of *WACs* in LA. They loved it, thought it was very smart and funny."

"Yes! It was sweet of them to come." Carrie waited for Meadow to say more, to say she had seen the film, but she found something to stare at in the space behind Carrie, her mind clearly somewhere else. "What about you, Meadow? How's it going?"

Meadow looked at her, the narrow smile again. "Not great, Carrie."

"Is it that stupid article?"

Meadow waved her hand as if to say "over it." But clearly she wasn't. She stared into the space beyond Carrie's shoulder again.

"It was stupid and pretty outrageous what they said about you. They would never call Errol Morris a goddamned handmaiden."

"I don't want to talk about it."

"Why don't you ever call me?" Carrie could hear the scold in her voice.

"I've been very busy, crazy. I want to make this movie about Sarah Mills. She's serving a life sentence for arson, and I think she's innocent. But I have to put it together. Figure out how to approach it. Because everyone seems to hate my work now."

"That's not true. You are so respected."

Meadow shook her head. Then she sighed. "Everything is so easy for you, an unbroken line," Meadow said.

"Really? It appears that way, maybe," Carrie said. She couldn't really argue that she hadn't been lucky. She worked hard, but things often broke her way. She knew that.

"And you have everything you've ever wanted," Meadow said, nodding at her belly. "Films. Family. Everything."

"Okay, listen up. Things aren't as uncomplicated as they seem. Should I tell you about my life?"

Meadow shook her head.

"For instance, I'm about to have a baby and my husband doesn't seem to want to sleep with me anymore, and I'm pretty sure he is having an affair." Carrie hadn't ever formed those words before, much less spoken them. She started to cry. Meadow looked away from her. "I am trying to finish this film, I am having a baby. I've had a very hard time."

"I'm sorry Will is being a dick, but I'm not surprised. Every marriage is like that, isn't it? At a certain point?"

"God! Why are you so unsympathetic to me?" Meadow smiled as if this were a joke. Carrie felt herself getting really angry at her. "You told that reporter you haven't seen my movie. Even if it were true, don't you think it hurts me to read that?" In the same *New York* article, Carrie had read that Meadow said this:

> "Most films just flatter their audience. Make them feel good about their moral compass. Reduce things. There are clear bad guys with a veneer of complication to lend it some sophistication." When

asked if she felt that was true about her friend Carrie Wexler's new black comedy, *WACs*, she shook her head. "I haven't seen it. So I can't say."

Carrie knew that the journalist had baited Meadow. But still it hurt. Meadow said nothing. She just looked at her hands. Meadow had sent Carrie a short, faintly positive email about her previous film. That's the most Carrie expected of Meadow as far as Carrie's films were concerned, and even that hadn't happened for this one.

"And you barely return my calls," Carrie said. "Is it something that I've done or what? I want to help you if I can, you know."

Meadow looked up at her, and her eyes were red. She said nothing. She wiped her eyes.

Carrie felt her anger melt to something else. She raced to figure out what she could do to soften the world for Meadow, make her happy somehow.

"I can help you make the movie about Sarah Mills. Your movie your way. With my production company. Let me help you."

Meadow shrugged. Took a sip of wine. "I honestly don't want what you have."

"When did you become like this?" Carrie said.

"I don't know." Meadow shook her head. "I don't know. Maybe I'm not a good person." Meadow's face crunched up and she put a hand over her mouth. Carrie had hardly ever seen Meadow cry.

"Jesus. Are you kidding? You're not different from everyone else, you know. Some good, some bad."

"Maybe that's why I make movies about people who have done terrible things. An apologist for moral deformities. 'Handmaiden to Monsters.' I don't even mind so much that I'm not good. I would just hate not to know it, to think otherwise. That seems important."

Carrie put her hand on Meadow's arm. Meadow was still lean and hard, but now Carrie felt the hardness in a different way.

"That's one of the insights in your work. No one is pure anything. Bad people are still human."

Meadow pulled out a cigarette. Carrie eyed it. "Of course I won't light up." Meadow laughed bitterly. "The thing is, that's precisely what I'm talking about. If everyone is good and bad, if everything is complicated, then nothing matters. But I also don't think the answer is to just give people what they want, tell them what they already know. If people cheer at your films, what are you doing?"

"You're being ridiculous. You're just trying to push me away."

"I'm sorry. It isn't just you. There's something sickening in what we all do. There is so much ego in it, and the rest is a veneer of something beyond self. A flimsy pretense that this isn't just self-aggrandizement. It is really an advertisement for my own intelligence and quality."

Carrie had seen Meadow do versions of this in the past. She was a woman of extreme positions. Her renunciations. This time Meadow seemed more desperate than Carrie had seen before, more rattled. Meadow kept the unlit cigarette in her mouth.

"I have to go. I am just fucked up with everything."

"Don't go," Carrie said. But Meadow was up and gone.

Later that evening Meadow called to say she was sorry. Sorry she hadn't seen Carrie's last film, and sorry Meadow was so hard on Carrie when really she was angry at herself.

"I know," Carrie said. She loved Meadow, and it would never change. She would find a way to the feeling she felt most comfortable with no matter what. The bad marriage made it all the more dire that her lifelong friend not leave her too. She would insist on the friendship, on the "best" friendship, no matter how shabbily Meadow treated her. Aren't friends allowed to accept each other on any terms? Unlike a marriage, which must be fulfilling and a goddamn mutual miracle, a friendship could be twisted and one-sided and make no sense at all, but if it had years and years behind it, the friendship could not be discarded. It was too late to change her devotion to Meadow, even if Carrie hardly ever felt it returned lately.

Meadow said she did want to do the film about Sarah, who had been in jail for twenty years—since she was eighteen. "Good," Carrie said. Meadow told her Sarah was in jail for the arson deaths of two people, her boyfriend and her daughter. But the evidence—that accelerant was found at the scene—was falsified by a corrupt DA. Sarah had confessed and pled guilty to something she didn't do. Maybe she could even help Sarah, who knows? Make the case for her innocence. Meadow wanted it to make some difference in Sarah's life. Not just use her, but help her. Carrie agreed to help produce the film.

After she got off the phone, Carrie wanted to make herself a grilled cheese sandwich. Will was out at band practice and she couldn't sleep. Carrie buttered the bread on the inside and out, layered in the cheese slices and fried it in a pan. She ate the sandwich with a bowl of thick-cut potato chips. When she was done, she ate a piece of carrot cake. The more she ate, the more she wanted to eat. She knew she would feel gross afterward, her flesh already pressing against her pants, her growing stomach and thighs. But it calmed her and she needed to sleep. Later as she lay in the king-sized bed, she felt more alone than usual.

Meadow began work on the Sarah Mills film, and almost immediately it fell apart. No one else knew about the Sarah Mills film because the Sarah Mills film was aborted.

Meadow brought Kyle, who was now her friendly ex-boyfriend, as her crew, and they planned to film Sarah at the Bedford Hills Correctional Facility. It would be their first conversation in person, and Meadow wanted Sarah to tell her story so Meadow could get an idea of what to film next. Although she was doing postproduction on her own movie, Carrie thought she would come for the first day of filming. She wanted to meet Sarah and give Meadow some support.

Carrie rode in the car with Meadow and Kyle up to the Bedford Hills prison. It was oddly situated, tucked next to wealthy Westchester towns, which made Carrie wonder how that ever happened, but maybe a women's prison wasn't as disturbing to the locals as a male prison. It also surprised her that so much of it was outdoors. They went through the initial security, which was elaborate even though they had prior approval to bring their equipment in. Carrie had a twinge of anxiety as they ran the hand-wand metal detector around and under her pregnant belly. She knew, and repeated to herself, that low-frequency electromagnetic fields were safe for pregnant women. After the meticulous searches they were stamped with an infrared number and then escorted through open-air passages lined by chain-link fences. At the top were gleaming spirals of razor wire. Then they ran their hands under a light to show their numbers, went through another security check, and were finally led to an open room that looked more like an elementary school classroom than the prison visiting rooms she had seen in the movies. One wall of the room was all windows. It was a sunny day, and the bright light warmed the room. At the back was a play area for the children of the inmates. A colorful mural of various animals was painted above the toys piled in boxes. The center of the room had brown laminate tables and purple plastic molded chairs. No bulletproof glass or bars between inmates and visitors. On the near wall, next to the guard's high desk, was a long row of vending machines.

"It's not what I expected," Carrie whispered to Meadow.

"It looks low-security, but that is for the comfort of the visitors. Every one of these women gets strip-searched after each visit. Can you imagine how humiliating that is? Even the elderly, honor-block inmates."

Sarah was already sitting at their appointed table when they arrived. She had a dog with her. Sarah ran an in-prison program in which inmates train dogs to aid the blind and also to work as therapy animals for people with PTSD. The unleashed dog sat obediently at her feet, and Sarah sometimes put her hand on his head or whispered to him. Meadow had told Carrie that Sarah earned her BA and a master's in animal science while she was in prison.

Over several phone conversations, Meadow had given Carrie the background on Sarah's case, and why Meadow found it so intriguing.

"I briefly dated this lawyer who works with the Justice Campaign, which is—"

"I know what it is. They use DNA evidence to vacate false convictions," Carrie said.

"Right, but also they reexamine evidence with current technology. In this case, fire engineering experts. Also they look at cases where the only evidence is a convenient confession, that sort of thing."

"She was very young," Carrie said.

"Yes, barely eighteen. She confessed to the arson charge and pled guilty. She is serving a seventy-five-years-to-life sentence, which means she can't even be considered for parole until 2054. Her public defender was incompetent, the DA was possibly corrupt." Carrie noticed that the DA was described as corrupt the first time, but now Meadow had qualified it with that "possibly."

"But the real reason she was, uh, *discarded* was because she was a big drug user, and she had a sordid and documented sex life, so she obviously was guilty."

"Why would she confess if she didn't do it?"

"Ha! Do you know how many people have confessed to murdering Elizabeth Short, the Black Dahlia killing? Sixty. No joke."

"Really?"

"It isn't hard to get people to confess to anything, believe me. We are highly suggestible creatures."

Sarah was exactly what Carrie expected: she was a small, pretty woman. Despite her green smock and baggy green pants, you could see she still had a shapely body. In the photos from the paper twenty years earlier, she looked young and sexy despite the fact that she was being led to court. Everyone noticed her beauty, and it seemed to work against her.

Meadow sat across from her at the table. She wanted Kyle to film them in a two-shot, in profile. She said that people have what is called a camera-perspective bias when only the suspect is shown in videotapes of interrogations. They are perceived as guilty, while if the interrogator and his questioning are also shown, the bias disappears. So Meadow wanted herself in the frame. She wanted Sarah to look at her and not into the camera. Carrie sat behind Meadow but out of the camera's frame. She could see Sarah directly as she spoke, the same as Meadow saw her.

"Do you think you can begin by telling us what happened that night twenty years ago?" Meadow asked.

"Yes. I haven't spoken to anyone about it in a long time. But I have made my peace and I am ready."

Sarah smiled placidly at Meadow, and then looked down at her hands on the table. She spoke slowly and deliberately.

"I was eighteen. Living with my daughter, Crystalynn, who was two, and Jason, my boyfriend. It was a snowy December night, two weeks before Christmas. I had put Crystalynn to bed after dinner, and by midnight, Jason and I were really gone. We had done a lot of pills and we'd been drinking. I had to get that way to make the videos you heard about, the sex ones."

She stopped and looked up at Meadow.

"I heard about those. You filmed some homemade sex videos to make money, right? Can you tell me about that?"

Carrie could not help but think that when Meadow constructed her film, she would make much of intercutting clips of badly lit, wavy-lined vintage porn video.

"The videos were not just sex. Other stuff. I'd be blindfolded, and he'd do things to me. At first I didn't want to make the videos, but it was good money and we always needed the money. It started out, the blindfold, because I was shy about being videotaped, and I had this stupid idea that if I was blindfolded, no one could see me. I knew that wasn't true, but it felt okay then. If he blindfolded me, and especially if he tied my hands, then I didn't mind being filmed. But the truth was that I started to really like it, the blindfold, I was into that, you know, feeling like it was out of my control. When you can't see or move, everything feels different, more intense. I tried not to think about who would watch the videos. But I did like the sex. The police called it rough sex. 'Rough sex videos.' Which wasn't true. Jason didn't hurt me at all in the videos. It was play. But when we weren't having sex, he did hurt me sometimes when he was angry—shoved me and pushed me, never punching but still hurting. That was what the police said was my motivation. He shoved me down the stairs that night, and my leg was badly bruised."

Sarah stopped, and her eyes looked to the side and back. She leaned over and rubbed the head of the dog next to her, then she looked back to Meadow. Her tone was emotionless, matter-of-fact.

"After we stopped shooting, we started to argue and then he pushed me. I don't remember what the fight was about. But usually it was Jason saying I cheated on him or wanted to cheat. Jason was like that—a lot of men are that way. They want you to be wild in bed, to get really crazy, but then they get freaked out like they blame you. I remember he slapped me and pushed me down the stairs and I ran outside. I was very drunk and high, so even though it was snowing and cold, I ran outside to the back of the house in my t-shirt and panties. Bare feet. This is when Mrs. Jamison saw me. I was screaming about Jason. Saying I would kill him. Crystalynn woke up. I could hear her shrieking, but I was too angry to stop. The garage door was open. I threw some stuff at Jason's car parked in the garage. I wanted to get him out there, but he was ignoring me. I never said anything about burning the house—that was Mrs. Jamison's mind. I was standing in the open garage, shivering, thinking if it weren't for Crystalynn, I would drive away from all this and start over. And then I calmed down, started to shake with cold. She stopped crying. I went back in the house. Jason was passed out on the couch. I went up to my bed, which is across the hall from Crystalynn's room. I fell into a wasted sleep. And sometime after that I woke up, maybe because I smelled something burning."

"So you never set anything on fire, not even by accident. You didn't leave anything burning?"

"No."

"Why did you tell the police that you set the house on fire?"

"I could've set the house on fire. I was a smoker, Jason was a smoker. We were so far gone, I could've passed out with a cigarette. I also burned food when I was like that. So it could've been."

"But not that night?"

"No. I was questioned by the police for hours and hours. I was young and scared. And they told me that the rough sex videos would be used in the trial and in the papers. And that Mrs. Jamison saw me. I was confused. I felt like it was all my fault. So after many hours of this, I said I set the house on fire to get back at Jason."

"There is evidence, suppressed at the time, that the fire was started by an electrical short in an overloaded outlet. In any case, arson requires intention, not carelessness."

"Yes," Sarah said, nodding. "I heard about that."

"But let's get back to the night of the fire."

"Crystalynn died," Sarah said, looking down.

"Can you tell us what happened?"

"Okay, I will tell you." Sarah looked up at Meadow and took a deep breath. As she spoke, her voice sounded flat, but she spoke very slowly. "I woke up. I was still high, the room—the world—was real hazy. I remember how I just wanted to go back to sleep. For many years I wished I had just gone back to sleep. The smoke and the smell came at me, I could feel my chest tighten. My throat was burning—the house was so hot, I couldn't breathe. I pulled myself out of bed. Jason was not in bed. He was still on the couch, and probably already dead at this point. I crawled to the hall. I could see the smoke coming up from downstairs and smoke over my head. I looked up at the door to Crystalynn's room."

Carrie had a premonition, an odd feeling, from Sarah's flat tone. She felt a wave of nausea.

"I never told this part before. They were too busy on how the fire was set, and so I never really got to talking about it much. I crawled to the door of her room and pushed it open. I stood up in Crystalynn's room, and there she was sleeping in her crib."

Carrie wanted to leave the room. But she didn't. Meadow looked frozen, listening intently. Carrie took a gulp of air and waited for what was to come.

Sarah's eyes looked up and back as if she could see the baby. Then she looked directly at Meadow. "I saw she was sleeping. I looked down at her, and I knew that she would die if I didn't pick her up and take her with me. It was a few seconds that I stood there. My eyes and nose were running, the smoke was getting worse and worse." Sarah nodded. Then she stopped nodding. "But I didn't pick her up and take her with me," Sarah said. "I didn't. Instead, I—"

"Cut!" Meadow said, her voice hard. Then, "Stop talking. Please don't say anything more." Her voice lowered to a whisper. "Jesus." She looked at Carrie. Carrie was clutching her stomach and crying.

"I thought you wanted to hear what happened," Sarah said.

"No, I don't want to hear any more. I'm sorry."

They packed up in silence. When they got into the car, Kyle drove as Meadow smoked and said nothing. After a few minutes, Meadow took the videotape out of the camera and held it in both hands. She put pressure on the plastic shell until it buckled and snapped. Carrie said nothing. Meadow turned to her left to face both Carrie in the backseat and Kyle in the driver's seat.

"As far as I am concerned, we never heard any of that. This movie is not happening. I am done with it," she said. "I don't want to hear about gently placed pillows, or the caress that snapped the tiny neck, or whatever the fuck."

"Should we talk to the lawyer?" Carrie said.

"No. As far as we know, she is a mentally ill woman making things up. And we are going to leave her alone."

"I agree," said Kyle. "We need to forget all about Sarah Mills. If she gets out for not committing arson, that's fine."

"She won't. She doesn't even want to get out, according to the lawyer," Meadow said wearily. "I was hoping—" Meadow sighed. "I don't know what."

When they got to the train station, Carrie and Kyle got out of the car, and Meadow switched to the driver's seat. Carrie leaned down to Meadow's window.

"Are you going to be okay?" Carrie asked.

"Yes," Meadow said. "I am just tired of confessions."

"You don't have to drive back tonight. Why don't you stay in the city?"

"I'll be fine. I want to get up there," Meadow said. And Carrie watched her drive away.

Carrie remembered that it was three days before Meadow's mother would call her and tell her about the accident.

DAMASCENE

I

In the 2015 spring semester, Meadow taught her class in DIY film, which always overenrolled. She attracted the students who disdained commercial filmmaking; they wanted to be like Sadie Benning, making disturbing videos with discontinued Fisher-Price PixelVision cameras they bought on eBay, or editing narratives out of found surveillance tapes, or using stop-action animation techniques for ironic nonchildish subject matter. She liked her students. They were finishing two weeks on the "LA Rebellion" of African American filmmakers of the 1970s. The anti-Blaxploitation films. Today they would discuss one of her favorite films, *Killer of Sheep* by Charles Burnett, which she had screened earlier in the week.

"*Killer of Sheep* was Burnett's MFA thesis. Think about that. Burnett made it for ten thousand dollars. Black-and-white sixteen millimeter shot with a school camera and edited in the school editing room. He made it on weekends over five years, using a number of nonactors from his Watts neighborhood, and filming in locations he grew up in. He says he wanted 'just the daily life of a person.' A scripted, fiction film that also contains a lot of real life, including the famous extended scenes of children playing. It is a beautiful film. The poverty of the neighborhood is everywhere, but Burnett treats it as something worthy of deep looking, with long takes, striking compositions, and lush music."

Meadow paused. "Today for small amounts of money we can buy a digital camera and edit film on our laptops. Or we can shoot and edit films using our iPhones. And yet. We should be overwhelmed with amazing outsider films, indie films, handmade films. Where are they? If technology was the barrier, and that barrier is gone, why don't we have some nerd in Albany making a homemade great American film like *Killer of Sheep*? Or like John Cassavetes? Instead we get bright kids doing super cuts of TV shows or selfie/vanity films made for Vine and Instagram. Fast and shallow."

She didn't mind that she sounded like a scoldy old person sometimes. The students looked up to her, listened to her. One of them, she was determined, was going to make something great.

"But maybe there are brilliant homemade films being made. How would we see them, find them, with all the visual static vying for our attention? Between all the"—Meadow paused, looked very serious, very stern, waved her hand—"cat parkour videos taking up all the available channels." The class giggled.

Afterward, as she was collecting her things, a student came up to her and waited until she looked up.

"Professor Mori, I saw your film *Children of the Disappeared.* I loved it."

"Oh. Good," Meadow said. "It was made a long time ago."

"I read Carrie Wexler's essay," she said. "And your essay." She made finger quotes when she said "essay" and smiled.

Meadow knew they would get around to asking her about that. Meadow smiled and then zipped up her bag. Meadow liked this student; she always listened and made interesting comments.

"Your essay was great—people were totally confused by it." Then, "I didn't realize you wrote fan fiction. And it is really cool that you did old fat Orson Welles, nobody does old fat Orson Welles. Plenty of people have done young slim Welles, but I don't think anyone has done what you did." The girl beamed. She appeared to be waiting. Meadow just nodded and waited back. "So, can I ask you something, Professor?"

"Sure."

"Since you are so passionate about cinema, why would you quit making films? If you don't mind my asking?"

"I don't mind your asking. I just haven't wanted to make any more films. I used to—" Meadow stopped, looked at this young woman's face. "But not anymore." The student nodded. "I'm afraid I have to get to a meeting now."

"Oh, sure." The student walked to the door and then turned to face Meadow. "You know what? I know you were joking, but there actually are cat parkour videos. It's like a whole subgenre of cat videos."

Meadow laughed and shrugged. "Of course!" When the student left the room, Meadow said, "Fan fiction? Oh my god."

When she got home, Meadow opened her laptop and reread Carrie's essay. Carrie had written that the accident had changed Meadow, which certainly was true. Of course Carrie knew more than that, and she had to leave that part out. But over the years Meadow saw the whole thing much more clearly. Your life changes, and it can seem like it bursts into the new life. A damascene moment, a conversion. But if she was honest, she saw it was a number of moments—significant events, one building on the other. All of them converting her, spinning her toward her new life. It wasn't a downward spiral, although it felt that way at the time; it was an inward spiral, a seashell spiral, a *spira mirabilis*, as if she were drawing the events to her, moving her closer to who she really was.

The first event was the phone call from Nicole/Jelly/Amy. It came long after *Inward Operator* had been released, when she was deep into the filming of *Children of the Disappeared.* Meadow got a message on her voice mail. She referred to herself as Jelly, not Nicole or Amy. Meadow called her back. She had no idea what was coming—she truly expected that the woman had seen the film again and was calling to say she liked it.

Jelly: I finally saw your film. The one you made about me.

Meadow: You did.

J: I didn't want to see it before because I was scared of watching myself, my life.

M: I can imagine.

J: You cannot imagine. *(A pause.)* You have no idea. The fact is that some women do not get love. And I knew that, I didn't need you to show me that. I didn't need the world to laugh at me. I did not need you to humiliate me. There is enough pain. Only Jack had a right to judge me.

M: I think you are wonderful, and I tried to show how interesting you are.

J: Don't condescend to me. I am not stupid, although I was naive to believe you. You had all the power, and you knew exactly what would happen.

M: I believed in you, I thought that Jack—

J: What?

M: I really thought that Jack would love and forgive you. That he would understand you.

J: You set me up to be humiliated. You knew how it would look. You filmed it.

M: I didn't know. I swear I didn't know how it would go.

J: You did this to me. You did this to me. It was a hard, mean thing.

M: I am so sorry.

J: You played me. And then when you saw what you had, you put the film out there. Not everything needs to be filmed. Not everything needs to be seen, to be public. What good did it do? What was it for?

M: I don't know. *(A pause.)* I don't.

J: I just wanted you to get the picture on costs. What you did and what it felt like for me.

M: Okay. I'm sorry.

J: Some people—you, for instance—are very lucky in this life.

Meadow never told anyone about Jelly's call, but it was impossible to forget what Jelly said. When Meadow later received a lot of criticism for *Children of the Disappeared*, she kept thinking back to Jelly's reproach. Meadow needed to do something different, which led to the second event: the aborted Sarah Mills confession. And her weird lack of affect as she confessed. The experience shook Meadow completely, which led to the third event, the accident. The stupid, careless accident.

After the three-hour drive from Bedford Hills, when she was just a few minutes from home, she realized she had no coffee or food for breakfast tomorrow. Meadow stopped at the Price Chopper to get groceries. She swiped her credit card and waited. She was tired, and she heard the girl say, "Thank you," and hand her the receipt. It didn't occur to her to say "thank you" back until she had already started to walk toward the door.

"Excuse me," she heard the girl shout. Meadow turned back and the girl was holding up her bag.

"Oh, my groceries! Sorry. Thank you so much," Meadow said brightly and took the plastic bag. Where was the car? She clicked her alarm button on her key to find it. It clicked and the lights blinked. Of course, there it was.

Sarah's hand had shaken a little, otherwise you would never know that she was fragile. It would be impossible to guess what she was talking about if you didn't speak English. She was so cool, even after twenty years, could someone be so cool?

Meadow turned on the car. She cranked up the heat. She turned on the radio, then she turned it off again. It was like that *Brother's Keeper* documentary. Wasn't there a scene where the old guy confesses on camera to killing his brother?

People will tell you anything. "I would confess," Meadow said out loud, and she was shocked at how her voice sounded in the car. She laughed. Maybe it is from watching so many confessions on TV and in the movies. Meadow's hands held the wheel lightly at four and seven o'clock. Her neck was sore; she put one hand in her lap and moved the other one across the steering wheel so she could control the wheel with one hand. The setting sun was in her eyes. She was driving into the dusk, and even with sunglasses it was too bright.

"I confess," she said. "I am a terrible, selfish person who just tries to make myself look smart," she said, doubtfully. "But really, I am just trying to make myself. Out of looking at other people. I have no real self, I think," she said. Meadow still couldn't see and reached to lower the visor. Just then she changed lanes, to get into the lane that was for her turn, the turn she had made a thousand times before. Meadow was already in her driveway when she made that turn, already walking to her bed, to the sleep that she needed so badly. She looked to her left, but she didn't look. She heard a horn, and she saw her car rushing toward the side of another car. She pressed the brakes, but her car did not stop, it swerved, and in the moment before contact, she knew this was a big accident, and she thought perhaps she would die.

When she hit the side of the other car, the front of her car crumpled and ripped away. There was an explosion, and her hands were pinned down as the airbag hit her face. Then it was over, just the burning smell. The airbag deflated, but she felt something sticking to her chin. She pulled the latch of the door and pushed. It creaked loudly but the door opened and she stumbled out.

"Are you okay?" a woman asked her. And Meadow nodded yes, but then she fell back against the car and the woman helped her to the curb.

"My face," Meadow said, and tried to touch her chin.

"Don't touch it. It looks burned from the airbag. And your knee, does that hurt? Don't move. An ambulance is coming."

The EMS people put a blanket on her. They made her lie down. They put something on her face. It was starting to hurt. The burning smell was awful, plastic and acid. She felt suddenly that she would be sick.

Only once she was in the ambulance did she think to ask.

"What about the other driver? Is the other driver okay?" The attendant nodded.

"They took her to the hospital. They are taking care of her right now."

"Oh my god. Was she hurt badly?" Meadow tried to get up. The attendant gently pushed her back down.

"I don't know, but she is getting care. Don't worry."

"What have I done," Meadow cried. "Oh god, what have I done?" Meadow started to sob, which hurt all of her face and her chest.

"It was an accident. Just an accident. You need to calm down. Everything is okay."

Meadow shook her head. She closed her eyes. *No. You don't understand. I am a terrible person, I do this all the time.*

It was true. Lately Meadow had been reckless in her driving. She slid blindly into traffic, she barely looked over her shoulder when she changed lanes. She drove quite fast, and negotiated turns with one hand loosely gripping the steering wheel. None of this was on purpose. None of it broke the surface of her conscious mind. It was only in the hospital, where she was kept for a day and a night due to her concussion, that she remembered how much she had been courting an accident. Her own desire to hit a divider and bounce off, or a tree, or an embankment. Not to die, but to make something hit her, shake her up. But never—she swore—did she ever imagine hurting another person.

Her victim was a thirty-year-old woman. Her injuries were not serious. A broken hand from her airbag and some bruises and a stiff neck. Yet Meadow knew that she was lucky. The cost of Meadow's carelessness could have been someone's life, and Meadow would have fallen into it without a thought.

Meadow's mother had flown out and was there to drive her home. Meadow was weak and unable to take care of herself. She needed to stay in bed and rest for two weeks. So here she was, at thirty-five, being cared for by her mother. She did not mind this at all. Her mother, as beautiful and familiar a person as Meadow would ever see, brushed her hair from her face. Her mother brought her a tray of food. Her mother helped her sit up with pillows behind her back. Her mother brought her books and ice water. Her mother helped her to the bathroom, and then stroked her face gently before kissing her good night. Meadow gave in to it. She had no resistance to the love. She was helpless, and her mother helped her. But still Meadow stared into space as she tried to sleep, her eyes wide open in the dark, and she knew it was not good—her life, the world, the accident.

Kyle visited. Carrie called her. Meadow told them all she was fine, just sore. Her face looked bad where the plastic had stuck to her chin, but even that would heal quickly. The second time Carrie called, Meadow told her, "Do you know why people change when they are sick? They have time to think about where they are. And how little they have left."

All of Meadow's life she had prided herself on her rigorous self-interrogations. None of this saved her from becoming a destructive person, a person who not only didn't make the world better, but a person who made some lives worse. She spent her last few days in bed taking inventory—wasn't this how it worked in those recovery programs? She made herself write in a notebook about her transgressions big and small, as if the precision about the small ones might let her sneak up on the bigger ones.

Notes:
My Transgressions

I flirted, drunkenly and outrageously, with a friend's husband. I remember touching his tie and looking into his eyes. The memory makes me flinch, though nothing came of it.

I did not return the letters of my aunt, who wrote in fine, even script of her admiration for my films. I meant to, but no.

I did not write to any of my teachers—not even Jay Hosney—to thank them for what they had taught me. Not once, though I think about it often. Gratitude unexpressed is no gratitude at all.

I cheated on the three serious boyfriends I have had, including Kyle. Some of it was discovered, but most of it wasn't. I would sleep with men the way I have driven lately: not intentionally, veering into a sloppy collision, finding some way to inhabit myself as I lied and omitted and cheated. It meant nothing, yet I had to admit it meant a lot because I went to lengths to do it. Finding myself away from home, going out to a party where I knew no one, fixing my attention on one receptive person and not wavering until they were in a cab or an elevator. A hotel room was ideal: no one belonged there and it existed in a space separate from both our lives.

Not watching all of Carrie's films, even though Carrie deserved better. Even though Carrie saw all of mine. Wishing, sometimes, that Carrie would not have success after success. Wanting, sometimes, people to fail. Not just people, but my friend.

Jelly in that fucking movie. That was the worst. I knew that Jelly would be humiliated. I put it in motion, and what for?

I lie all the time. To my parents, to my lovers, to my subjects, to myself.

I spend money. I have money from my parents, and I spend it on my art, my vanity. I gave a pittance to various causes related to my films, but that was all self-serving. All to show what a good person I am. All to mitigate the narcissism that was in evidence in everything I made.

I made

Meadow gave up. Her litany of self-recrimination was absurd. It did no one any good. Even her guilt and inventory were an exercise in narcissism. A way of proving that she was a certain kind of person. Part of her already saying, "Everyone behaves badly, but I am special because I admit it." Meadow hurled the notebook off the bed and pushed her face into the pillow, which made her wince from the scab on her chin. She finally slept, and when sleep came it fell on her all at once, dreamless, long, and deep.

Meadow's mother brought her juice and a white pill. Meadow took the tablet, put it on her tongue, and then the swallow of the juice. She looked up at her mother. Her mother said, "You need to eat something. Try some toast." And Meadow picked up the piece of dry toast and bit into it. She chewed, looking at her mother and not speaking. She swallowed, which hurt a little.

"Good," her mother said. Meadow took another bite and slowly chewed. She ate the toast.

"I think you need to take a shower. I will help you walk to the bathroom."

Meadow swung her legs over the side. She was stiff and sore, and she needed her mother to keep her steady. She lasted only a few minutes in the shower before the hot water made her feel faint. Her mother held a towel around her and then helped her into a robe.

"Put your arm in here. Good," she said. "Let's brush our teeth before we go back to bed."

Meadow brushed her teeth and looked expectantly at her mother.

"Back to bed and rest," she said, and her mother helped Meadow walk back to bed. She helped swing her legs up one at a time and lie down. She pulled the sheet up and then the blanket. She turned out the light, kissed Meadow on the forehead. Meadow didn't make lists or cry or throw anything. She thought of nothing at all except her mother saying, "Try to rest now." And she did what she was told to do.

After her body healed and her mother had left, Meadow hoped she was different. She ate, she slept, she read the paper, she exercised. She had no idea what to do next. She moved through her old life with both deliberation and detachment, as though she were waiting for something to happen.

DAMASCENE

II

Money was complicated for everyone, but for Meadow it seemed that the older she got, the more uneasy her wealth made her feel. It had been Meadow's habit—her whole life—to give money to people who asked her for money. People on street corners, a hand with paper cup held out or just a hand. The men standing by the streetlight or highway entrance ramp holding a piece of cardboard with a message written in Magic Marker: "I am a vet. Please help me. I have no place to live." Sometimes a grubby teenage girl with piercings and a vacant look in her eye. "Excuse me, ma'am, can you help me get bus fare home?" A man on the subway or the bus with a ready-made speech that made everyone look away, or stare at the ground or the paper with steely absorption. The speech was always impossible, the weariness in the voice already making it seem rehearsed and insincere. She wanted them to stop, didn't want them to perform their need. What difference did the speech make? You gave or you didn't for whatever reasons, but not the speech. She pulled out some money as soon as they began.

Tiny, meaningless amounts of money, for which the person was always grateful and Meadow was always sheepish and embarrassed. The moment was always the same: she holds out the money and knows that she does not want to touch the person asking for money. So she forces herself to press it into the person's hand, forces herself to make eye contact, smile, however fleetingly, lets her fingers brush the dirty rough fingers of the person. And in this moment she gets a glimpse of living on the streets, of dirty layers of clothes, of what skin must feel like unwashed for days and weeks at a time. And always Meadow feels shame. A shame that she must force herself to touch and see them, ashamed of how grateful they are, but mostly ashamed about how measly and self-gratifying the gesture is. She hates to do it: it is sentimental and self-serving and a sop to her guilt. To use another person's need to make you feel as if you are good, even to use another person to remind you of your own luck and privilege—this is shameful.

But here is what is also true:
Meadow feels momentarily good despite the shame. It feels good to lose her indifference, to move outside her own experience for an instant, however complicated it is. At least there is a glimmer of truth in admitting that she has had great good luck in this life. Admitting that, confronting that.

And:
As problematic as the giving could be, she cannot abide the alternative. Ignoring the person. Looking away and hurrying by. Saying no (in a barely audible voice as if the conversation hasn't actually happened or shaking a head slightly, also not wanting to give it full engagement or open up any avenue of discussion). So awful does it make her feel that on the occasions she has ignored someone (because the light was changing, because her hands were full, because—oh god—she was in a rush, perhaps a bit late), she has ruminated and felt the sting of her

own selfishness so acutely that she has even circled back to find the person (driven around the block, walked back to the corner, put her bags down and located her wallet), apologized as if they have even noticed her passing them (what do they want with her apology, she is forever making it more awkward, more undignified, her apology only to repair her vanity about her own generosity, her own porousness), given them five dollars or ten dollars and hurried away before the thank-yous, which are too much, much more than she deserves. (Sometimes she feels that it is entirely transactional: she pays them so they will thank her. She is buying a feeling of gratitude from them.)

But of course there is also this:

They want the money and need the money. About the want and need there cannot be any doubt. They have asked for it because they desperately need it. They want the help, even if futile. It serves them as well. She knew they would buy food or drugs or drink or all of those things. Maybe some cigarettes or a thick sweet cup of coffee somewhere indoors. Maybe some Handi Wipes, toothpaste, a room with a shower. Whatever can be bought that is needed to endure the day. And so it cannot be refused. All of that came to her if she thought about it, which she did. Yet she also, like most people, soon moved on to whatever else occupied her. But then came this particular incident, with this particular woman, and Meadow saw that she was changing in ways she was still discovering.

Meadow had pulled into the post office parking lot. The line would be long. The lot was nearly full. She reached over to the passenger side and grabbed the package off the seat. Why would 10 a.m. be a crowded time at the post office? She felt her coat pockets as she locked the car: phone, wallet, cigarettes.

A tall woman with stiff dark brown curls reached the glass door just as Meadow did. The woman stopped as Meadow rushed forward (always in a rush!), and then there was a slight hesitation between them before the woman stopped and held the door open for her. Meadow said, "Thank you." The woman looked at her, large brown eyes, wide gleaming smile, and then looked at the ground. She looked very something. She looked young. Meadow passed her and then worried about being ahead of the woman in line. The woman—a girl, really—had almost deferred to her. Apologetic or something. Did she have a mental disability? Meadow stopped at the doorway to the main room, held the second door open, and waited for the tall girl to pass her. The girl again hesitated, and Meadow gestured with her hand toward the line. The girl flashed a smile, eyes open and bright. She took her place ahead of Meadow in the long line.

It was a muddy, salty, cold day. The girl undid her scarf and unbuttoned her gray overcoat, and then she took off her coat. She was slim and tall in polyester navy slacks and a sweater. A plastic bag of clothes hung from her wrist. Meadow watched her carefully roll her coat into a bundle and then walk out of the line and place the bundled coat in the corner of the post office's main room. She neatly tucked it there, placed her stuffed plastic bag on top after removing a small zipper pouch. She then walked back to the spot in front of Meadow. The bottom cuffs of her pants were crusted with mud. Could be homeless. But she looked so clean otherwise. And would a homeless person trustingly put her coat and bag in the corner and leave it? She was young, pretty, clean. Not living on the street. But she walked a long way in the street to get here. With no boots and her stuff in a plastic bag.

The line moved slowly. By the time the tall girl was at the front of the line, Meadow had her wallet out. Meadow looked at the package in her hands and read the name she had written, checked that the package was sealed. Checked in her wallet, checked the time on her phone. She waited. Two service windows opened at the same time. The tall girl with the muddy pant hems went to one, and Meadow went to the one next to it. The postal clerk in front of her was taping her package and then weighing it. The clerk at the next window, helping the tall girl, spoke in a loud, clear voice.

"Hello! Good news. I called the refugee center, and they said you can stay there and receive mail while you sort out your visa issues."

Meadow stole a side glance at the girl. Of course. She was foreign, not American. She held a green passport in her hand. Meadow handed the clerk her credit card. She did not turn toward the girl, but she could hear the other clerk speak to her.

"What you need to do is send this passport by express mail to the embassy in DC and they will return it overnight. But it costs twenty dollars each way, so forty dollars to send it." There was a long pause. "Sorry," the clerk said, "but that is what you need to do to be sure it gets there and back."

The postal clerk sounded kind. Meadow admired her. She could feel the line restless behind them. Meadow waited for the clerk at her window to give her a receipt.

"Four dollars?" the tall girl said with a British accent. Meadow looked sideways and saw the girl's zipper wallet open in her hands.

"No, four-tee dollars. Four zero." The clerk wrote the number on a piece of paper.

The tall girl smiled and shook her head at her wallet.

"I know, I am sorry," the clerk said. "That is what it costs. There is nothing I can do about that. You can go to the center and see what they say. And then come back here . . ." The tall girl stood there, saying nothing. Meadow shoved her receipt into her own wallet, and saw two twenties in the cash section. She had exactly forty dollars in cash in her wallet. Exactly. She pulled them out of her wallet, and felt her heart start to pound a little, like she was going onstage.

Meadow walked toward the tall girl at the window and as she passed she looked down and placed the two twenties on the counter next to the girl's hand.

"Do it. You should send it express," Meadow said, not looking, not stopping really. But Meadow turned her head and looked back at them for a second as the money registered, as they understood. The tall girl looked up and said, "Thank you," in a high voice. She smiled, so broadly her mouth opened, and the clerk laughed. "Welcome to Albany, young lady!" the clerk exclaimed. The line was behind Meadow, but she could feel them watching. Meadow walked faster and did not look back again. She was in the parking lot, rushing toward her car.

She got in, flushed, heart pounding in her ears. She sat there. The tall girl looked so surprised and happy. It was no big deal, the money meant nothing to Meadow. Forty dollars was spent without blinking. Hardly an act of generosity or charity. Her heart continued to make its beats felt in her ears. She could hear her own excited breaths. How small and easy a gesture. How satisfying. Meadow sat in the driver's seat, holding her keys. She put her hand to her forehead, lowered her chin, and let out a soft sob as she began to cry. She felt the tears blur her eyes and slide down her cheeks. She opened her palm across her forehead and let her head rest for a second. It calmed you, a palm, even your own. She let herself keep crying, and the sounds vibrated in her ears. Meadow took her hand off her forehead and sat up. She found a tissue in the glove box and held it to her nose, which had began to run. It felt, she thought as she inhaled and sniffed, so calming. She pressed the tissue to her nose. The crying, the gesture, the action, the moment, the smile. It was stunning how good it felt.

She should leave. She didn't want to be lurking around there when the woman came out. Her hand trembled as she inserted the key. She felt so giddy—almost high. She breathed in deeply. Wow. But leave now.

Meadow turned the key and started the car, felt the blast of the heat and the radio. She lowered the volume. She felt different now than she had before. Ridiculous, as if she could change. She clipped her safety belt. She felt for her wallet, her gum, and her phone. She backed out.

Meadow remembered an article she had cut out of the paper about Zell Kravinsky. When she got to her studio, she went through her files until she found it. "An Organ Donor's Generosity Raises Question of How Much Is too Much." Zell was a millionaire who one day began to give away all his money except for a modest house. Why should he have extra when others didn't have enough? That was a very simple question. Then he went even further, why should he have two kidneys when some people were waiting for transplants? So he gave one away to a stranger. The article speculated that his generosity was some kind of pathology, a mental illness. His generosity was so extreme that it was almost grotesque to the writer, and presumably to a reasonable reader. But what Meadow admired was that it wasn't emotional—it was moral logic, duty, a deliberateness on Zell's part about doing good rather than harm.

How to be good? Maybe she would never be a good person. But she could do good things. Meadow would not give away a kidney, but she could change her life. It was quite clear. Rearrange it until it was a net good.

Money, for starters. She always had more than most people, but what good was it?

She talked to her father, and with the trust fund he had given her, she arranged to buy a tiny house on a small piece of property in the green hills between Gloversville and Albany. It was a perfectly intact nineteenth-century saltbox, with a fireplace and only eight hundred square feet of living space. All she would have to pay were the taxes. She got rid of her place in Washington Heights. She got rid of the warehouse studio. All of the remaining money from the trust would go to causes she identified. One of the biggest donations was given to the Justice Campaign.

She felt liberated. The further she went, the simpler it became. Slowly she sold off her belongings so she could give away more money. She wore thrift store clothes; she stopped eating meat. She got her expenses down to a minuscule amount. She liked how this felt, but she didn't let it go too far. She did not starve herself or swear off all bodily pleasures. She kept her DVDs and her books. She took measure of herself. She would not become like Kateri Tekakwitha, the Lily of the Mohawks. She wouldn't let herself go to an extreme in which deprivation became its own excess.

Carrie occasionally called, and Meadow was cryptic about her life. But eventually Meadow told her what she had been up to.

Without hesitation, Carrie said, "Sell the house. Sell the car. Sell the kids. Find someone else. Forget it. I'm never coming back. Forget it!" This from *Apocalypse Now*. They both laughed. "You have pulled a Kurtz."

"Kurtz doesn't say that, you know," Meadow said. "It is a recording of Lieutenant Colby."

"I know, I know," Carrie said. "But everyone remembers it as Kurtz." There was a pause. "But you are okay, right?"

"I'm trying," Meadow said.

Was it possible to be truly humble? No, but she could tread lightly, quietly.

What did she have to give? What was hers to give?

She adopted two dogs from an animal shelter. She volunteered her time. At a women's clinic for underserved communities. At a literacy center for adults. At a group for environmental advocacy. She didn't have any particularly useful skills, so she mostly made phone calls and asked people for money. She knew that for things to get truly better, systematic change was needed, not charity and gestures. But she urged herself to do whatever small good she could think of, right now. It made her life tolerable, and she could sleep at night.

After three years of this penitent life, Meadow decided to take a job teaching film at a college in Albany. It was a BFA program, and she was a professor of practice. She didn't care to teach filmmaking, but they let her teach film studies. Film studies classes for filmmakers, not academics.

Meadow taught whatever films she wanted to study. It was like being twenty all over again. Her first semester she taught a class devoted to film noir in its weirdest permutations. Of course she taught nonfiction film. Then she taught the European New Wave, with a focus on the lesser-known films. But her favorite thing to teach was the Orson Welles section of her Innovators class. Welles was considered obvious and overrated by her students. She liked to show them exactly why he was her favorite. When it worked, when they understood that, and when she got them excited, she knew this also was a good thing.

PART FOUR

JELLY AND JACK

Jack called her number one night and left a message on her voice mail.

He was so goddamned sick of the well-wishers and the caregivers. He just wanted to sit with his hound dog Sandy and look at the beach. He didn't want to hear any more about options and palliatives and comfort.

Sandy was a perfect comfort: she was the same as she had always been. Sandy expected him to walk and feed her. She lay sleepily on the couch next to him, her chin resting on his leg. Everyone else was either talking about the illness or not talking about the illness but still thinking about it. His daughter winced when he lit a cigarette or made a drink, even though his diagnosis had nothing to do with these vices. What for, all this concern, when it was a fait accompli?

On a whim, he realized he wanted to talk to someone who didn't know his prognosis, just knew him, and then he realized he would like to talk to Nicole.

After their disastrous meeting, and the film's release, he thought he was finally over her. She had left two voice-mail messages for him, apologetic messages, one right after the film was shot and one a few months after that, but he never called her back.

He felt different now, less wounded. Leave it to a fatal disease to make you feel healed. She called him back, and they talked like old times. He didn't tell her he was dying. But he did tell her some stories, and he played some music for her. She told him what she thought, and she was as kind and brilliant as ever. They were back to talking on the phone every day now. They discussed the movies they had watched, just as they had before, and sometimes she even told him about her life, her real life.

CARRIE GOES TO THE MOVIES

Rehearsal is going super long. I'm really, really sorry, but can you go without me?

Her son, Dash, texted her in complete sentences with punctuation. It was condescending, mom-texting, the equivalent of speaking really slowly to an old person. She wanted to text back:

but we ALWAYS go 2 a movie on Dec 26!!

They were going to see *Manformers*, a big action blockbuster, which was also part of the tradition, seeing a big cheeseball of a movie. Instead she texted:

no worries! c u later

She actually didn't want to see *Manformers*, not at all. She did feel like seeing a movie, though. The Film Forum was showing a restored print of Vera Chytilová's *Daisies*, a film she had heard about but never seen. Meadow had emailed her about it earlier in the week. Just a link and a sentence that said, "One day only to see this on the big screen. Want to go?" Carrie was amused that Meadow still used "on the big screen" as an incentive. Nobody gave a crap about big screens anymore. Besides, Carrie owned the Blu-Ray Criterion Collection *Daisies* DVD and could watch it on a pretty big screen in the comfort of her home anytime she wanted to, although she hadn't gotten around to it yet. She had written back that she would love to go, but it was her movie tradition to go to a blockbuster with her son on the day after Christmas. She also said she hoped to see Meadow soon for dinner or lunch. It was the first time Carrie had heard from her since she put her essay online. She had no idea if Meadow had read it—but of course she must have.

Carrie took a cab to Sixth Avenue. It was already getting dark at 5:00. She paid for her ticket and headed into the theater. She saw the place was half full, and she snuck curious looks at her fellow New York City cineastes. The world was out shopping, and here the hardcore cinema lovers were waiting to be transported to the world of the Czech New Wave. And then she heard Meadow.

"Carrie!" Meadow was sitting toward the center back, all by herself. She waved Carrie over, and Carrie smiled and walked toward her.

"I thought you couldn't come?" Meadow said as they performed an awkward hug standing in front of the narrow seats.

"He blew me off!" Carrie said, shrugging. They sat, and Carrie filled the space between them with updates about Dash and his band. Then the lights started to go down, and Meadow leaned over to her.

"I read the essay you wrote. It was very generous," she said.

Carrie whispered, "I was worried you would be mad." Meadow scrunched her eyes and shook her head no.

As the previews played, Carrie felt the giddy wave of excitement that she got from being in a dark theater watching a big screen. No pausing, no looking things up on her phone. It was indeed different than sitting at home, on her couch, falling asleep. Sitting in a theater with other people giving their full attention to the film. It was devotional, and sometimes she forgot how much she loved that.

The film is about two young women in a fantastical tableaux of shifting, rhythmic Pop-colored filters. In interludes throughout the film, the girls are seen in bikinis as a clock's ticks on the soundtrack drive the jump cuts. Sometimes faster than life and sometimes slower than life—both delineated and dismantled time. The "plot" concerns the two girls running amok. They go out to dinner with middle-aged rich men. Then they eat hilariously large portions of food, horrifying and sometimes splattering the older men with various kinds of food spray. "I love to eat," one girl exclaims, and Carrie could not help but laugh. After the girls eat, drink, and smoke to disgusting excess, they ditch their dates at the train station. In between dates, they burn things, steal, trip people, wear bikinis, crank-call people ("Hello? Die, die, die.") and lounge around in cutesy-girl outfits. All of this was very funny, but it was the end of the film that floored Carrie. The final prank shows the two women demolishing an overladen banquette table by shoving food into their mouths in an orgy of slurps and food-crushing noises and images. Next the film abruptly cuts to the girls atop the table, stomping across the plates and glasses and carcasses in high heels, smashing it all. It was absurd and dizzying in a very specific Eastern European way. But the final scene was like nothing Carrie had seen before. The girls return in bondage suits made from newspaper, and in a frenzy of fast motion they reset the table with the broken glasses and dishes, chanting in unison whispers, "We are good and hardworking. We shall be happy and everything will be wonderful." Carrie yelped with delight, and then she turned her face to her right and glanced at Meadow, who stared at the screen, smiling. Carrie looked back at the movie, where the girls molded the smashed, spilled cakes and meats into disgusting mounds on the platters as they continued to whisper-chant, "We'll do everything and we'll be good and happy and beautiful. And happy again." Carrie felt Meadow's hand on hers. Meadow squeezed her hand, just that, and Carrie squeezed back.

KINO-GLAZ

And Meadow?

She taught her classes. She watched the films, watched her students' faces. One day she showed them Tarkovsky's *Andrei Rublev.* She remembered when she'd first seen its black-and-white images, and how she thought that this was what films made in the fifteenth century looked like. And she remembered Hosney saying that Tarkovsky wanted to use images to make us feel the infinite, find a form to express the infinite. That's all! She thought it worked like this. His films made you regard a person in a landscape, the beauty of the composition drawing you in until you lost your impatience, your preoccupation with temporality, with the next thing, drawing you in until you stayed there with him, and the material world and the mystical world became one. He used conjure and artifice to show what was true.

What else?

One day after class she sat at a table and ate her lunch. It was cold, but the sun was bright. She could smell the coming spring in the air. She closed her eyes to the sun and saw the red light through her eyelids. Then she opened her eyes and stared at the blue sky.

Several streaks of cloud matched the line of the horizon, and bright rays back-lit the clouds in light-lined rows like a Tintoretto painting. More filmic than real, she thought. She watched the sky and the light, and then Meadow closed her eyes again and imagined a kaleidoscope of images: waterfalls, towering trees creaking in the wind, the arc of a looping bird toward a river and back, electric-skinned amphibians in a glistening jungle, a muted pink glow as snow fills the dusk sky, the sharp glint of the moon on a glossy lake. Then she heard a steady sound, the rhythmic sound of a heartbeat, or a computer hum, or even the sound of a machine, the clack of a train? She tried to listen to it by sitting with her eyes closed on the bench, and she felt small but also connected. She thought of her images again but with slow motion, almost stop action, with distorted sound, with a crane shot moving her up, the view levitating, and then the camera flying forward over all of it. She thought of wide angles and deep focus, a posthuman or prehuman landscape, a film like a long lyric mist. But not only that. She imagined that a person shown in the right way could meet this, this glimpse of the sublime. Can an image convey something unnameable, impossible, invisible? What is an image if not inflected by a consciousness, a noticing? Something quieter and simpler: a person with an open face—any person, any face—sitting alone. How plain could an image be, how humble? Something to make her refutation or resistance give way. She imagined making this film, but also knew and hoped that everything would change in the doing. Change her vision, and change her, again.

THE PRISONER

In the early morning, Sarah Mills kneeled in her prison cell. Sarah was not religious, but she was spiritual. What else could you be when the actual world offered so little? She prayed, but not to God. She prayed to her daughter, Crystalynn.

She did this every morning as soon as she woke. She kneeled, closed her eyes, and pressed her palms into her closed eyes to block out all the light. She waited and then began to compose her senses. The sister told her about composition of the senses, and about Saint Ignatius of Loyola, a Jesuit priest, who created the practice. To pray on something, you used each of your senses to create a direct experience of it. Jesuits used composition of the senses to experience the life of Christ. Sarah had her own version.

She stared into her pressed eyelids and she conjured what the house looked like. *The living room with the black leather couch striped by cat scratches. The Christmas tree, plugged in so the lights and tinsel sparkle. I had cooked spaghetti with red sauce from a jar and scorched the sauce when I left it on the stove, so the house already smelled of something burnt. I sat on the couch and smoked, the menthol tasting like a dry, rough mint in my throat, but the cigarette smoke was so constant that it hardly smelled at all to me. I stared at the tree because the pills I had taken made the blinking bulbs linger in my eyes until I felt I was in a trance. I was fixed to the couch. I felt very good at this point. Also sitting by the tree was you, Crystalynn. You had wispy white hair, and you didn't like to have it combed. It was sticking up, wasn't it? You were sucking your pink binky and staring at the tree. You wore blue footed pajamas with the top snap undone. There were no presents under the tree, but you loved the ornaments. I watched you in my daze. You reached your finger out and swatted a red bulb. I did nothing but stare. You giggled and swatted it again even harder, and then I said, "Look don't touch, Crystalynn!" The bulb swayed and spun, the lights moving in its shiny surface. You laughed, and I could hear it, can hear it perfectly twenty years later. Next I put you to bed, how heavy you felt when I lifted you. The weight in my arms. I carried you, and I felt wobbly on my feet. I was barefoot, and my toes gripped the carpet on the stairs. Your room was a mess. I unzipped your pajamas and checked that your diaper was dry. You squirmed as I zipped you up, and it smelled like plastic and baby powder. You cried when I put you in your crib, so I went downstairs and took a bottle of juice from the fridge. Jason came in, and I stopped as he walked over to me and put a hand on the back of my bare thigh. He moved his hand up, and I arched against him, leaned into Jason. You started to yell from upstairs. I still had the bottle in my hand, and I groaned—I did, a tired sound in the back of the throat. I went up the stairs. You stood in your crib, crying, big tears rolling down your red cheeks. I gave you the bottle. You instantly stopped crying and held the bottle with both hands as you sucked. I reached into the crib, put my hands under your arms, and picked you up. I pushed my lips to your cheek, hot and soft and a little wet from your tears. And when I pulled back, I could see you smile with the bottle's nipple in your mouth. I swung your legs back and then laid you on your back in the crib. You were so very tired, and your eyelids already started to droop. I pulled the knit blanket up. I said, "Go to sleep, baby." And I touched your cheek, felt for a second its fullness.*

I smelled apple juice, baby powder, and my own cigarettes. I turned out the light, and I closed the door to your room.

Sarah stayed on her knees, her eyes closed, her hands pressing her eyelids.

The last time I heard you, I was in the garage screaming at Jason. I heard you crying, and I wished that you would stop. I did not go to you. I was yelling, and Jason was ignoring me. I wished that everything would stop. I was sobbing, and I was in pain from my fall. My leg was red, and my thigh throbbed. I was in my panties and a t-shirt. I was shaking from cold and from the combination of drugs. My jaw was grinding in my mouth, and more than cold and sore, I felt angry. I threw a shovel at Jason's car. I threw his bike pump against his car.

The last time I saw you, I was in your room and you were asleep. The smoke was burning my throat. I could feel the heat from the floor below. I stood over your crib, and you looked asleep. You were not crying, and my eyes and nose were watering. I could not tell if you were alive or not. I did not check. And I did not pick you up and run out of the house with you. I did not. I thought of doing it, and in the second I stood over your crib, I decided no.

In the early years, when she first began this exercise, Sarah used to think this litany during this part: *I decided no. So you wouldn't be like me, like my mom, like all of us. A bust. Like I was. So you wouldn't find out about this life, that money would always be short, and without money, everything was too hard. So you wouldn't turn that perfect body into a thing to fight against. So men wouldn't hurt you. So I wouldn't hurt you. I didn't think those words, baby. I felt it in my tired body, and the only words in my head were, "Leave her be."* But then Sarah began to strip back the reasons, the story of why she thought she did what she did. Because even if it were true, it only served the self that she wanted to discard. She must simply contemplate what she did.

The smoke was choking me, and I went to the window of your room and opened it. The air, the cold night air, made me want to breathe, so I pulled myself out the window. I left you in the smoky room, and I moved toward the air until I woke up on the grass with someone giving me oxygen and loading me in an ambulance. This is what I did, Crystalynn.

Sarah stopped there. She no longer needed to add this part either: *It was the wrong thing; it was a terrible bad thing and I am so very sorry that I did not save you.* This was not her confession. This was her life in her cell, alone.

Sarah stayed kneeling, stayed pressing her eyes closed. Every day she did this, went over her last hours with Crystalynn. Every day it would come back, and every day Sarah must remember it. This was important, Sarah made herself remember, and then she could let herself go. She was on her knees and she felt now something like forgiveness. Not by God, or Crystalynn, or anyone else in the world. She felt forgiven by her own insignificance. She saw herself from the outside, on her knees in the cell, and she was gloriously insignificant. So much so that she was just air. What she wanted, what she thought, what she knew, didn't matter.

The repetition of the days did something to you. You knew the monotony, but you couldn't fight it. You had to invent your own repetitions to meet it. A ritual. This early, barely awake kneeling was hers.

She looked deep into the black of her closed eyes. Stared into the dark. When your sense of vision has very little stimulation, it invents images. Sarah doesn't know the name for this is the Prisoner's Cinema. It is a trick of the mind, blindness turned into glorious sight. Isolation turned into hallucination. After enough time, she saw a series of lights. The false images are called phosphenes, which means "show of lights." But all Sarah knew was that it gave her vibrant colors of great depth, and patterns like a mosaic, like a tiled church floor or sometimes like the spiral of a shell. These visions did not absolve her of her time, her duty, and her deeds. Instead these visions took her through the limits of who she was and what she had done, and for this she felt gratitude, and with this, at last, consolation.

ACKNOWLEDGMENTS

I am indebted to *Exploding the Phone* by Phil Lapsley. "The Miranda Obsession" by Bryan Burrough and Miranda Grosevnor inspired elements of the proto-catfishing in this novel. I derived part of Meadow's analysis of the scene from *Barry Lyndon* from Martin Scorsese's take in *A Personal Journey Through American Movies*. I took a line that imaginary Orson says from an appearance Orson Welles made on *The Merv Griffin Show* the night Welles died. The idea of re-creating lost films came from Guy Maddin. James Benning's *RR* belongs on Meadow's list of train films, but it was made too late to fit into the chronology of the book. His work also pointed me toward this book's epigraph.

Thank you to Melanie Jackson and Don DeLillo for the support they have given this novel. Thank you to my editor, Nan Graham, for her intelligence and passion. Thank you to Roger Hallas, Laki Vazakas, James Rasin, Robert Polito, Tom Luddy, Sam Green, and Bennett Miller for so much help on aspects of the film content. Thank you to Jim Hosney for emailing me answers to my film questions and allowing me to name him in this novel as an homage. Thank you to Cody Carvel for reading and commenting on the phone phreaking sections. Thanks also to Kelley Rourke, Eric Bianchi, Christine Healy, Scott Healy, Sterling Youngman, Marie Lorenz, Sarah Harwell, Rachel Kushner, and Judith Clark for comments and conversations that helped my work here. I am grateful to Syracuse University and its Creative Writing Program for giving me the time and support to work. Thank you to Susan Moldow, Katherine Monaghan, and Daniel Loedel and everyone at Scribner for supporting this book. Thank you to my mother, Emy Frasca, for reading this novel and giving me such helpful comments. I cannot thank Jonathan Dee enough for his constant support of my writing.